Empire of the Void
The Director's Cut

The Empire Marathon: Book 1

By Andrew Valenza

Valenza Publishing

Valenza Publishing

Hadley, NY 12835

First published in 2023
Second Edition, 2025

Edited by Dr. Stephen Hull

ISBN: 979-8-9919345-3-4

More from Valenza Publishing

Andrew Valenza

Empire of the Void
Lost World of the Void

Three Short Horror Stories

Ella M. Hayes

Bookends
Witch's Brew

J.T. McGee

Thrall
Enthralled

Jamie Norton

The Second Act Comeback

Praise for
<u>Empire of the Void</u>

"Truly never read anything like this.."

"A great sci-if story with just the right touch of inter-personal relationships and interactions."

"This has so many things happen for a novel of its size! It has a love story, it has plenty of action, betrayal, and redemption! Valenza's world building is amazing, so much so that you can picture these planets as real places. A must read for any sci-fi fan!"

"Reminded me of the 50's science fiction movies on TV Friday nights when I was a Kid."

"Whether you are a science fiction fan or not, this book is a great adventure. I enjoyed every minute reading it.. ready for the next adventure!"

Praise for

Lost World of the Void

"LOST WORLD OF THE VOID is another fantastic addition to its series and will leave you on the edge of your seat, ready for the next book. It combines elements of suspense, science fiction, and drama with just the right touch of humor to craft a narrative as entertaining as it is thought-provoking."

-Chris Jones, Overly Honest Reviews

"...has all the flavor of early Asimov stories with a little more romance, but all the same intrigue and plot twists."

-Goodreads Review

"...even better than the first!.. A book you won't want to put down."

-Jade Nioma, author of "Fate's Tether"

Dedication

Dedicated to my Dad for raising me on incredible films like Star Wars, Planet of the Apes, and Aliens; and my Uncle Lawrence for helping me really understand both the history and weirdness of cinema.

Prologue

"It is Day 400 of our journey aboard the *Silent Horizon*. I'll bet our compatriots back on Earth reckon we've gone crazy by now. Up here where nothing ever changes, a year feels like a decade. I guess that makes my upcoming anniversary with Lacy feel that much more meaningful. It's almost like we've spent a lifetime together already." Dex turned to gaze at his wife asleep in the bunk against the port-side wall. The starboard-side bed hadn't been touched since their "unofficial" wedding night, and had accumulated a fair amount of dust.

"Yes sir... who would have thought it would only take us seven weeks to give in to each other like that. To be fair, after that one date before launch, we agreed to wait until our return to Earth to carry on our romance. I bet the boys back on the ground had money on us succumbing to our passion like that sooner. That's why we were picked for the mission, right? If anything is to happen, worst-case is we restart the human race on a new planet. Well, congrats boys. Hope you're sending another ship out with our anniversary gifts. Never got the Christmas one, must have been lost in transit." He paused the recorder and laughed to himself. Would he ever celebrate Christmas again back on Earth? Would there ever be a Christmas gift again for that matter?

He resumed the recorder. "I'm hoping that by day 500 we'll have at least some sign of another planet. We've passed beyond the scope of what our friends on Earth can see, and thankfully, the terror of flying blind like this hasn't quite set in yet. I'm not the only one getting antsy either. Lacy's spending half her time at the computer watching the radar rather than piloting this craft. I'm beginning to think she's had enough of me-"

Dex was cut off by a hand falling gracefully on his shoulder. He looked back and saw Lacy's blue eyes looking down lovingly into his. She then leaned into the microphone, and said with a playful smile, "*Lieutenant* Lacy Prullen has not had enough of you quite yet." She paused the recorder then said to Dex, "If I want to find a planet now, it's just so we can build ourselves a bigger home than this ship."

With his eyes still on her, Dex resumed the recorder one more time. "It seems as though this is my signal to close out today's log. Captain Dex..."

"And Lieutenant Lacy Prullen, signing off."

Lacy sat on the edge of the console, arms crossed and chin raised just a bit, her smile now a smirk.

Dex spun his chair in her direction. "Something on your mind, L.T.?" As a tease, he added, "These logs aren't important to you anymore?"

"These logs are between you and everyone back on Earth. And with so little to report, I think you can ease up with the daily ritual."

"Have something else in mind we can be doing?"

Lacy's smirk pursed as if she was keeping a secret she wanted him to pry from her, and arced her eyes across the ceiling as if to say, *I had a few ideas.*

Dex took the bait.

He gave a small chuckle, and asked, "What is it this time?"

She looked back down at him, then took a seat on his lap and placed her arm around him. "I've been thinking. By the time we get back to Earth, how much time will have passed?"

Dex thought for a moment, exhaled deeply then answered, "I don't know. Orders say we're allowed to turn around if nothin's found in five years. But, let's say we're back on Earth ten years after we left. Given the fact that time works differently in space, relative theory and all that science nonsense, who knows how much time has passed for them? We could have missed the whole rest of the century and land in... I don't know, 2021!"

Even with the miracles of science they left behind in 1958, even thinking of the possibilities of what 1980 would bring boggled their minds.

"Can you imagine?" She asked. "2021. By then maybe the colonies will be extending far past our solar system. Travel might be a hundred times faster than what we're capable of in this beautiful ship."

"And robots will be enslaving all mankind, or evil aliens assimilating us! Yeah, that'll be the day." They laughed together and Dex kissed her forehead.

Lacy got off Dex's lap and took seat at the right side of the console.

"More than likely there won't be an Earth to go back to," Dex continued, his tone shifting from the playful banter to one of slight melancholy. "Either another race will overpower us, or we'll destroy ourselves."

"Very optimistic." The smile began to fade from

Lacy's face.

Dex wasn't deterred. "The world we left behind was great, but even this mission just goes to show the end is near. We're racing to get off the earth. This craft is beautiful, yes, but the energy we harnessed to make this? It could wipe out half the U.S.S.R in an instant." Dex cast his eyes out into the void. In the distance on the port side was a nebula swirling green and purple stardust, as if he were looking from the sky down into a whirlpool.

"Yeah, I'm glad I made it out when I did. And more than that..." he reached out to hold her hand. "I'm glad you made it out with me."

When the smile returned to her face, Lacy's blue eyes gleamed more beautifully than all the nebulas and all the mystical colors of all the infinite number of galaxies in the universe could ever dream to be.

"Call me a pessimist about the fate of Earth, but looking toward the future of this mission, and the infinity of what's out there waiting for us... all I see are infinite ways to make happy the woman I love."

"Well, with all that pessimism, what if we don't go back to Earth?"

"What?" Dex was taken aback by the idea, but not completely against it. For some time now, long before they'd ever begun the mission, Dex had developed somewhat of an aversion toward the big blue ball.

"Oh, I was only thinking, darling. As you said, there might not be an Earth to go back to. How bad would it be if we just found a new home out here?"

"You and me?" Dex laughed.

"Me and you. Just a thought." The words glided off of Lacy's lips like a soft breeze, and she leaned in to kiss him.

Their future together truly would be far beyond what anybody they left behind on earth could possibly imagine.

1. Happy Anniversary

The *Silent Horizon* drifted through space at a speed just below light's. It was a small two-person ship, with a cabin only about twenty-five feet in length, and eight feet wide. The outside of the craft glistened with a material like silver that had been discovered on one of Saturn's moons. To all beholden to its passing glory, it gave the ship an image as that of a star piloting itself through space. The bow of the ship was tipped with a long needle that housed the main antenna. About three feet behind that was the viewport, a single glass pane that wrapped 180 degrees around the command console. Moving to the rear of the ship, the passengers had a cabinet with a fold-out table, chair, and their full supply of provisions. Down further were their bunks, with drawers on the bottom for their clothes. Compartments on top were for storage of their personal effects, mostly scientific tools for when they found another planet, medical supplies, and a bottle of wine for if they ever found a habitable planet. A locker stood beside the bunks, housing their red with gold trim Planetary Exploration Suits, field packs with emergency gear, and the standard white spacewalk suits that had seen far more use than the P.E.S's. These suits had no independent oxygen tanks but were fed air through a tube that ensured they wouldn't drift too far away from the ship when doing repairs on the hull. On the port side of the back wall was the latrine, and on the starboard side was a hallway that had three doors. The first was a greenhouse in case they found any plant life to bring back, then the engine room, and along the back wall, the airlock.

To call it a small home was an understatement. Yet they had enough to stay busy. The ship's computer was equipped with a database of films, books, and music from Earth. Their fold-out tables were equipped with a vast library of board games that could be projected onto the surface.

Thanks to the artificial gravity on the ship, Dex and Lacy had been able to keep up with some moderate physical activities to keep their muscles from total atrophy. They still worried though, from time to time, about how their bodies would treat them if they did ever find a planet or return to Earth.

Conversations never went stale as their interests in media consumption differed greatly, but they were both curious about each other's thoughts on what they were currently invested in. Dex explored the library of films and was into swing music and the new wave of "rock and roll" that was gaining popularity before their mission began. Lacy was far less of a film enthusiast. She would indulge him with a movie night here and there, but otherwise had the vast majority of the book library all to herself and would keep Dex up at night talking about what she'd read and the issues all the characters were facing. Musically, she greatly preferred classical symphonies and jazz. Growing up, swing music was played too much in her home and she grew to hate it. But since Dex loved it, she would dance around with him to his favorites, and he in turn would suffer through her symphonies. The jazz collection he was more tolerant toward. Specifically, "Rhapsody in Blue," because how could one not love it?

The one physical book they did have was Dex's pocket Bible. It was a gift his father adamantly gave him from when he served in the Army. Abner Prullen wasn't the most religious person but carried the Bible at all times while deployed for a sense of comfort. He'd hoped it would give Dex the same comfort as they drifted into space.

All things given, this was enough for Dex and Lacy. Additionally, they had a better view than any of their old neighbors from Earth.

* * *

Day 416 began with a soft beeping coming from the ship's computer. It was almost an hour after the beeping began that Lacy woke. She heard the sound coming from the console and tried to ignore it, thinking it was some part of a dream that kept with her as she came back to consciousness. Eventually, the beeping could no longer be ignored. She navigated around Dex's body and climbed out of bed.

As her head became more clear, she realized they hadn't heard a sound like this one since they left Earth's solar system. An unidentified ship had drifted too close to them. It had turned out to be a private space-yacht that was knocked way off course, but the computer was alert for any mass not yet programmed into it. Planet or ship. Once things began to click for Lacy, she became as alert as the ship's radar.

"Dex!" she yelled over her shoulder. "Dex, wake

up!"

Dex lifted his head the smallest bit and let out a groan, "What is it darling?"

Lacy raced back to the bunk, and grabbing her husband by the hand, yanked him out onto the floor.

He jumped to his feet, thoroughly annoyed, but instantly recognized the excitement on his wife's face. "What happened?"

All she could do was smile and jump like an excited kid with a secret they were dying to tell the world. "Happy anniversary!" She jumped into his arms and kissed him as hard as she could.

Dex kissed her back but his eyes were focused beyond her, on the console. Slowly he put her back down. "What do you mean? What's going on?"

She took his hand and led him to the console. Lacy pressed a button next to the large central computer screen and Dex slowly understood. After so much time staring into emptiness, Dex had begun wondering if the *Silent Horizon* was incapable of traveling far or fast enough to find anything in the vastness of space within their mission window. It seemed, thankfully, that he was wrong.

"How far out is it?" he asked, mindful not to let his imagination run too wild.

"About 8 hours. It's 0430..." She looked at the screen again, "37. So we have plenty of time to get all done up before we land." She turned to rush over to her dresser under the bunk but was stopped by Dex's hand on her forearm.

"Is this a planet or ship?" His voice held firm as his eyes remained locked on the screen.

"What? I-"

He turned to face her. "Lacy, this is very exciting, there's no doubt about that. But there are protocols for something like this."

Lacy pulled her arm away, but tried to meet his caution with optimism and grace. "Dex, no matter what protocol says, it has never been put into practice. This is an incredible moment for humanity. The first object found in space outside of anything we've ever been able to see!"

"Which is why protocol is so important. It won't mean anything if we're never able to report what we found. Be excited, please, I love to see it in your smile," he said as the backs of his fingers grazed her blushing cheek. "But we have to be smart about it too."

Lacy lowered her head in acceptance, but couldn't stop the excitement from creeping into her smirk. "Okay. I'm going to shower, then let's eat and figure out a plan." She turned and walked to the latrine.

Dex decided to use this time to try to boost the ship's sensors in an attempt to see if he could pick up any hints about what this new object could be. He diverted power from as many of the other computer functions as he could spare. When that wasn't enough, he began looking for ways to divert power from other parts of the ships, at one point forgetting about Lacy in the shower, and eased up on the artificial gravity. She gave a shout of surprise, and shouted his name in playful annoyance, and Dex quickly restored power. No matter what he tried, the object was too far outside the scanner's reach to identify anything other than the fact that something was sure as hell out there.

The next best course of action he saw at the moment was to document this discovery and keep tabs on it.

He turned on the recorder and adjusted the microphone. "Day 416. Lacy and I received a nice anniversary gift today from the universe. Which is great because I did not get her anything. So hopefully she'll enjoy this one." He paused and heard the water stop. After over a year, how much of their recycled water was actually keeping them clean?

Dex went on into the recorder, "According to Lacy, we discovered the signal at around 0430 this morning, but we don't know how long it has been going for prior to us waking up. Maybe from now on taking shifts wouldn't be a half-bad idea. I've done all I can to boost the ship's scanners but it's still too far off to get a good reading on anything."

Lacy was back in her standard-issue underwear (guaranteed best choice for true American astronauts) when she stepped out of the latrine and rushed around with excitement to get dressed.

Dex continued after a quick glance back at her, "We're... optimistic about what this could be. My guess is, with how vast space is, our odds of finding intelligent life by chance are nigh impossible. It's most likely an asteroid, but even that can hold incredible potential for us. Still, we have our blaster just in case. I'm sure it'll be ready for anything. Hasn't been touched once since it was loaded with the rest of our gear, and I hope it doesn't have to be."

Behind him, Lacy was now dressed and opened up the food cabinet and unfolded the table. The food was less than a meal, really only a massive supply of pills. One was taken for each meal to give them all the nutrients they needed. Romantic dinners had died a long time ago for this couple.

"Hopefully within another two or so hours, we'll have a better read on this thing. By hour five we should have visuals, given a constant speed, and know if this thing is stationary. We'll record another log when we have more information." Dex turned off the recorder and swirled his chair around toward Lacy, who was about to swallow her breakfast pill.

"Thanks for the little thrill in the shower. Thought we came on that thing a few hours too early." She swallowed her breakfast and chased it down with a small glass of water. The only drink they'd had in over a year.

"Sorry, got a little ahead of myself with the controls."

Lacy shrugged. "I heard a good amount of the log. No need to brief me on your... findings."

He gave her a small laugh.

"Just an asteroid you think?" She asked, her lips curling in doubt.

"Just an asteroid. Still, it'd be a good idea to prep the gear. Make sure no mice or aliens got into anything," Dex joked.

"Well, I think we may have really lucked out here. I'm betting it's a beautiful world with a bright blue sky just like back on Earth. Rolling mountains and vast oceans, and quiet. Imagine if it's just plant life. No animals except for you and me when we land!"

"No animals? After all this time I wouldn't mind a nice alien steak."

She laughed now, "Oh come on, we've got all the gourmet meals we need right here!" She tossed one of the pills toward him like candy, which he caught in his mouth.

He swallowed and almost instantly the pill sent

waves through his body that told his brain he tasted bland pancakes with soulless maple syrup, then a second wave that had the simulated taste of the powdered eggs that men like his father had to eat during World War II and the Eurasian War.

"Ah. Goddamn delicious," he said with as much sarcasm as he could muster.

* * *

Three hours later, the computer was able to give a better reading of what Dex and Lacy were approaching. It was a solid mass, just under 100 kilometers in diameter.

"That's... that's smaller than, what? Long Island maybe?" Lacy asked.

Dex typed something into the console. "Yeah," he said. "Just about."

"We may be too far out," Dex said, "but not picking up any atmosphere. Won't be larger than your thumb until we're right on top of it. And with a rock that small, gravity will be real low. Gotta be careful when we land, no jumping around. Might drift too far out."

Lacy giggled at the thought. Of course she would be safe, but the idea was so silly to her.

* * *

Another hour passed and the computer was able to bring up an image of the rock.

"Looks like Earth's moon but... it's so smooth. Strange, isn't it?"

Dex studied the computer screen. "May be small,

but maybe it's denser than expected. Could have a stronger gravitational pull." He looked at his wife, "Helps smooth it out."

"So jumping around is allowed again?"

He smirked with a coy look in her direction, and held back from making too many promises he wouldn't be able to keep. "We'll see how much celebrating is allowed when we get there. If nothing else though, there's still the ship."

* * *

Hour five crawled slowly toward them. Far off in the distance, they saw the smallest speck, differing from all the other stars in the vastness of space only by the intensity of the light bouncing off of it and its size, slightly larger than the stars themselves.

"There it is, baby. Your moon," Dex said. "And seeing as you're the one that found it, it's only fair you name it." He reached across the gap between them and took her hand in his.

Lacy, sitting at the co-pilot seat staring out into space at the moon, heard his voice but barely noticed his touch. "Who'd've thought... Us, of all people, would one day be out among the stars naming our own celestial masses?"

Dex's smile faded to only a smirk. "Don't get too excited. It's a big rock drifting along. An exoplanet. Not even a moon with a real planet to orbit around. Chances of finding anything past dust is almost null."

She looked up at him with a gleam of eagerness in her beautiful blue eyes. "Yes, but where there's one, there's another. And another."

Dex looked back down at the console. *Not necessarily,* he thought to himself, but would never say that out loud to her. Still, there was nothing on the radar except the rock. He wanted to bring her back to reality but now didn't seem like the right time. Not on their anniversary.

"So, what about a name?" He asked.

"Darling," she giggled, "This could potentially be one of the greatest finds of human history!"

"Or a rock."

She scoffed his comment away. "There's no way for me to come up with a name for it on the spot like this. This rock, as you're so keen to remind me, whether desolate or the home of some material that could somehow save Earth from whatever end you're thinking of, is a first step in the expansion of the human race past our own solar system! It needs a name to match its awesome importance."

They both sat in silence for a moment, thinking of a name worthy of such a major moment in human history.

After some thought, Dex reached out his right hand for the button on the console that presented the keyboard. "Prullen-1. Putting it in the log."

With a laugh, Lacy reached out to pull his hand away. "Dex! There's no way we're calling it that!"

"With all due respect, Lieutenant, you were taking too long."

That smile could disarm anyone, she thought.

Dex held his left hand above the now-present keyboard. "Well?"

"Can we change it later at least?" Lacy pleaded.

"Only until we find Prullen-2."

Lacy let go of Dex's hand and slumped back in her

chair. The minutes continued to slow.

In their minds, the excitement told them time should be speeding up, that it would pass in the blink of an eye. But with such a focus on the coming discovery, the entertainment on the *Silent Horizon* lost all appeal. The music and film library seemed dull in comparison, and neither one of them could keep their focus on reading for more than a hundred words before their thoughts brought them back to the rock.

* * *

Hour six. Prullen-1 was only fractionally larger, and the anticipation was killing them.

* * *

Hour seven. Out of the ship's viewport, Prullen-1 was only half an inch large, but in the grand scheme of their exploration, it was growing quickly.

To Lacy, it was inviting, but the more Dex observed the readings he was getting from the computer, the more hesitant he was to land the ship.

"This can't be right," he started.

Lacy was sitting in the seat to his right. The anxiety in his voice did nothing to bring down her spirits. "You're worrying too much. We're so far outside the reaches of what we used to know. Why should this rock have the same laws as Earth or... heck, any of the planets of our solar system?"

Dex looked at her with hardened eyes. "Lacy, it's a rock that's half the size of Long Island but just about the gravitational reading is all... hazy. It's like I'm getting interference."

"It's just a rock, darling." Her tone was half teasing, half reassuring. She put a hand on his shoulder.

Dex looked out the viewport at the slowly growing rock, then turned his head back toward her. Gently taking her hand, he raised it to his mouth and kissed her fingers.

"Promise me you won't drop your guard." He commanded her, with a touch of loving concern. Never had he really commanded her before. Even with the official rank they held, at the end of the day he only ever treated her as his wife.

"Yes, sir." Lacy knew when to respect the rank, but this far into the voyage, emotions held the highest rank. To break the tension she puffed up her cheeks.

Dex recognized instantly what this was and followed suit. Early in their romance, there had been a night they shared the shower and Lacy being playful showed him "how guppies kissed." Puffing up her cheeks and when their lips met then raspberried. The resemblance was more like a pufferfish than a guppie, but that was part of the silliness.

They both had their cheeks puffed up, then raspberried out when their lips met. "Guppie kisses," they said in unison.

An odd thing.

* * *

Hour eight. Dex was handling the flight controls manually. Lacy was in the rear preparing their gear. She laid the Planetary Exploration Suits on the starboard side bunk, then looked through the storage container above, planning out what to take.

"What should I pack with the P.E.Ss?" She asked. Dex cocked his head slightly to the right but kept his eyes forward. "Pack light," he said. "I don't think we're gonna have a whole hell of a lot to explore. Maybe a cave if we're lucky. But I still don't see any readings for life on the rock. Plant or animal. Just load up both the flashlights and some water. And grab the laser cutter. I wanna get some samples of whatever it is this rock is made of."

Lacy did as she was asked.

As they approached Prullen-1, Dex felt the controls get tougher. It took more and more strength with every passing moment for him to keep the ship steady.

He called to her, trying to hide the strain he was feeling at the helm, "Baby, I'm going to need you up front!"

Lacy dropped what she was doing and jumped to her seat. "What can I do to assist, sir?" She asked, trying to make up for the tension in his voice with a little playful heart.

"Prepare the landing gear. We might be coming in a little hot." On any other planet, and at this speed, this would have been the point where Dex and Lacy would be seeing heat coming off the bow. Dex did what he could to reduce speed, but the gravitational pull got stronger by the second, faster than he was able to adjust.

"Landing gear is good to deploy," Lacy announced.

"Not yet, don't want to crush them on landing. Just want it ready to go."

"How about some mood music?"

Dex shrugged, "Whatever sounds best to you."

Lacy flipped through the library quickly. "How

about this?"

Pines of Rome by Ottorino Respighi began to play.

Dex laughed awkwardly, but his lightheartedness was broken by a jolt in the ship's controls.

They were nearly on top of the rock. Sweat started to break out on Dex's forehead, but he was doing all he could to keep his cool. Partially for his own sake, but mostly because in his mind he was still trying to impress Lacy with a calm and collected demeanor. As Prullen-1 got closer though, he couldn't help but worry more. He had decent control of the ship, but it was hurtling toward the exoplanet far too quickly. They had to reduce speed quickly or their anniversary would be cut far too short.

"Shift all thrusters in reverse." He commanded Lacy.

"Righto, preparing to-" she began but the ship lurched violently and Dex cut her off.

"Don't prepare, just *do* it!"

She was taken aback, and for the first time that day, her smile dropped. Her training kicked in, and she reverted to her military bearing. She did as was commanded by her superior officer.

Lacy punched in the commands to shift the thrusters, but without time for them to adjust, they felt a massive *CRUNCH!* from somewhere in the rear of the ship. The lights in the main cabin flickered for a moment. Through the viewport, they could see fumes and the tips of the flames of the forward thrusters shooting out ahead of them.

"We're losing speed," Dex announced. "Should be on the ground in less than two minutes."

Just then an alarm went off that sounded almost

loud enough to destroy both of their ears. They both looked toward the center console. A red banner flashed quickly telling them, "FIRE IN THE ENGINE ROOM."

Before Dex could say anything, Lacy was out of her chair and racing to the engine room. "I got it!" She called to him. "I'll be back for the landing gear, just try to hold it steady till then."

She hadn't noticed, but as soon as Dex read the fire notification, the sweat started streaming more profusely. Lacy had no idea how hard he had been fighting the controls. One wrong move and he was sure to throw them off their course. They would most definitely make it to the surface at this point, but on which side of the ship would it be? And how much damage would there be to fix? And at the speed they had been going, would they even be alive to fix it?

That last problem may have been solved, but now with the engine on fire, how badly had that been damaged? Would there be enough working parts to get off this rock? Would Prullen-1 be their doom?

Happy anniversary, he thought to himself.

In the engine room, Lacy was scrambling to put out a fire that was slowly crawling toward the rear wall. Between two drawn out bursts with the extinguisher, she smacked a hand on the wall intercom to send a message to Dex.

"Captain! Captain, can you hear me?"

Dex responded from the command console but kept his focus on the descent. In another minute and a half, they'd be on the ground in any condition ranging from moderately okay to totally and completely screwed.

"I hear you," he said. The strain was more than

apparent in his voice.

"We have to vent this place! The fire's too big! If we want to save anything on this ship we have to vent, now!"

A minute twenty left. If they vented, the engines would be inoperable for too long. They would surely crash fatally with this trajectory. If they didn't vent, he knew, they'd land most likely in one piece, but they'd never get back off the rock.

A minute ten. "Dex! Dex what are your orders?" Lacy screamed through the intercom over the sounds of the raging flames.

Dex was lost. Either choice was the wrong one but he had to make one. An idea clicked. "Lacy! Baby, get out of there! I'll vent!"

"I copy!" Lacy called back. She gave up on the extinguisher and dashed out of the room, locking it behind her. She ran up the hall, ensured the door to the main cabin was locked behind her, and raced back into her seat.

Fifty-five seconds until impact. Lacy strapped in but Dex couldn't afford to take his hands off the controls.

"Venting now," Lacy announced and put in the commands on the console to vent the air out of the engine room. The next window she brought up showed live feed from the room and outside the ship. The fire was diminishing with the lack of air. But it was at this point Dex truly lost control.

Dex looked over at her screen and saw exactly what he had hoped for. "We just might make it out of this one," he told her.

In the center of the console, she saw the gyroscope had recognized a gravitational pull from Prullen-1. Ever so slowly, their angle of descent was increasing, and they were listing slightly to the left. "What's happening?" She asked Dex.

"The vent is angled. The force of the flames and air ejecting is nudging the trajectory. With any luck, we'll land on our side instead of the nose, and save the engine."

Twenty-five seconds. The surface of the exoplanet was taking up their entire window now. Lacy grabbed Dex's hand as tight as she could. So much so, that it began to hurt, and her nails were digging into his skin. But he pulled her hand to his mouth and kissed it again, and this time he prayed, *oh God... please save our goddamned butts!* As soon as pseudo-prayer was thought and given out unto the universe, they noticed the smallest sliver of black space creep into the window.

Fifteen seconds. The sky was coming on slowly and the horizon was angled but just maybe they would make it.

Ten seconds. What happened next came in a stroke of lightning. The computer announced the venting was complete and the fire extinguished. Lacy pulled her hand away from Dex's and rushed to get the engine running again. It had to warm up but Dex couldn't wait. Seeing what Lacy had done, before she could make it back out of the hallway, Dex steered the ship upwards as hard as he could with the controls. Lacy was thrust against the cabin floor with the sudden increase of gravity, but she pushed on, almost crawling to her seat, until gravity lightened and she could reach something to hold onto on the wall.

Their angle of descent leveled out just the littlest bit more. Dex screamed through his gritted teeth with determination as he tried to save them from their doom. Lacy threw herself behind the starboard side bunk to brace for the crash, and covered her eyes.

Impact. With a deafening boom, they hit the surface. Lacy screamed in terror and felt her full weight press against the bunk wall; her stomach rising in her throat. A rock slammed into the window and left a small crack.

As they hit the ground, Dex slammed with full force into the console, hitting his head on the edge of the computer screen, leaving a gash in his forehead just above his left eyebrow.

Lacy was struggling to breathe. The pressure on her chest from the sudden decrease of motion to almost a complete halt and her racing heartbeat nearly threw her into an anxiety attack. She tried to slow her breathing and gradually came back to a calm state.

Dex, slowly coming out of a state of shock, with blood dripping along his face and into his left eye, felt relief at least that they never put the landing gear down. It would have been completely torn off or torn to shreds on impact. Now the bay doors for the landing gear would be jammed or wrecked, but at least fixable.

They slid for maybe a half mile before the *Silent Horizon* came to a full stop. Alarms were going off like crazy in the main cabin. The feed from the engine room showed that a fire had started again. Dex began to stand up to take action, but Lacy was up faster than him and called across the cabin for him to stay where he was. She would get the medical kit on her way back.

As he moved, he felt a jolt of pain in his core. *Most likely a broken rib*, he thought.

The fire in the engine room was much smaller this time. Lacy used the extinguisher to douse it and, once the smoke had cleared, she saw the thick glass pod that covered the engine had a chunk missing. Small pieces of glass were all over the place. A terrible smell was coming from the engine itself, and though it was spinning, its motions were about to go ape, sputtering viciously here and there. She knew it was fixable, but it would take time. Right now though, she had to care for Dex.

She walked cautiously back to the cabin, but her legs were shaking and she had to keep a hand on the wall to keep her balance. Her breathing still felt restrained, but she didn't know what condition Dex was in. She retrieved the medical kit from the locker where the space suits were kept.

Kneeling beside Dex, she unwrapped some of the gauze and applied it to his forehead.

"Hold this," she said tenderly.

"I'm sorry," he breathed, as if every word he spoke threatened to tear his lungs apart.

She felt his core for broken ribs. "For what?" she asked, trying to force a laugh like none of this was a big deal in the slightest.

"I shouldn't have yelled like that."

At that, she didn't have to force the laughter. "Darling, right now I don't think your tone in that whole... mess, is our biggest issue. But you *can* apologize for that god-awful landing."

He laughed back at that but was cut off by the pain caused by his broken ribs. "At least we landed. This rock can't break us that easily."

Lacy smiled but said nothing.

"Hey." Dex reached out a feeble hand to lift up her chin.

Lacy looked up to lock eyes with him.

"Happy anniversary," he said.

As Lacy applied medical aid to her husband, something below the surface was alerted to their crash.

2. Prullen - 1

Dex dictated his log into the ship's computer between painful breaths of air.

Lacy was in the engine room cleaning up from the explosion while Dex finished his oh-so-important Captain's Tasks before they could get out and explore the rock. The room still felt about 120 degrees due to the fire. At least five times a minute, she would wipe the sweat from her face with the blouse she'd taken off and tied around her waist. She tried not to think too much about what was waiting outside for them, but there was far too much excitement in the air. But in the meantime, she could clean up and get a reading on how much repair the *Silent Horizon*'s engine would need.

The outer hull was almost entirely destroyed, though, that wouldn't hinder the ship's performance. The *Silent Horizon*, and other spacecraft of its kind, had been designed with an inner and outer hull. The outer protected the craft from hazardous space debris and small-scale asteroids, while protecting the inner hull which prevented oxygen from escaping even if the outer hull was damaged, as well as other fumes that could be recycled back into the ship's engine.

The engine itself, however, had been strained nearly to a breaking point in their landing attempt. It would run again, but only after what Lacy estimated to be another day.

Covered in sweat, and hands stained and cut up by glass and grease, Lacy decided she'd waited long enough. She was now more than just itching to get outside their claustrophobic ship for the first time in over a year. She wiped her hands on her pants and then called to Dex through the intercom.

"Hey, baby, I've done what I can for now. This thing won't be able to fly for at least another day or so. And since we're in no real rush... are you about ready to go for a walk?"

Dex paused the log when he heard her voice. Activating the comms on his end, he responded, "Just about. Was almost done recording, then we can get suited up." He sat back.

"Dex, if you're not up to it... If you're in too much pain, it's okay." She was trying to sound considerate.

"Think I'm gonna let you have all the fun, darling? This is a moment that'll go down in the books. We'll share it together. Just let me finish this up, take some painkillers, and we'll get going."

Instead of words, he heard the sound of her blowing him a kiss over the comm. He smiled to himself then spun his chair around to retrieve a pill bottle from the nearby cabinet. Dex popped two pills in his mouth, then a third after feeling a sharp pain in his side.

After waiting half a moment for the pills to kick in, Dex resumed his log. "It seems we're about to leave the ship for the... harsh... desolate... awe-inspiring and soul-crushing plains of Prullen-1. Maybe by the time we get back, we'll have a better name for this rock."

The hallway door opened, and Lacy walked

through. Dex swiveled around in his chair. He saw her there, wearing just her skivvies on top, a blouse wrapped around her hips, and covered in sweat. Exploring out on the exoplanet suddenly seemed much less interesting.

"Sure you don't wanna spend just a little more time on the ship?" He stood to walk toward her. "Who knows what dangers are out there?" he said with a smile as he put his hands on her sides to pull her closer. "Could be the last moment like this we have together."

As he went in for a kiss, she put her hand on his chest and bit her lip just the littlest bit. With a light, airy voice, she teased him, "Sounds like fun but..." She rotated her body toward the P.E.S. laid out on the bed but kept facing him. "This sounds like a lot more." She tipped her head up slightly and teased him with her eyes as she walked away to suit up.

"Not even gonna shower first?" He asked.

"Baby, right now nothing could stop me from going out there." She unwrapped her blouse from her hips and then slid down her pants. Dex followed suit, and soon they were checking each other's gear to make sure everything was squared away and in the right place on their belts.

"Water pack full?" He asked.

"Check."

"Flashlight?"

"Check."

"Laser-cutter?"

"Check. Guppie kisses?"

He gave her a guppy kiss. They laughed together for a moment, and he kissed her forehead. Then he looked over her suit. "You're all squared away. Nothing unsecured. Check me?"

He rotated slowly as she inspected his suit. "You're all set. You sure you don't want to bring this?" She handed him their one blaster. "You've got better aim than I do. You got lucky with that score on range qual day, but you also did better than I every time before then."

"No sign of any life on this rock."

"Prullen-1." She corrected with a smile.

He exhaled with fake annoyance.

"There's no sign of any life on Prullen-1, Lieutenant."

She giggled and saw her breath fog up her helmet just in front of her mouth.

Dex continued, "Just extra weight. We'll save our storage space for all the cool rocks we find."

She shrugged and placed the blaster back into the storage container above his bunk.

"And when we get back," he reached out to a medical scanning device in the container and held it up in front of Lacy. "Full scans. I don't want to carry anything toxic or radioactive back to Earth with us."

"Roger, sir," Lacy said with a joking salute.

Dex took a deep breath, which hurt just a bit because of his broken ribs, then said, "I guess it's time to head out."

* * *

The airlock opened with a hiss. It wasn't as regal as Dex and Lacy had hoped it would be. No onlookers were watching the arrival of the aliens. No fireworks or parades to welcome them. Without a show, and with a bad crash, Dex found their first steps onto Prullen-1 disappointing.

The ramp that ejected from the base of the airlock was designed for a level surface. With the nose of the ship stuck in the ground, the base of the ramp hovered about a foot over the surface.

Lacy was the first to leave the ship, followed closely by Dex, who held her hand. The sensors on the gloves of their P.E.S.s simulated the feel of each other's hands, so it felt like they weren't wearing gloves at all. As a husband first and an astronaut second, it was one of Dex's favorite advancements in modern technology.

Lacy was speechless from the view, now unobstructed by the ship's window. On the ship, they may as well have been watching television, or one of those virtual reality roller coasters on Coney Island. But this truly was stepping into a brand new world. Though the surface was bland and wavy like grey sand dunes, she knew in her heart this exoplanet was the beginning of something incredible. Whether it was the first in a long string of planets they were to find or, as she believed in her heart, Prullen-1 itself held all the mystery they were looking for.

Dex was as far on the opposite end of the spectrum of imagination as one could be.

Lacy turned her head to look back at him. As she did, a distant star reflected on her visor. It sparkled in her blue eyes just as they locked with his. His care for the exoplanet or what would come next disappeared. He was here, far from all other life, far from all worries. Nothing in his whole universe mattered except for the woman he loved. And oh, how beautiful she looked. He fell in love all over again.

They said nothing but exchanged a small laugh, the kind that's more of an exhale than a laugh, but both parties involved know that's better communication than any combination of words.

Dex and Lacy stepped off together down the ramp. The gravity was not so very different from Earth's. They felt about ten pounds lighter, but Dex still helped her down from the edge of the ramp.

The sands of Prullen-1 felt so peculiar to them from the moment they stepped down.

"You feel that?" Dex asked.

Lacy knelt and scooped up a handful of the sand. "It's got the right consistency of Earth's sand," she said as she sifted it through her fingers into Dex's hand.

"If it's sand, why does the ground feel so... spongey?" They both looked at their feet, where they noticed clear indentations in the ground like they were stepping on the world's largest mattress.

"E-tool?" Lacy asked.

Dex nodded. He did a 180 and a small hop back onto the ramp, then walked toward the airlock.

Inside the ship, he rummaged through the storage above his bunk to find the E-tool, a highly convenient tool that worked as a shovel or blade - or weapon if they were truly desperate - and folded into itself for easy mobility.

Just a minute after leaving Lacy, Dex was back outside, but there was no sign of his wife.

"Lacy?" He asked the empty world and received no response.

He jumped off the side of the ramp and landed comfortably on the spongy surface, sand flying up to about knee height around him.

"Lacy, where are you?" He asked, concern growing steadily in his voice.

She stepped out from behind the port side of the ship. Her steps made the softest sounds in the sand.

"Dex? I'm just over here!"

He spun toward her. "Sorry, I thought-"

"Thought what?" She smiled with her hands on her hips. "Thought I'd already gotten lost?"

They walked toward each other, Dex ducking under the high end of the ramp.

"Possibly," he said. "Could've rushed off into one of this planet's many lush forests."

Lacy brought her hand up to the part of her helmet in front of her mouth and laughed.

"No," she said. "I don't think we'll be traveling very far. Especially with the ship in this condition." She pointed her hand toward the base of the ship. "We're gonna have to do a little bit of digging on top of engine repairs before we fly again. Never thought I'd find myself actually lodged into a planet."

Dex let out a deep sigh. "Thank God we got one of the smaller ships." He began to walk around the perimeter of the *Silent Horizon*, inspecting the damage to the hull, led by Lacy.

"Really, the damage is only cosmetic," she told him. "Scratches here and there, but no tears. This sand isn't as coarse as it is back home. The nose is the real problem." They bounced forward, taking advantage of the slightly lower gravity. She pointed to the antenna, their biggest problem. "The metal housing on the antenna is strong enough, but it's deep in there, almost the full three meters. I don't know if it really is damaged. It's not like we can test it out and call home. So that's gotta be dug out before we even boot up the engine. If it's only being held together by a thread, I can probably fix it, but if not, no communication with Earth until we're back on it." She looked up at him for some sort of acknowledgment.

He thought for a moment, then asked, "Is there anything in such critical condition that it needs immediate attention? Antenna's not going anywhere, right?"

"No, it's nice and cozy stuck in the ground." She told him with her hands on her hips.

"Copy. Well, tonight you start working on the engine again, and I'll stay out here digging this out and pulling security."

She crossed her arms and raised an eyebrow at the idea.

"At ease, Lieutenant. You're too cute to be giving me that look when we're supposed to be professionals."

She smiled. "Roger, Sir. So does that mean it's time to go out?"

He placed his hands on the sides of her helmet as if to touch her cheeks. The sensors picked up the texture and coldness (automatically adjusted to be a more comfortable temperature by his gloves), and he wished it could sense through that and simulate the feel of her skin. He then leaned in as if kissing her forehead.

"Time for an adventure."

An hour and twenty-seven minutes after "landing" on Prullen-1, Dex and Lacy began their journey across the grey sand of their own private rock. Nighttime didn't exist here. The planet was cold but illuminated by the vast sea of stars that surrounded them, and some small suns far and away. No matter how long they walked, they never got over the strangeness of the ground just below the surface layer of sand.

They had dug about three feet deep around the antenna before leaving, but found nothing except more sand. If there were something below the surface, creating the spongy mattress effect, it wouldn't have been that far down. Dex was more and more determined with every scoop to find something, but Lacy was itching to leave. She believed with every fiber of her being that something was out there beyond the dunes.

For the first three miles or so, nothing. They had stopped once to have a drink. On the suit's right forearm was a series of buttons. One to magnetize their boots in zero gravity situations, one to activate their internal comms, one to clear their visors if they got foggy, and one to activate a straw in their helmet that ejected from the liner on the neck and came perfectly to their mouths.

In the lower gravity, it was taking less energy to walk over long distances, but Dex couldn't get his mind off the repairs the ship needed. And with nothing else happening on Prullen-1, it was hard to think of anything else. The initial excitement had worn off a mile back.

Lacy, though, was still enthusiastic. After every dune they crossed over, she would call to him, "Just one more dune! I know we'll find something!"

He never had the heart to tell her that he had his doubts. But now he was beginning to consider that maybe she was right about there being other planets close by, now that they'd found the first. And there were hopefully better odds that they'd find the others more interesting than this one.

Another two miles before they turn around, he told himself, realizing they'd probably circle the whole planet before actually retreating. And then once that lap was complete, she'd want to circle the perpendicular lap.

Under Lacy's optimism, though, one thing nagged at her mind she wasn't quite comfortable with sharing yet. *Someone's watching*, she thought. Maybe that was why she was so confident in carrying on. From the moment they'd left the ship, she'd felt eyes on her. And they didn't belong to her husband. But there were no sounds, no shifts in the sands or winds from any direction telling her who or what was watching. Maybe a satellite farther off into space. The eye of a distant alien spying on them from another solar system. Whatever it was, though, the tiniest voice in the back of her mind told her she was in someone's line of sight. But the optimism and excitement of discovery overpowered it. The warning voice was muted down to nothing more than a dog whistle to a young adult. It was just barely a perceptible frequency.

Just before mile four, at the top of one of Prullen-1's many dunes, Lacy stopped in her tracks.

"Find something?" Dex asked, trying to hide the sass in his voice with fake optimism.

"Dex, I know you're tired of this, but I think your patience has finally paid off."

Dex took a few steps to catch up with her, and when he did, he was overwhelmingly... disappointed. More sand.

More... God damned... SAND. He shouted internally but kept a calm face.

"Do you see it?" Lacy asked with the widest eyes.

"No, Lacy," Dex replied, the irritation seeping through his feigned curiosity. "What is it I'm supposed to be seeing?"

"Oh, come on! Look! Tell me you don't see it!"

Dex studied the landscape for half a minute before he began to understand what Lacy was talking about. How she was able to notice it so quickly was beyond him. His eyes began to widen all the same. Over the miles of Prullen-1's surface they'd inspected, the dune's size, shape, and frequency had been as natural as hamburgers and beer on the Fourth of July. But here, there was a clearing, perfectly rounded with what seemed to be one continuous dune. They looked into the crater of sand and were amazed by the ecological anomaly.

"It has to be man-made," Lacy said.

"Well, not man-made," Dex corrected. "But I suppose it is unlikely this formed naturally. I mean, if it's a crater, you'd expect there to be some debris in the center that pushed all the sand away. But even then, the perimeter is so perfect."

"Think it's time to dig again?" She held out a hand for Dex to hand her the E-tool. "Maybe something did crash."

"If something did..." He looked her dead in the eye. No romance this time. If anything, she thought she caught a glimpse of fear. "Who buried it?"

Trying to alleviate the tension of Dex's ominous question, Lacy tried to laugh it off, but for once, even she felt truly uncomfortable in their situation. The laugh came out weak and did nothing to help them feel better.

"Well," Dex started, looking back into the crater. "What are we here for if not to explore?" He took the first step into the crater and Lacy withdrew her hand.

The ground felt the same as the rest of the planet, but now it was like stepping on holy ground. A chill came over Dex, which nearly caused him to lose his footing. The crater itself was only about three feet deep from the top of the perimeter, but had a diameter of about ten meters.

As Dex neared the center. He looked back and saw Lacy waiting patiently at the top of the hill to see what would happen. He gave her a nod, signaling all was okay, then unlatched the E-tool from his belt and extended it. At full length it was only about two feet long, and he had to kneel to use it.

Dex stabbed once into the ground and lifted a small mound of grey sand. Some of the surrounding sand slid into the hole he'd made, but it was a start. He stabbed again and excavated more. Nothing. Another scoop, and another, and another. Nothing. No debris, no rocks, no nothing, no how. But it was the first sign of anything remotely interesting on this planet. Though Dex was losing patience, he didn't want to let Lacy down or give up on her hopes, so he kept digging. He scooped faster and faster, channeling the growing annoyance he had into the power of his scoops until one thrust too hard into an unexpected guest.

Pain shot up through his right arm. He could have sworn it was an electric shock.

Lacy shouted behind him in shock and raised her hands to cover her mouth, forgetting her helmet was in the way. "Dex! Are you okay?" Panic quickly rose in her heart.

Dex gritted his teeth and the pain dissolved. "Fine! I'm fine! Just stay up there. I think I found something, but... just stay for a sec."

It couldn't have been electric, he thought. *Just too much force into a hard surface.* Regardless, whatever he hit was unknown. And if it was dangerous, he didn't want Lacy around to get hurt.

Instead of digging more, he collapsed the E-tool and re-clipped it to his belt. He then brushed away the sand to find what he'd hit. About two feet under the surface, he found he was wiping sand off a hard metallic surface. Inspecting it, he realized the E-tool had made no dent or even a scratch on the metal. Even more amazingly, it was smooth. Unnaturally smooth and perfectly flat.

He brushed more sand away and eventually scooped some more up with his hands to reveal more of the surface area of the strange sub-surface metal until he revealed a line. A perfectly straight and deep line in the metal.

"Lacy!" Dex shouted.

"What is it? Can I come down?" Dex considered. He wanted her in on the discovery, but he knew something was wrong. Nothing this perfect came naturally. He needed to know it was safe before she came down.

"No! No, not yet, just... just toss me the laser cutter."

Lacy unlatched the laser cutter from her belt and tossed it toward Dex. For once, her time on her high school's softball team paid off.

Dex caught the perfect throw and lowered the tool to the metal. Just a few inches before making contact, Dex felt another electrical tingle like a forcefield trace up his arm. He retreated a few inches and then pushed through. The electric sensation started up again, but he needed to know what was causing it. Right on top of the surface, he activated the laser, and a bolt of pain shot through him again, this time knocking him on his ass, and sending the cutter flying a few feet away.

He cursed in pain, which Lacy took as a sign to

help him. But as she took her first step into the crater, the ground moved. No, the planet moved. They were both knocked to the ground and heard creaking and booming underneath them.

Dex got to his feet as quickly as he could and raced toward Lacy.

"Get out of here!" He shouted, but after the first few steps, he felt the ground moving underneath him. It was pulling him closer toward the center.

He could no longer run; the sand was shifting too much underneath him. Looking back at the center of the crater, Dex saw that where that perfect line had been, there was now a bigger one, reaching the whole length of the crater into which the sand fell. The ground was opening underneath them, and Dex couldn't pick himself up.

Lacy didn't fare any better. As hard as she tried to crawl back up the perimeter, the sand kept pulling her toward the opening. She screamed in fear, and Dex could do nothing to help.

The crevice was drawing closer to him, and he could see on the opposite side of the growing crevice that as the sand on top of the metal began to diminish, poles were coming out of the metal that gave him the immediate thought of a bank vault.

It can't be! he thought, and the thought had cost him. He hadn't realized in the time it took for him to stop and think, he'd fallen back with the sand that was at the lip of the pit. He came to the realization just in time and before he fell, grabbed hold of the empty slot the poles had come out of.

"Lacy! Get out of here! Run!"

But she couldn't hear him over the sound of the

machinery working underneath them. She was still doing all she could to just keep her balance. When she was able to stand, she realized there was no longer a slope up to the perimeter anymore, but a wall left behind from all of the sand that had fallen away. She couldn't escape, and now there were only about five feet between the wall and the edge of the pit. She had to work fast. If it were a door, it only opened so far, and it was fair to assume the perimeter of the crater was that endpoint. She pushed away the sand as fast as she could until she found a raised platform. When there was enough space, she stood on it and prayed to keep her balance. With the door moving closer to her, she saw her husband hanging on for dear life and realized then just how fast a heart could beat without exploding.

The door came to a halt. There was Dex, hanging on to the inside of the door, and Lacy, on a one-by-one platform just above him. The wall of sand around her was still about four feet high, and the wrong move would send her down into the abyss from an avalanche.

"Dex! Just hold on a moment, I'll get you up!"

"I'm holding! Just be quick!" The gloves were doing nothing to help his grip. They were designed for basic protection and accessibility in unknown environments, not rock climbing.

Lacy moved quickly, first activating her magnetized boots from her forearm pad. Then she began knocking away the sand to her left, pushing it into the abyss. It was a fast process, and the one-by-one space soon became a one-by-two.

"Lacy, hurry!" Dex was never one to win a weightlifting competition, but in times of crisis, most people will find untapped strength within themselves. Dex was finding this strength, but it was diminishing quickly.

Back on top, Lacy had cleared enough space to safely kneel. "Okay! Grab my hand!" She reached toward him, but Dex wouldn't reach back.

"I- I can't!" He shouted. Lacy reached further down, trying to grab his hand, so desperately clinging to life. As soon as she made the slightest contact with his right hand, it shot up and grabbed her forearm.

"Okay, work with me now!" She said, trying to be gentle. The adrenaline had helped, but now Dex was feeling the pain in his side. He took deep breaths, trying to ignore the pain, but it was flaring up too intensely. Under the helmet, he was sweating profusely and fogging up the visor.

"Almost there!" Lacy reassured him.

Dex's heart beat rapidly. Vertigo threatened to take over him as they struggled to pull him up to safety.

Once in a safe place, they both took a moment to breathe and clear their visors.

Dex was the first to break the silence. "I guess I should have thought of the boots sooner, huh?"

Part of her wanted to hit Dex for being so casual after almost plummeting to his death, but it was a laugh of relief that escaped her. Lacy fell into his embrace and laughed with him, as a few small tears leaked out.

Neither one of them knew how to comprehend the situation. What do you say after such a thing?

Hey, honey, want to check out this deep, dark vault that someone obviously lives in? he thought to himself. *Why not? Could be fun!* Or if they went back to the ship, *Well, that was fun, good mission, darlin', now back to Earth and tell them we bailed at the first sight of anything!*

Dex put his hand at the base of her helmet, what would've been her chin, and raised her head. "Everything's going to be all right now."

Dex knew it was a lie, for as soon as the words came out, a voice from across the pit shouted, "Identify yourselves!"

3. Royal Void Outpost-19

They couldn't believe their ears. There was no way someone was actually talking to them! Lacy shook her head nervously, her terrified expression toward Dex unbreakable. But the voice came again.

"Identify yourselves or we will fire!" It was a deep artificial-sounding voice, like someone was speaking through a megaphone.

Dex pulled Lacy in closer toward him, shielding her eyes from whatever was there with them. He looked around and in the center of the now open crater, he saw a large hovering platform with three figures occupying it. They looked like robots to Dex, wearing all-black suits of armor. The only color was a thin purple strip across the face, where he could only guess was how they saw anything. Otherwise, there were no identifying marks on their suits. They were so polished and clean. There were no breaks or joints, it was like the suit was their whole being. There wasn't even a holster for the blasters they held pointed at them.

"This is your final warning!"

Without hesitation, Dex mustered all the courage in him and raised his hands in surrender. "My name is Captain Dex Prullen! Pilot of the *Silent Horizon*! With me is my wife, Lieutenant Lacy Prullen!"

There was a moment of silence from the dark figures, then, "From what colony do you hail? Answer quickly or be annihilated."

Dex and Lacy exchanged a look of confusion. "No... no colony... sir!" Dex eked out.

The robotic figure who led the others looked at the two others as if in confirmation, but their blasters never fell away from Dex and Lacy. A moment of silence passed, then a bridge extended out toward where they stood.

"Step toward us. Move quickly," the lead said.

Dex and Lacy stood their ground. Lacy fell back a little behind Dex's arm. "How about you identify yourselves first!"

Instantly, Dex regretted his words. The figure to the lead's right flicked a switch on the blaster with his thumb and pulled the trigger. A surge of pain rang in Dex's head crippling him. He fell to the ground on all fours. Dex thanked God the bridge had come out to meet them, or he'd surely be falling to his doom.

The leader spoke again. "This is your final warning."

Lacy helped Dex to his feet. His legs felt brittle, with tiny prickles running along the soles of his feet and up his calves.

"Let's do as they say, darling," Lacy warned quietly. "I'm sure we'll be alright. Let's just go."

They stepped toward the dark figures slowly. The blasters maintained their focus on their heads, not even swaying an inch. When they reached the robot-like figures, the two on the sides moved in a flash of lightning.

Their blasters were lowered to their hips and assimilated into the suits. They both placed a hand on Dex and Lacy's shoulders and shoved them onto all fours.

The leader spoke, "In the name of the God Emperor of the Void, you are under arrest for trespassing and laying siege to Void military territory."

The descent into the abyss was brief but pitch black. Once it had begun, the door closed above them, and they could only now see the purple lines across their captors' visors.

Lacy opened her mouth to speak to Dex, but their captors sensed it coming. Before a single breath escaped her lips she felt the butt of one of the blasters crash into her spine.

Her body spasmed as pain shocked her entire system.

Dex's initial instinct was to fight off his captors, but he was kept restrained on the ground. Instead, he mouthed to Lacy, *Don't worry, we'll be alright.*

Even the act of mouthing the words had become pointless before his lips ever moved. As he did, he watched their captors put a device on Lacy's helmet and felt a little bump against his own. It was a small metal cylinder, about two inches long, with a suction cup device sticking to the helmet. As soon as it was attached, he realized he was unable to make any sound. And not only that, but when he looked at Lacy's mouth, it seemed to be clouded over. Like he was looking at an out-of-focus picture.

"Prisoners will refrain from speaking unless given permission."

They were terrified. Dex saw a tear stream from his wife's eye. It was a certainty that their captors had complete dominance in this situation, but a small part of him tried to convince the rest of his mind to fight back, though he knew it would only get them killed more quickly if that wasn't the plan already. And that thought alone fueled his fear and quelled his delusions of grandeur.

He had to stay brave for her. If he couldn't tell her, he could show her, everything would be alright without resorting so quickly to violence. Unable to speak, Dex softened his face so that Lacy could see the calm in his eyes.

Lacy was quick to pick up the expression on his face and what he was trying to tell her, but her breathing was slow to match his calm.

The platform came to a halt, and a door slid open in front of them. A blinding light came in, and there stood another of the robotic figures behind a tall desk, with the same black suit and purple line across their eyes.

Dex and Lacy were lifted by their captors and shoved forward.

In the same semi-robotic voice as the rest of their captors, the desk guard asked, "Identification?"

Unable to give a name or title to this new foe, the first connection Dex and Lacy had made was to military police officers stationed at the gates of army posts they had once worked on. This did nothing to comfort the two Earthlings, and if anything, made them resent the "gate guard" by association.

"Spies, or saboteurs. From a region called *Silent Horizon*. They refused to answer further."

The gate guard typed something into a panel on his desk. The captors waited patiently for a response, and Dex and Lacy's eyes darted back and forth. They stood in a tunnel that seemed to be made of pure light. He then looked back up. "Take them to cell block 1138. The next transport back to Golloch is in two days' time. Until then,

I'll schedule them for interrogation. Carry on."

The leader stepped forward past Dex and Lacy to lead the way. The two others shoved them forward down the corridor.

There was no end in sight, and no markers on the wall telling them where to go or where they were. Eventually, the lead just stopped, did a right-facing movement, and placed his hand on the wall. A blue light appeared as an outline of a door, then was pulled back and slid up. He gave Dex a shove in the back, ordering him to move.

Dex knew he couldn't speak to Lacy, so he did the first thing that came to mind. He swirled his head quickly to lock eyes with her, then puffed up his cheeks. It told Lacy everything she wished she could hear. *I'll be ok. I'll see you soon. I love you.*

Dex was shoved again and followed by one of the black-suited figures through the door. It shut promptly behind them. He tried to rush to escape, but his captor raised a hand and, like pushing over a child, shoved him to the ground.

"Stay down," the electronic voice told him without any emotion in its voice.

Dex tried to shout, but the device on his helmet wouldn't allow for it. He instead tried to stand, but faster than he could get to his feet, the guard drew its blaster from his suit.

"*Stand down!*" The voice shouted now. It felt loud enough to shake the room. Dex clutched the sides of his helmet in pain, trying to cover his ears, and again felt his ribs hurting him. "Now, disrobe. And don't try anything."

As if this was any crazier than anything else that had happened to them, Dex was still taken aback by the demand.

"None shall wear the Emperor's colors. Remove them now or suffer more," the robotic man ordered, gesturing his weapon at Dex's scarlet P.E.S.

Dex complied and was happy to do so when it meant the voice suppression device would come off. He twisted his helmet an inch to the left and air hissed out, telling him it had come far enough. He lifted it off his head and, though he didn't want to risk trying it, he knew his voice had come back. He then continued with the rest of the suit, taking off his belt first, then zipping down from his left shoulder to his right thigh. After taking his arms out of his sleeves, he let the suit fall to the ground and kicked his feet out.

Standing there in his skivvies, he realized just how cold it was. There was no cot in the cell to sleep on, and no blankets. Not even a toilet.

Without a word, the robotic man picked up Dex's P.E.S. and left the room.

There was no indication of just how long he would have to wait for... for what?

Interrogation? he thought. *Torture? What do I have to hide? Did he really call me a spy? Who in the hell would I be spying on? And Lacy... if they hurt her, I'll... I'll tear this whole place apart!*

But what could he do? He was standing in an empty room with nothing but his underwear, against enemies who most likely weren't even human, and moved with incredible speed. If only he could get his hands on one of those suits. He thought that maybe he could knock one of the robotic men out the next time they came in. If it were just a suit, he could wear it and try to break Lacy out of this prison. But once they did, how would they get back to the ship? What was to say these guys didn't already get to the *Silent Horizon* and start scrapping it? So many questions were running around in his head, but most importantly, he wondered, *Where's Lacy?*

* * *

As the door to Dex's cell shut and disappeared back into the wall, Lacy was shoved forward by the two robotic men. They walked about another fifty feet before stopping, and a door appeared for them. Lacy entered without having to be pushed, followed by one of her captors, and the door shut behind them. She was given the same orders as Dex and put up less resistance.

Scooping up her clothes, the robotic man turned to leave. The door opened as he began to move, as if it had sensed he was coming.

Lacy wanted to say something, ask about Dex, or at least be told what was happening to them, but she held her tongue, not wanting to instigate her captors further.

* * *

Once the doors were closed, time became irrelevant. The lights in their rooms never turned off. No outside noises were creeping their way in, and though they banged on the doors and walls, no one ever answered. It was like they had been abandoned in this pristine prison. The only sign of time passing for Dex was a five o'clock shadow. If nothing else, they would let their bodies do the work telling time for them, granted they let their sleep cycle take and release them naturally.

Lacy was the first to go. She had recognized after the first few hours (though it felt like a full day), they would be attended to on their captor's time. Dex, on the other hand, wanted to stay alert to whatever would happen next. It was his idea that their captors were monitoring them, and if they came back, it'd be while they were asleep. *Easier to handle once we've given up*, he thought. He only hoped Lacy was feeling the same way.

And he had been right. Dex was pushing his body too much, what with the broken ribs and the stressors of being taken prisoner by an unknown enemy. Though he tried fighting it off, his body eventually shut down. Ironically, it was one of the best sleeps he'd had in years.

A short while after he passed out, his cell door opened, and one of the robotic men entered.

* * *

When he opened his eyes again, his retinas were burned by light flooding in. He flinched and immediately felt hands-

Human hands!

press down on his shoulders.

"Easy now," a stern but educated voice said. It brought back a memory for Dex, of a cocky officer he trained alongside back on Earth, whom Dex always detested. That unwanted connection alone made Dex not trust the man. "Just calm yourself, let me do my job."

Dex didn't know what to say. Was it a dream? Was he back on Earth? He slowly began to realize how strange his core felt. Dex began to lift his head, but the voice's hand gently pushed his head back down.

"Trust me, you don't want to see this quite yet," the voice told him.

Dex was regaining full consciousness quickly. "Where... what's going on? Where's Lacy?"

"Not to worry about that now. Once we've finished up here, you'll have plenty of time for questions."

Dex felt a chill on his core. No, not on it... He lifted his head quickly this time and wanted to scream in terror.

He was in an ER. The walls were like the hallway he'd been escorted through, and in each corner was one of the robotic men. Directly past his feet, there was a window where a man, a real flesh-and-blood being with human features, watched the proceedings. But it was what the doctor was doing that scared him the most. Standing on four legs on his abdomen was an empty frame through which Dex looked to see his internal organs.

Dex felt a cry for help stuck in his lungs, and again his head was thrown back by the surgeon's hand.

"Keep quiet now," he said. "You'll be alright, I'm just about through."

Though he wanted to, the scream wouldn't come out. But he was barely able to squeeze out a rough, "What are you doing to me?"

"Helping, sir," the surgeon said. "You've suffered a serious injury, and if you'd *permit me*," he said sternly, "I'm trying to fix you." The surgeon turned to grab a tool that looked like a chrome pop bottle, with a trigger on the top. He pulled the trigger, and a mist sprayed on Dex's now mostly repaired ribs.

Dex felt like screaming again, but realized he felt nothing.

"What is this... thing?" He asked.

"Just a coating," the surgeon replied. "I've done what I can to fix the bones, this just holds everything together until the glue dries." With this, he gave Dex a disingenuous smile, then pressed a button on the top of the framed device.

Dex looked down and saw that within the frame, his skin seemed to grow back.

"Or did you mean this?" The surgeon asked.

Dex nodded.

The surgeon laughed quickly, "Ha ha, modern science at its best, is what it is. Just because you're a spy doesn't mean we won't treat you with respect. No, you'll be in the best shape possible for your interrogation." Another smile, though more ironic than the last.

"Spy? I'm not a spy."

"Of course! Don't worry, I'm just the doctor, you can say whatever you'd like to me, but it won't matter in the end. If you'd like my advice, though, stop fighting the Zar-Mecks." He took a moment with a deep breath. "Well, I've done all I'm good for. Good luck out there, you're in the hands of the Emperor now." He looked over at the window and gave an "all clear" gesture to the man behind the glass. "Soon you'll be off to meet him."

"Him? The Emperor? Who is this Emperor?"

The surgeon turned off the overhead light he'd been using, and Dex was able to get a good look at his face. He had mostly human features, except for his eyes. They were overall the size and shape of his, but the irises leaked into the whites of his eyes like an egg yolk flowing into the whites. "As I said, I'm just the doctor. No need for spy games with me; won't get you anywhere."

The man behind the glass was gone, and the

robotic men, Zar-Mecks as the surgeon called them, drew in close. The surgeon was now holding a data pad and typing something. "You'll be escorted back to your cell until we are ready for you. Good day."

Two of the Zar-Mecks grabbed Dex by his arms and lifted him off the operating table, onto his feet.

He turned his head back to the surgeon to speak, but as soon as his mouth opened, one of the Zar-Mecks punched him in the jaw. "YOU WILL NOT SPEAK UNLESS TOLD TO, SPY." It wasn't a shout, but his volume was intense.

"Excuse me! Gentlemen!" The surgeon again. "Please refrain from your brutality. I just gave all that time mending him, would you be so kind as to not break him again?"

The Zar-Meck who punched Dex was silent for a moment, then turned away to face the wall. An outline appeared as it had with the cell.

Just after they stepped off, a piercing alarm sounded. The Zar-Meck guards holding him showed no reaction past stopping in place, but the sound was brutal for Dex and the surgeon.

The Zar-Meck stood in place like they had fallen asleep standing up, then after ten seconds started walking again, escorting Dex through the doorway and down the hall.

Once through the doorway, a voice came over an unseen speaker system. "INTRUDER... INTRUDER IN SECTION 1-9-7-7... INTRUDER..." This repeated, every phrase separated by about three seconds, then "INTRUDERS... INTRUDERS IN SECTIONS 1-9-5-6... 1-9-6-8... 1-9-7-7... AND 1-9-8-0... INTRUDERS."

At 1-9-7-7, the two lead Zar-Meck raised their blasters from their thigh "holsters." Dex had an idea that he understood what this meant. He was either about to be saved... or killed.

They kept walking, but off somewhere, buried under the blaring alarm, Dex could swear he could hear blast sounds.

The source of the blasts was getting closer until an outline on the wall appeared. A door opened, and in walked a line of clunky grey robots. These were nothing like the slick Zar-Mecks. They stood on two, sometimes three feet, and they looked hobbled together from scrapyard junk. Their arms were massive tangles of wires and metal, and they had tiny heads that were no bigger than Dex's fist, with one antenna sticking out of the top with a green light, acting as an eye. In each hand, they held the biggest blasters Dex had ever seen. They looked like .50 caliber turrets his father manned in the Eurasian War, but they were handled by the robots as if they weighed no more than a .45 Magnum.

As soon as the first of the robots had walked through the doorway, the two Zar-Mecks in the front opened fire. Their aim was incredible, every shot hitting its target. But the blaster bolts seemed to do as much harm as a BB gun. Burn marks stained the junkyard metal, but it did nothing to hinder the behemoths approaching Dex and his captors.

In sync, the Zar-Mecks adapted their aim to fire on the antennas, but as the bolts came close to their target, they ricocheted off a blue shield wrapped tightly around the head of the robots. Nothing was stopping them.

The Zar-Meck in the lead raised its arm, and a

protective barrier ejected from the wall, leaving four small openings for the team to shoot through.

The Zar-Mecks holding Dex's arms stepped in front of him, now acting like his bodyguards, and then they too opened fire. By now, three more of the junkyard bots had entered the hallway on the other side of the barrier. And though they couldn't fire on their enemies, they were determined to kill.

The first junkyard bot to come through ceased its firing. The guns it carried slid up its forearms, and in their place, a metal shell covered its fist. The bot raised its right arm and ran with all its force into the barrier. With one punch, it left a dent extending at least five inches deep. With force like that, Dex thought less and less of his chances of being saved.

Punches kept coming, and the door was beginning to show signs of breaking. In response, one of the Zar-Mecks held out its palm upwards, and an orb grew out of its hand. He tossed it through the hole in the wall, and the four of them ducked in sync. Dex put two and two together and fell to the ground with them.

A blast from the other side of the barrier shook the hallway. The pounding stopped momentarily, and all they were left with was the sound of the alarm.

At that moment, Dex didn't feel like he could carry on. There was too much going on that he didn't understand, and he knew he was caught in a fight between two enemies that probably both wanted him dead. And where was Lacy in all of this? In his confusion and fear, he'd forgotten all about her. Had those junkyard bots gotten to her already? Was she already on her way to this Emperor that the surgeon had mentioned? What was he going to do about it?

With his mind racing, the pounding started again, and he made his choice. The Zar-meck stood up to begin firing again and dropping more grenades through the holes. By now, the other side of the barrier was clouded in smoke, but the Zar-Meck's attention was stuck on it. Dex saw the opportunity and took it. In a flash, he was up on his feet and running in the opposite direction.

All four Zar-Mecks noticed this immediately. One in the rear of the small fighting formation flicked a switch on its blaster, and a blue beam shot out after Dex. He dropped to the floor, dodging it, but immediately after, he felt the Zar-Meck on top of him, boot in his back.

"STAY DOWN." The Zar-Meck ordered.

Adrenaline pumped too quickly for him to sit by idly any longer. The thought of Lacy being in danger made him act. Dex rolled to the right and grabbed the Zar-Meck's leg, yanking him down. When he hit the ground, the right side of the purple visor chipped, and Dex could see an organic eye that looked devoid of life, with white pupils that leaked into the rest of the sclera. He was shocked, but couldn't let it get to him.

A few yards back, the rest of the Zar-Mecks and the junkyard bots were continuing their fight.

Both Dex and the Zar-Meck raced to their feet. The Zar-Meck quickly holstered his blaster in his thigh and removed a small, two-foot-long baton instead. He jabbed first into Dex's gut. Dex attempted to dodge the blow but was too slow and was locked back against the wall. Another blow was coming, this one Dex did manage to dodge. As he did, he grabbed his attacker's forearm with both hands and pulled with all his might to slam the Zar-Meck into the wall, and on impact, the entire moon base shook.

It was enough to break Dex's focus momentarily, knowing that it wasn't he who had caused it.

Back at the barrier, the others took notice of the fight. One of them flicked a switch on their blaster and fired a blue beam at Dex.

Dex, still holding the Zar-Meck's arm, pulled him in close and rotated around to use it as a shield. The beam hit the Zar-Meck, and Dex saw the pure white eye sputter then droop. Its body then slumped over unconscious on top of Dex, with the baton falling to the ground.

Dex pushed the unconscious body off and saw the three remaining Zar-Mecks had traded their blasters for batons.

At least they want me alive, for now, Dex thought to himself. The only saving grace was that the barrier looked like it was about to give in at any moment. The junkyard bots might have wanted Dex dead, or at least were complacent with him being a casualty of war, but they would have to go through the Zar-Mecks first.

But the Zar-Meck's priorities were clear, and this was an unwinnable fight with no good outcomes. Dex turned to run in the opposite direction, but another barrier closed between the Zar-Mecks and the junkyard bots.

The Zar-Mecks descended on Dex. A single blow struck him, shattering the bones in his left hand as he tried to block. The sound of it, for as painful as it was, was too loud for a baton. After the blow, the three Zar-Mecks turned around, switched out their batons again back to their blasters, and opened fire. The junkyard bots had broken through.

The sound of the blasters, on top of the alarm still

going, was torture to Dex. He had nowhere left to run and feared the bots as much as he did the Zar-Mecks. But he wouldn't fear them for long.

The bot's aim was good and began quickly tearing through the Zar-Mecks who had trapped themselves in a corner. Dex saw their armor blast off their bodies where they were hit and thought he saw pale flesh underneath it. Even as they fell to the ground defeated, they continued firing their weapons aimlessly. They were silenced when the junkyard bots crushed their heads under their heavy feet.

Dex stayed where he was, lying on the ground, holding his broken hand.

One of the bots retracted its weapon, and in its place, three long fingers extended toward Dex. In a fully artificial voice that seemed to come from the core of the machine, Dex heard it say, "Prisoner, you will come with us."

Dex didn't move. Why trade one captor for another?

"You will come with us," the bot said and grabbed Dex by wrapping its hand around his chest. He felt like Fay Wray and was carried off down the hallway. His nerves had gotten the better of him at this point, and with the adrenaline slowing, he felt himself going into shock.

* * *

From her room, Lacy heard the alarm and what sounded like explosions coming from down the hall. She sprang to her feet and put her ear to the door.

Running! She heard people running!

"Help!" she called out. "Somebody help me, please!"

The sound of the footsteps drew closer but never slowed as they approached her door. Lacy pounded and screamed for help as loudly as she could, but the sounds of people or robots rushing by paid her no mind.

No one would come to save her.

All alone in her cell, Lacy was afraid.

* * *

Dex was coming to grips with the fights breaking out around him. The junkyard bot had let him walk on his own, and when he tried to flee, one held out its massive arm in his way and asked in its electronic voice, "Please don't run, we will transport you to a safe area."

He was surprised by the attempt at politeness, but didn't want to test the extent of it. He'd been beaten too many times today to open his mouth out of place again.

The group of six bots and Dex made their way down the hallway, cutting through Zar-Mecks as they did. Dex had no sense of direction or location, as every hallway looked the same. When a door appeared on the wall and they walked through, they would just be in another identical hallway. The only difference was that the Zar-Mecks had begun to up their game.

The Zar-Mecks switched up their tactics. Instead of focusing on recapturing Dex and stunning him with their batons, their weapons morphed into blades, and they attacked the junkyard bots.

The bot's armor was thick, but the build was gangly and amateur, and weak points were found easily. For a moment, the tide of the fight seemed to be turning. Two of the bots were taken out briskly, and a third nearly joined them, but threw a plated arm wide, knocking back two of the Zar-Mecks.

The next moment, one of the downed Zar-Mecks threw up a hand to shut a barrier between itself and the rest of Dex's party. The strategy was clear: contain the enemy while the Zar-Mecks regroup and could launch another attack.

Unfortunately for the Zar-Mecks, Dex's new protectors had no intention of being contained. The bot closest to Dex rushed to wrap itself around him, while another threw itself against the barrier. Dex couldn't see what happened next, but he heard what sounded like a hundred pounds of dynamite had just gone off.

The barrier had almost completely blown away, leaving just bits of sharp, hot metal along the edges, with the rest having been blown down the hall or sticking out of the Zar-Mecks.

The bot wrapped around Dex let him go, then told him, "This is where we start to really move." It wasn't much, but the three remaining bots were pushing themselves as much as their weight would let them. If a Zar-Meck got in their way, they used their mass to ram into them, hopefully doing enough damage to temporarily incapacitate them.

"We are almost there." The bot told Dex.

"Where? Where's there? Did you find Lacy?"

The bots gave no answer. They only continued knocking aside the Zar-Mecks.

As they ran, one of the Zar-Mecks swiped the dull side of its blade at the back of Dex's knee. It missed, but in the worst way. Instead of the blunt force hitting the knee, the tip cut across his calf. A chunk of flesh hung down, and blood began to pour out profusely.

The junkyard bots took a moment to notice this, and when they did, the Zar-Mecks were already back on their feet, racing toward him. As one of the Zar-Mecks descended upon him, the closest bot ejected its bulky arm, propelling it through the air, over Dex, and crashing into the approaching Zar-Mecks. It held out its remaining hand to Dex, but he brushed it aside and limped along at their pace.

Instead of helping, the bot motioned its already extended arm upwards, and a barrier closed between them, but it wouldn't hold for long.

Thankfully, it didn't need to. The next door they passed through led them back to the desk of the gate guard, who was now dead and lying next to its desk, and the vault door, with more of the bots waiting for them.

"Go," the one-armed junkyard bot told Dex, "You are almost safe." It gave a gentle push, and Dex did as he was told, limping along much more willingly than before thanks to the choice of language.

Standing on the platform that would bring them back to the surface, one of the bots that had been waiting held out a black box. "Put this on." It told Dex.

Dex gave the box a confused look, and the platform began to ascend.

More sternly, the bot told him, "PUT THIS ON. The airlock will open momentarily."

Without hesitation, Dex reached out to grab the box, and instantly it began to crawl across his skin, covering every inch of him. It immediately gave him a sense of relaxation and warmth. He knew a normal reaction to a strange fluid covering his body should be striking fear in him, but he also realized this must be what the Zar-Mecks were wearing. As his face was covered, a purple visor opened in front of his eyes. Hovering in front of all the bots were numbers; he guessed IDs. There was even a full heads-up display with a heart rate monitor, and a notification telling him he had taken damage in his left hand and right calf (as if he needed a reminder).

The bot spoke to him again. "You may want a blaster for this."

Dex had no idea how to access the blaster or any weapon in the suit, for that matter. Before he could find it, the door opened, and Dex immediately heard the sounds of all-out warfare going on outside. They crested over the doorway, and the once dull gray desert had become a battlefield.

Robot carcasses and Zar-Mecks lay scattered all around. Missiles flew across the sky and erupted on the ground with such force that it felt like the whole planet was shaking. All around the surface, bunkers had popped up, occupied by Zar-Mecks providing covering fire to their fellow soldiers facing the junkyard bots head-on in melee combat.

Though outnumbered, the junkyard bots had managed to outmaneuver and overpower the Zar-Mecks. Mixed in with the tanks that had taken Dex were smaller, more nimble bots. These bots stood no more than two feet tall and attacked in packs, racing up to a single Zar-Meck and tearing it limb from limb. The blood being sprayed by the Zar-Mecks was a deep blue and gave the exoplanet some of the only color it would ever see.

What stuck out the most to Dex was that there

was no rhyme or reason to any of the forces' tactics. The junkyard bots were attacking and moving in any and every direction. The Zar-Mecks, on the other hand, were organized into fire teams, working as one mind to defend their positions.

The one-armed bot put a hand on Dex moments after the platform stopped moving. "Our transport is almost here."

Dex looked around, and over the horizon came the largest ship Dex had ever seen. The saucer-shaped ship was at least half the size of Earth's "Grand Central" Space Station, and fifteen times bigger than the *Silent Horizon*. It moved with incredible speed. In no time, it was right on top of them, taking up the whole sky as it hovered thirty feet above them.

Dex was again struck with awe over what this new world was showing him.

Overhead, a bright light appeared. Dex shielded his eyes, and through his fingers, he could see a ladder descending.

It was then that a voice called out as clear as day with a real sense of urgency and care, "Climb! Climb for your life!"

Dex took only a moment to gather himself, and with some help from the bot, attempted to climb. He had been so eager to reach safety, he'd completely forgotten about his injuries. When he grabbed a rung of the ladder with his left hand, a jolt of pain ran through him, and he nearly fell back into the bots.

The voice called to him, "All right, just hold on right there! This is gonna be fast!"

The introduction of the ship had not been stealthy

in any sense of the word. The Zar-Mecks on the battlefield began shifting their aim toward the ship, and the ladder especially.

The ladder was fast, though, so fast he almost lost his grip, but he held on for dear life, and in no time he had shot through the porthole the ladder had come through. Before he crashed into the ceiling where the ladder was stored, a hand grabbed him off and pulled him to the floor.

"Drop the decoy!" The strange voice shouted to an unknown recipient.

Though Dex couldn't see it, a corpse was dropped from the porthole he'd climbed out of.

"All right, we're good! Punch it!" The voice shouted. The ship lurched forward, and Dex no longer heard the sound of the battlefield.

Dex now lay on his back, looking up at the room he was in, with a man standing next to him. A very human man, but with the same leaked-iris eyes as the surgeon.

"Surprised we made it out of that one so clean! Come on, let's get up," the man said, extending his arm.

Dex raised his right hand to meet the man's, and through the pain in his right calf, got to his feet.

"I'm sure you've had enough excitement for one day, so I'll wait to ask questions." He raised an eyebrow inquisitively toward Dex, "Unless... you've got any?"

As soon as it came out, Dex knew it was the wrong question. He wanted to know Lacy was safe, but the first thing that came to mind was, "What... the *hell!* is going on?"

Though the pain rushed through his body, he grabbed his savior by his jacket and pushed him into the wall of the small cargo hold they stood in.

"Easy, guy, easy!" The man held his hands up in a

feigned surrender. "Calm down, all right! I'm just here to help!"

Dex was breathing deeply. His heads-up display in the suit told him his heart was racing too quickly and he'd been losing too much blood. It also warned that he may be about to overheat. He thanked God for the suit, hopefully making him look more intimidating than he would have been without it.

"My name is Korr," the man said gently. "Korr Montori. All right? Good place to start, eh? I saw an alien vessel on my radar and decided I'd do better with it than the Empire. Fair enough?"

Dex lowered his hands. "So... so you're just like them. We're your prisoners now?"

"We?" Korr asked.

4. Prisoner

The alarms and sounds of battle had ceased nearly an hour and a half after the initial attack on the outpost. Another three hours later, Lacy's isolation was ended by a single Zar-Meck at her door. She sat huddled in the corner with her arms wrapped around her legs. As she raised her head, the first thing she noticed about the Zar-Meck was that it was holding a folded-up olive green jumpsuit.

"Put this on," the Zar-Meck told her in a cold voice, then tossed the suit her way.

She did as she was told without question, just feeling relieved to finally have clothing again.

The suit was basic, with two zip-up breast pockets, a thick rigger belt, pant pockets, and soles built into the feet of the suit, with straps that tightened over her feet and just above the ankle. Once the suit was on, she attempted to roll back the sleeves, but the Zar-Meck stopped her.

"Come with me," The Zar-Meck told her in a flat manner as that of a nail being struck into wood with a single hard swing of a hammer, and Lacy followed.

Lacy sat now, alone again, in a white room. It was not unlike the ones she and Dex took their psychological evaluations in when being recruited for the mission. She was upright with her hands resting on the long grey table in an attempt to show resolve in case anyone had secretly been watching her. Lacy had noticed earlier that when she stood up to stretch her legs, the table rose with her to maintain its height relative to her, but it didn't follow her around the room.

Eventually, her patience was rewarded. No footsteps were heard building up to it, but a door opened across from her, and a man walked through. He was a man with very human features, save for irises that leaked into the whites of his eyes.

He wore a dark grey uniform with navy blue trim. The blouse was buttonless, instead folding over across from the right side to more of a third of his body, where it was held together presumably by a magnetic strip within the lining. Over his left breast was a single horizontal white line about an inch long, and on his lapel he wore a gold pin that looked like a crown. Under his right arm, he carried a black tablet and held onto it tightly with his left hand.

The man walked briskly toward the table, and a chair rose out of the ground to meet him. As he sat down, he placed the tablet on the table. Lacy saw nothing on its surface but noticed the small white dots dancing around in his eyes; a reflection of what he was seeing on the tablet.

Eventually, he looked up from the tablet and spoke to her, "I understand you go by the name First Lieutenant Lacy Carradine Prullen."

Lacy hadn't spoken a word out loud since they were taken captive on the surface, save for her brief cries for help in her cell, and was still a little bit afraid to speak.

"Don't worry," the man said, his lips cracking into a forced but polite smile. "You're granted permission to speak. Please confirm your name for me."

Lacy placed her hands on the table, fingers

interlocked. "Yes. That's my name."

The fake smile dropped, and he responded quickly with an accusatory tone. "Real or alias?"

"Excuse me?" Lacy leaned in slightly.

The man sighed and tapped on his tablet. "You have permission to speak, but I'd advise you not to test my patience."

"It's my name. My only name, Lacy Prullen."

The man squinted his eyes, looking back at the tablet, and spoke without looking back up at her. "Explain the rest of this to me, then. If 'First Lieutenant' and 'Carradine' aren't your names, what does it mean?"

"'First Lieutenant' is my rank." Lacy declared with some pride in her voice.

The man's eyes widened. "Ah! So you are here on military terms!"

Lacy realized she would now be treading water with every answer. "N-" she paused, then clarified, "No. Not exactly. Coming here was a mistake, see-"

"Oh, I'm sure it was, Ms. Prullen."

"Mrs." She corrected, again, with some pride.

He continued tapping on the tablet like he was typing out notes. Then, like he hadn't been interrupted, "I suppose it's just luck then, that you happen to land in restricted sectors of the Empire. Probably happens every other day, is that right?"

Lacy gave him an inquisitive look. "You misunderstand. We weren't searching for this place. It came up on our radar, and all signs said it was uninhabited."

"Do you expect us to advertise our presence?"

Lacy was silent for a moment.

"I've been reviewing your ship's log. Baffling

encryptions, I must say."

An analyst, Lacy thought. *Great.*

"Your cover is... interesting... but ultimately laughable."

"How do you figure that?" Lacy asked.

"Sending two life forms into unknown space in hopes of discovery. Ma'am, that's a job for a cruiser or a probe. So why don't you tell me why you've landed here? I promise the pain will be much less unbearable if you cooperate."

"You think I'm a spy, don't you?"

The Analyst only gave her a look to say that much was obvious.

"My husband and I came here as explorers," Lacy told him. "We were seeking out new worlds to expand our race."

"Your..." he reviewed notes on his tablet, "Earth... Empire, correct?"

Lacy smiled at the misunderstanding. Even with how awful the situation was, there was no way Earth could ever fall under just one Empire. At least not in her lifetime. "No, not an empire, none for a few decades. Many different nations."

"All on one planet?" The Analyst asked, now showing the smallest hint of genuine interest in his voice.

"Yes, all on one."

"And you're able to refrain from war?" He was nearly glowing. Literally. His skin began to radiate a golden color. It was barely noticeable, but if he were in a pitch-black room, it would be obvious.

Lacy could almost smile. If she kept his interest, maybe she'd have a way out. But what should she tell him?

What would keep him going? Lie, she decided. Tell him whatever he wants to hear. "Yes, it took some time. Many, many wars, but we've accomplished peace."

The Analyst had all but forgotten about his tablet, he was leaning much closer now.

"We fought three wars nearly back-to-back on a global scale, but we were able to come together by uh.." She had to keep the story going quickly, but couldn't think of any figures or names that would make sense. What does it matter? It's all a lie anyway, and he wouldn't know the difference anyway, she told herself. Thankfully, she didn't have to think of a name.

"Flash Gordon? It was Gordon who united them, correct?" The Analyst asked eagerly.

"Yes!" Lacy exclaimed, "Yes, it was Gordon! He overthrew the evil dictators of the world and brought us all together. Earth has lived in peace ever since!"

The Analyst's smile shifted devilishly, "And that's why they sent you out to explore the universe? No wars left on your Earth to fight?"

Lacy gave pause to think. "Y-yes. You know, don't need us for fighting anymore, why not?" She tried to laugh it off playfully, but she saw his interest was shifting.

"I see," the Analyst said as he picked his tablet back up. "And, who was one of these dictators Gordon overthrew?"

Lacy was at a loss for an answer. The Analyst hadn't likely had time for a deep dive, but he mentioned the name "Flash Gordon" because he'd done at least some research now and was testing her to make sure her story lined up with whatever information he thought he had. But Dex was the film buff. She knew he'd definitely mentioned the Flash Gordon serials from the ship's computer at least a dozen times, but right now couldn't remember a single thing about them. She sat there thinking for too long. The Analyst was the only one in the room with her, but she felt like a hundred pairs of eyes were locked onto her. A bead of sweat formed at her hairline and slowly fell down the side of her face. It was all the Analyst needed.

"Ming." He said. "Funny. Emperor... Ming."

Lacy fell back in her chair.

The Analyst sat back in his chair. "It's strange. Earth hasn't had empires for 'decades,' as you said, but your last war, the one you say Gordon fought in and defeated Ming, ended just three years before you left on your planet." He scoffed. "The database in your ship's computer is totally incoherent. Fascinating, but incoherent. And because of that, it's so easy to tell when you're lying. Clearly, you haven't had enough time to take in your situation, spy."

Before Lacy could stand in protest, she felt an electric shock run through her body. She screamed out in pain, but couldn't pull herself away from the seat, and her eyes felt like they were about to pop out of her head. The pain lasted a lifetime in her mind, but as suddenly as it began, it ceased. The first thing she saw when she was able to focus again was the Analyst's face. His smile was completely gone.

"Ms. Prullen, I have no qualms with making your existence as painful as rákingly possible. I'll continue to go through your ship's computer, but as I said, it's very difficult to decipher, so if you'd please cooperate... well, I can't promise this will be over any time soon, but it will be less painful." He waited a moment for Lacy to respond.

She sat there, her heart beating heavily, and stared

at him. She felt paralyzed in her chair.

"Hm... maybe I went a little too far with that," he said, sounding almost disappointed that she didn't have the strength to move or say anything in return. "How about this, I'll scale back the shock level and you tell me if it fits you better." He began tapping something on his tablet, and the lights again flickered in his eyes.

Lacy was terrified of what was to come and managed to squeeze out a "... wait..."

The Analyst stopped what he was doing and met her eye.

Lacy was trying with all her might to sit back up in her chair.

He said with a grin, "At'a girl."

"It's... It's not real."

The Analyst's disappointed look returned to his face. "A lot of suspense to tell me again your story was a lie." His fingers hovered again over the tablet.

Lacy saw his hand move and shouted as loud as she could, "The *tapes*!"

Now the Analyst stopped, "Tapes?"

"The files on my ship's computer." She stopped to catch her breath. The mental strength it took for her to try to put words together was starting to make her nose bleed. She felt it trailing down her nostril, but it hadn't yet made it out. "They're just movies. It's not real..."

At this, the Analyst showed real confusion.

Lacy recognized the look. "You know, stories. It's just entertainment. Fiction." The blood crept out of her nose.

"My my my," the Analyst began. "So many questions do I have for you."

Lacy wiped her nose. "They filled up the computer with movies and books so we didn't lose our minds on the journey. We had no idea how long it would take to find another planet we could land on."

"So... what you're saying is, your ship is full of..." The confusion had passed, and now he looked offended. "Lies? You are a sick, unholy breed." He stood up, and his chair disappeared into the floor. "It's no wonder your instinct is to lie. Even in the face of torture!" He was shouting now in anger, "You blaspheme your own history! And you *dare* to bring the Emperor's colors where they DO NOT BELONG! It's clear that a being of your... distinction... has only one place in this universe." The Analyst attempted to calm himself down, breathing deeply. He then picked up the tablet and placed it back under his arm. "You will be terminated."

Her eyes widened in shock.

"And dissected."

Horror.

"It's clear there is nothing you can tell me that I should trust."

She rose again in protest by instinct and was caught by the shock of the chair. Again, she screamed, and as she did so, she prayed that he would truly kill her.

5. Ships That Don't Exist

Dex and Korr sat at a table in a cafeteria that looked like it hadn't been used in decades. The Zar-Meck suit Dex had been given was in its cube form, on top of the long table they sat at.

Korr had placed a device, similar to the one the surgeon at the outpost had, except smaller, over the top of Dex's broken left hand. It had first sprayed an alcoholic-smelling chemical on his hand, then opened up his skin like it was a window to reveal the broken bone. Next to his hand was a first aid kit that Korr was using to operate on Dex with.

"So is this a common find in any household around here?" Dex asked.

"Miracle of modern science, jarrmin box," Korr told him. "We can't fix everything. But most things are pretty easy. And the best part, no pain." He finished up the job and tapped a side of the small jarrmin box.

Dex's flesh closed over the insides of his hand. As Korr had said, he felt no pain.

"Need something to eat? Drink?" Korr asked as he stood up.

They were sitting close to the wall near the cafeteria entrance, and just behind them on Korr's side of the table was a serving counter, and behind that, a kitchen. Even before Dex nodded, Korr was on his feet and bounded over the counter toward the kitchen facilities. He opened one of the tall, silvery containers, and cold air rushed out. From the refrigerator, he took out two cans, which made Dex think of a nice cold beer, but Korr didn't bring them back to the table. Instead, he warmed them up on the dinkiest hotplates Dex had ever seen. When Korr had served it, Dex was hesitant at first. The beverage had no scent, and it looked like bile, but Korr insisted he'd feel better.

Dex took one sip and almost vomited. He hadn't realized until too late that this was the first thing thicker than the water he'd had in over a year, and his body wasn't keen on trying new things quite yet.

Slowly, just a few small dabs of the tongue first, then little sips, he was able to get it down. It was warm and tasted like spiked hot chocolate. Just the thought of it nearly gave him a mild buzz.

After a few sips, Dex pleaded with his new host. "We need to turn around, we need to get Lacy."

Korr didn't say anything for a moment. He only dropped his head slightly in discomfort.

"Did you hear what I said?" Dex asked. "We have to go back!"

"I'm sorry, my friend, but we can't. It's too risky," Korr told him. "A quick attack here and there? Sure. But believe me, if they weren't on high alert when I came in before, we can expect an armada this time."

Dex dropped his head and spoke gently, trying not to push too far with his host. "I just don't understand any of this. We weren't hostile. We didn't even know anyone was there for Christ's sake!"

"Who's sake?" Korr asked.

Dex waved it off and took another sip of his drink. This time, he knocked it back like he'd just gotten off the longest shift of his life, then dropped his head into his free hand.

"Look, I think I'll be able to clear the air a bit," Korr said with sincerity in his voice. "Just tell me your story first, and hopefully I can fill in the pieces."

Dex lifted his head again, thought a moment, and began to speak, but caught himself and slowly pushed his drink away.

"What's wrong?" Korr asked and tilted his head, trying to hear if something was amiss.

Anger boiled in his chest at the tone-deaf question. "What's wrong?" Dex pushed away from the table and jumped up violently. He shouted again, "What's wrong? My *wife* is being held prisoner somewhere in the middle of space! What's wrong is you came in with some cobbled-together army and still managed to leave her behind! And you want to talk it out over warm beer? Why should I trust you? I don't even know who you are! You kidnapped me just like they did!"

Korr stayed seated, but his face hardened at the disrespect of his guest. "Wait a minute now, I saved you!"

"Yeah, and left my wife to die! What, are you just taking me to sell off to someone else? Is there a bounty for the discovery of new aliens out there? Is that what I am?"

"Dex, sit back down, now," Korr warned.

"I think I'm fine right where I am, and maybe you should start talking!" Dex's hand shot out for the Zar-Meck armor box, but Korr was faster.

Korr was leaning back in his chair, with his feet

planted on the box. He'd lifted his hand in a finger gun gesture. "I wouldn't do that if I were you... friend."

To Dex, he looked like a gunslinger, Gary Cooper or John Wayne, if they'd forgotten their side iron at home. He wanted to laugh, and that did a bit to calm his nerves a bit.

"Easy now, just have a seat."

"Why? Gonna shoot me?"

As the words came out, Korr's hand morphed into a silver blaster barrel protruding from his forearm.

"Jesus Christ!" Dex shouted and jumped back nearly a full yard.

"I might," Korr said coolly before the blaster morphed back into his hand. "Dex, I'd like to help you out. Please, just sit."

Dex did as he was told, but with reservations.

Korr leaned forward again, feet on the floor, and let out a deep sigh. "All right, how about I start?"

"Yeah," Dex agreed. "Start with why you felt the need to get me out of there."

Korr pursed his lips to the right, then began. "Here's what I'll tell, and all you need to know. I grew up on Wiccar, and my life was dedicated to the Emperor. As soon as I was old enough, I began studying at my planet's military academy. There are lots of paths for servitude where I'm from. I mean, I could have been like my mom and gone into the priesthood. But my father was in the army. I hadn't met him until I was nearly an adult, but I'd grown up hearing the stories of how the Emperor's army had liberated and developed so many planets. I thought that was a true honor, bringing more souls into the Emperor's keeping." Korr laughed to himself, laughing at a buried pain, then locked eyes with Dex. "I don't know where you're from, or what gods they have there, but they're nothing like the Emperor." Even with the resentment that came from his words, there was still a lingering reverence in his voice.

"Well, our gods don't usually come down to our planet and tell us how to do things," Dex said, as he took another sip of his drink. "Usually just some lunatic says he had a dream, or something like that."

Korr scoffed. "Well, mine does. Come down *and* talk to the crazies in their dreams."

"So, which side is he on? Yours or those..." he gestured to the cube between them. "Those guys, the Zar-... the robot guys."

"Zar-Mecks. That's his army, his ground troops at least."

"But you still accept him?"

Korr tried to hold back frustration. Not with Dex, but with himself. "Evil is one side of a coin, my friend. And I've seen that coin with my own two eyes." He leaned in further and pointed to his broken pupils as he said it. "It's hard to deny things like that. I accept that he's real, and maybe he is a god. But not a benevolent one. Wherever that one is, he hasn't reached our borders yet."

Dex registered the pain in Korr's voice. "Okay, so, you saw something bad and a bunch of you took off? You guys some kinda rebellion, saving guys like me that wander in?"

Korr shook his head. "No, just me."

Dex leaned back and took it in. "But, hold on, all those robots that broke me out of that prison... You couldn't have done all that yourself!"

Korr laughed politely, "Well, you'd be wrong." Stood and walked back to the cabinets. "Smoke?"

Dex thought he understood, but thought that there was no way they were on the same page. "What, like..."

"Like smoke. Do you smoke?" Korr rose again and this time walked around the counter back to the kitchen, and opened one of the cabinets from which he pulled out a small box with what looked and smelled like real Cuban cigars. He walked back and put the box on the table for them both to enjoy.

Dex picked one up, smelled it, and let out a sigh of relief. "It's just like back home!" The butt was already cut, and Dex put it in his mouth.

Korr reached over, and the tip of his thumb popped back, revealing a small flame to light the cigar. "Glad you like it," he said.

Dex reclined and took a deep draw of the cigar, then laughed out a hard cough. "Oh, yeah, no, I love it. I remember when my dad gave me my first cigar right after I got my commission."

Korr smiled politely but clearly had no idea what that meant. He then lit a cigar of his own and puffed it.

"Okay," Dex began again. "So you saw some things you didn't like and you got out of dodge."

"I guess. I had to bide my time, which was by far the hardest part. You see, you won't find anyone under the Empire's thumb that doesn't give themselves completely to the Emperor."

"But you can't be the only one in history that's ever left."

"Maybe not. But if so, the Empire does a great job of finding you before you can make the choice. I've never known anyone who's defected. The people of this universe give themselves completely to the Emperor. It's an honor to die for him. The poorest people either become priests or officers of his army." He laughed, "There's so much demand to serve him, most do it for the bare minimum. He's proved himself time and again, and the people will never stop following him."

"It's just one man, though. Right?"

Korr waved the remark away and tried to speak, but Dex kept going.

"Back when my world was young, there was a country called Egypt. They had their gods, but they also had human rulers. The belief is that when they died, they became gods, but at the end of the day, they were still born, still died, and lived a normal human lifetime!"

"The Emperor is no mere man. He's not mortal. The Emperor has existed long before even the planets formed, and he'll live long after they die."

Dex tried to laugh it off, "But... but that can't be. Everything dies eventually."

"Not him. His followers won't allow it."

At this, Dex was able to laugh, "That's too bad! I said I wouldn't let my dog die when I was eight, but he did anyway, it's nature!"

"The Emperor doesn't care about what's natural."

Dex stopped smiling.

"This is what I saw that made me doubt. The Emperor has survived for so long because he feeds on the people. Not their bodies, their energy. Their very souls. My second duty station was as a deck officer on one of Wiccar's temples' transport ships. A priest or priestess would bring their offering to the Heart of the Void, the center of the

Empire. These offerings were people. Volunteers who would give their lives to extend the Emperor's. Dozens of ships go out each year, with hundreds aboard, all going to their deaths. But I saw what these feedings look like. When the color leaves their skin, and the life leaves their eyes, there's no peace. All they leave behind is pain and regret. I've seen men die in battle. When they die for something they believe in, they're at peace. But when you realize everything you believed your whole life was a lie, that your life has been stolen, and fed to a... I don't know... god, I guess. All I know is their souls will never find peace again. Not in this world, or whatever comes next."

There was silence between them for a full minute. Korr rested his chin in his hands and looked down past Dex as if he were no longer there.

Dex felt it was best to let Korr have his moment, but after that, he knew it was time to get back on track. "Korr, I'm sorry for what you've been through. I can't imagine what it's like to have your world turned on its head so disturbingly."

Korr didn't lift his head, but he did raise his eyes to meet Dex.

"But I do know what it's like to leave everything you've ever known behind," Dex continued. "It feels impossible to start again. But once you find something to fight for, once you have a purpose again, it's easy not to look back." At this, he stood. "Now I know this is a lot to ask, but my wife is still out there. With or without you, I will get her back." He held out his hand in an offer of fellowship. "But I don't think of all the paths in the universe to cross, I came by yours just by luck."

Korr looked at Dex's outstretched hand, then back

to meet Dex's eyes. He then stood. "I'm sorry, but I can't help you like that." He then turned to walk away down a featureless white hallway.

Dex grabbed the Zar-Meck cube and followed after Korr. With annoyance in his voice, he asked, "What do you mean you *can't?* You broke me out once! Why can't you do it again?"

"I don't have the resources!" Korr exclaimed without turning back. "On paper, I don't even have this ship. The Empire believes that it, and everyone on board, including me, was destroyed. All records of it say so, and no one has had any reason to argue otherwise. I made sure of it."

"Yet, here I am, courtesy of your efforts."

"You're not the first undocumented life form to land on the Emperor's doorstep. I have to pick my fights. Building up my force takes time, and when I go in, I have to go with everything I've got. So right now, I'm empty."

Dex grabbed Korr's left shoulder and forced him to stop.

Korr's reaction was quick. His right hand shot up and grabbed Dex's hand, as he spun around and threw it off. "Don't mistake my hospitality for weakness, Dex." With that, he turned and continued down a long, narrow hallway.

This hallway had the resemblance of the pristine nature of the outpost's style, but looked a bit more worn down. The walls were all still white, and where Dex figured doors should have been, were just lazy paint jobs a different color from the wall and marked in writing what was behind the door. Dex thought back to the hallways of the outpost, how the outline of the doors only appeared when the Zar-

Mecks approached or activated them.

As they walked, Korr continued. "If the Emperor's officers follow protocol, they'll realize she's an undocumented species and they'll bring her to an audience with the Emperor. She's probably on her way already."

They reached the end of the hallway and faced a blank wall. Korr pounded on it as if there were something past it. "Come on, damn busted door!" He lifted his hand to chest level, and his fingers shifted into an array of strange, small tools.

Dex watched as a port near the corner of the wall opened, and Korr's mechanical finger messed with the circuitry inside. "What does that mean? An audience."

"Well, I don't know how to put it nicely. Every species carries different levels of energy with it, right? A bug is much more insignificant than a being like you or me. So if that's the case..." A shock ran from the circuitry to his cyborg's fingers. Korr shook his hand to get rid of the pain, then continued to work. "Stupid door. Anyway, the Emperor will use her to figure out how powerful your race is. How much your kind can sustain him."

"You mean, she'll be killed? Like all those others?" The fear in his voice was clear.

The door opened, but Dex didn't register what was behind it; his eyes were fixed on Korr with anticipation and doubt as to what he dreaded Korr would say next.

Korr turned to Dex and said the words that Dex didn't want to hear. "Yes, she'll be sacrificed."

Dex was speechless. His eyes went wide, and the words he wanted to say were caught in his throat.

"I can't attack another outpost, Dex. I can't put myself out there and help wage a two-man war on the

Empire. And I know that I won't be able to stop you from whatever it is you're thinking. But... I guess I can at least offer some courtesies." Korr gave a small smile and stepped through the doorway.

It took Dex a moment to put together what Korr was saying, but it all made sense once he realized what was in the room just beyond them.

It was a large room, most likely an old hangar. A handful of robots moved around, hard at work. But what caught Dex's eye was a magnificent, though slightly bruised and worn-out, white cone-shaped ship, with a viewport that took up most of the bow and a long antenna that looked like it could serve as the world's largest rapier. In front of him stood the *Silent Horizon*.

"H-... How did you get this?"

Korr stood off to the side, so as not to obstruct Dex's view. "As I said, I go in with full force. I can't say I saved it completely, though."

Dex walked up to his ship and ran his hand along its hull.

Korr continued. "When my robots got there, it was crawling with Zar-Mecks and technicians of the Emperor's army. Chances are, whatever information your computer had is in the hands of the Empire now. But with the bulk of the Empire's forces focused on the main entrance of the outpost, getting the ship out was the easy part."

"Korr... I..."

"I know it's not a fleet," he raised his hands apologetically. "But, maybe you can get your bearings from there."

Dex couldn't speak. He only stood with eyes wide, and a smile slowly crawling across his face.

Korr waited a moment for a response, then, when he knew it wasn't coming, said quietly, "You're welcome, by the way. It was no trouble."

When the lump in Dex's throat disappeared, he burst, "Korr, this is mighty fine! Just... well, real damn swell." He laughed to himself in disbelief, then took a step closer to the *Silent Horizon*.

"I don't know how to thank you."

Korr slapped Dex's back, the cyborg's hand hitting harder than Dex had expected. "All I ask is that you don't rat me out when you get caught."

They laughed together.

"Never, Korr. For something like this, I owe you my life."

"Keep it. Better yet, give it to your girl."

"Right!" Dex stepped closer to his ship but kept his attention on Korr. "Guess I'd better get going then. Don't wanna keep the missus waiting!"

Korr just smirked. "Well, I wouldn't recommend going off just yet."

Dex gave him an inquisitive look.

Korr stepped past Dex and motioned his hand toward the robots. "My crew took a look at your ship. They relayed to me just before we got you aboard that your ship is outdated, I guess we could say."

Dex knew he agreed, but still gave Korr a look of offense.

"All I'm saying," Korr continued, "is that compared to our tech, your planet has a long way to go. I admire your determination to save your wife, but there's no way in Maoul you'll catch up with an Empire ship."

The disappointment returned to Dex's face.

Korr recognized it and was quick to save himself. "But! But I guess we could shift course."

"To where?" Dex asked.

Korr motioned to the nearest junkyard bot. The bot hobbled over to his master, and Korr ordered, "Bring a message up to the bridge computer. Re-route for Reechi. Moorak City."

Without a word, the bot nodded and hobbled away.

Dex couldn't help but be amazed at the setup Korr had. "What's Reechi? Is that a planet?"

Korr smiled. "Yeah, one of the oldest ones in the Empire."

"Sounds like they'd have a big presence there. Nowhere else we can go?"

"Only other option is Areeno. Desert planet without much activity. But that's much further out of the way."

Dex considered his options. "So you do have allies out on this... Reechi?"

Now Korr had to laugh. "No! Ha, ha, I wouldn't call them that. If they knew who I really was, I'd never be able to set foot on any civilized planet again. I just have good enough cover. Definitely not allies, but I know some people who can help you out."

"So Reechi's close to wherever they're taking Lacy?" Dex asked.

"If all things go well, you should be at the Heart of the Void within a day or so."

Dex knew well enough to be grateful for even a slim chance of hope. "I don't know how to say 'thank you,' Korr."

Korr raised a single hand in protest. "I do," he

said. "All you need to do for me... is leave me out of it. I can bring you there, introduce you to my contact, but if anything goes down, I'm out of there, and you never knew me. Deal?"

Dex nodded.

"Great. Want me to show you where you can bed down?"

Dex looked back at the ship. "I think I'll be fine once I'm in my old bunk again."

Korr motioned toward the ship as if to say, 'Be my guest.'

6. Transport

Three hours after her interrogation, a pair of Zar-Mecks arrived at Lacy's cell. For the first two of those three hours, she contemplated means of escape. The Analyst had told her execution and dissection, and she could only imagine what Dex was going through at the moment. Had he been threatened, too, by the Analyst? Once away from her captors, how would she be able to find him? More than once, Lacy gave a thorough inspection of the wall to find air vents she could crawl through, but the cell was a perfect prison. Air flowed in and out of it, but for the life of her, she couldn't find where from.

For the third hour, she resigned herself to the Analyst's plans. Now was not the time for escape, but somewhere along the path from her cell to the chopping block, she would have to make her escape.

When the Zar-Mecks entered the cell, Lacy jumped to her feet and pushed herself up against the wall. They would likely beat her if she spoke out of place again, but she wanted them to be well aware that she still had some spirit in her.

"Follow," the Zar-Meck demanded in its synthetic voice.

For all her spirit, she still shuddered at the Zar-Meck's voice, how fake it sounded; an unnatural middle-ground between man and machine. And though she was forcing herself to stay strong, she was still able to think with reason. If she were to be argumentative or hesitant there, pain. She wouldn't make it far with a broken leg if that was how far they were willing to take it. Her fear of immediate punishment for disobedience overpowered her fear of possible termination, and she followed the villain out of her cell.

Hooking a right, they walked about a hundred feet, then turned left through a door that only appeared when one of the Zar-Mecks put their hand to it, then crossed a foot-long platform into a small glass room. It was clear by looking through that no part of the room made contact with the shaft the room was in. It was just floating there like an elevator unattached to cables. And that turned out to be just what it was.

When they stepped in, one of the Zar-Mecks put its hand up against the wall. On contact, a faint blue light rippled across the glass. The room moved to the left a few feet, then dropped suddenly down the shaft at full speed.

Lacy could feel herself getting lighter, the elevator moving faster than she was falling, but her captors stayed perfectly cemented to the ground. She also realized that, although she knew she should be floating, falling with the elevator slower than it was moving, her boots stayed firmly on the ground. She wasn't just descending, but was pulled down with the elevator car.

Within moments, they fell into an imposing spherical room, with portals littered across its walls covering nearly half the surface area. Other elevators came and went, with either Zar-Mecks or humanoid aliens, reaching the center of the room, turning, and shooting up another shaft. They all moved with such speedy precision that there were no cars waiting or jamming up. As they reached the center of the sphere, the elevator came to a stop, and Lacy's momentum almost forced her to the floor, but the Zar-Mecks at her left and right held her up. When they grabbed her, she realized something.

There's no gravity here, she thought to herself. *This must be the center of the rock!*

Just as quickly as they reached the core, the elevator rotated itself and shot upwards through another shaft.

They rose for almost as long as they'd dropped, and soon Lacy saw a light growing larger above them. When they passed through the top of the shaft and came to a halt, Lacy was amazed and terrified by what she saw.

The elevator parked itself along a wall, facing toward a hangar bay Lacy assumed was larger than the National Mall in Washington D.C., and from one end to the next were rows upon rows of hulking saucer-shaped transport ships. Both Zar-Mecks and humanoid beings like the Analyst were moving with purpose; boarding ships, loading them up, off-boarding, or unloading them. Smaller ground transports were scurrying about, usually carrying large, clunky robots that looked like they'd been through hell and back, or other Zar-Mecks and machinery that didn't fare much better. Above the hanger was no ceiling. Instead, Lacy could see clearly into the sky through a transparent but grainy blue screen. Small saucer-like ships were constantly dropping into the hangar through the screen, dropping scraps of the robots and Zar-Mecks down onto ground cars, then flying back up and out of sight.

As the elevator doors opened, the Zar-Mecks next

to Lacy pushed her forward in the direction of the closest large ship.

Approaching an entry ramp, Lacy saw at its base the Analyst.

He stood firmly with his hands behind his back. His face betrayed no hint of emotion. When they met, he raised a hand in dismissal for the Zar-Meck.

"That will be all," he told them, and they turned to leave. The Analyst then shifted his attention to Lacy. "Mrs. Prullen, I'm greatly looking forward to our journey together."

"Where are we off to?" Lacy asked, trying to hide her relief. If she was going to be executed as a prisoner of war, why fly her off to another planet to do so? And even if they would go through all that trouble, that still gave her more time to make an escape.

Lacy glanced around the hangar and was quick to notice smaller aircraft being loaded onto the large transport ship with the rest of the cargo. She quickly cast her gaze away as if she hadn't noticed it at all.

She added quickly, "I thought you were to have me terminated."

The corner of the analyst's mouth dropped the slightest bit, but Lacy could discern the annoyance he was struggling to hide.

"And dissected," she added again to deepen the wound.

"New orders," he said plainly. "You will be brought to an audience with the Emperor. So, given that you'll have at least another day or so to live, I decided we shouldn't waste the time we have to learn more about your planet and..." he looked her up and down, noting again the similarities between them as a species, but still disgusted by the culture he perceived from studying the *Silent Horiozn*'s logs. And now she wore an imperial-made outfit, further muddying the waters. "... people. Now, please, follow me." He turned and walked up the ramp.

Lacy hesitated a moment, and the Analyst could feel it.

"Now is not the time to run," he said and swiveled his head to look at her through the corner of his eye. "I am not allowed to kill you, but I *can* make you suffer. Again."

The memory of the chair returned to her so strongly that she almost felt the pain shooting through her. Lacy agreed it would be best to cooperate. She would bide her time and wait for the right moment to make her escape. With a deep breath, like she was about to jump off a cliff, she took a step onto the ramp, closer to her fate.

* * *

Her room was much more accommodating than the one she was forced into back at the outpost. In this one, she at least had a small bed, a toilet, and a window stretched across the width of one wall. It curved upwards from the floor, and she watched their ascent into space in that way.

Barely out of view at the top of the window, she watched the blue film warp around the ship as they passed through it. From the sky, one would never realize there was a base hidden under the planet's surface. The blue film was gone, and all she saw was the exoplanet's surface and the damage from the battle. Lacy realized then that the blue film was a cloaking device-slash-shield.

That must have been what we were standing on, Lacy told herself. Just below the very real sandy surface of the exoplanet, she and Dex had been walking across a shield that was solid enough to keep them out, but soft enough to absorb and disperse impact.

As the transport ship drifted off, Lacy sat on the bed, staring out into space, legs wrapped in her arms. Her body told her to lie down and get the comfortable rest she'd been dying for, but her mind told her to wait just a little longer. Maybe since she didn't see Dex when she boarded the ship, he had already made his escape. That would explain the loud noises and the battlefield she'd just seen. Any moment now, he'd be flying in to rescue her.

But no one came for her.

No ships swooped in to rescue her. Dex was lost, and as much as she fought against it, a nagging thought crept into her mind that she'd never see him again. No, if she was ever going to taste freedom again, she'd have to get it herself.

Some time passed, and a small ash-black robot, no more than two feet tall, delivered a tray of food to her room. The robot held it up above its small, half-dome-shaped head like an offering, but made no noise.

She took the tray out of the robot's arms, and it walked away on two stubby legs. The door slid shut behind the robot. Lacy didn't even have time to say thank you.

The meal was a stew in green broth. None of the "vegetables" were recognizable, and the meat in it looked like beef but had the taste of ham with way too much salt. It was hard to eat at first, but the smell was at least decent, and this was the first meal she'd had since being taken prisoner. She'd wished after all the time taking meal pills, her first would be something closer to a five-star restaurant seafood platter, but this would have to do.

When she finished eating, Lacy placed the tray at the base of the door, and almost instantly, the little robot returned to collect it. This time, while the door was opened, even though it was only momentarily, Lacy focused on any other sounds in the hallways. Thankfully, there were none.

For the rest of the day, Lacy sat by the door. She kept her mind focused on any and all sounds outside her room, but heard nothing all day until, somewhere between six and eight hours later, a light stomping quickly approached her room. Lacy put her ear to the door, hoping she could make a guess at the size and speed of whatever it was outside. Whatever it was, it was definitely small. The suspense didn't last, as the door opened and Lacy fell onto the little ash-black robot, spilling a tray of oatmeal-looking food back onto the robot's body.

Lacy's body lay perfectly centered on the threshold of the door. Immediately, she realized she was alone in the corridor, save for her personal waiter. The heat of the moment took her, and she was on her feet, sprinting in whatever direction she happened to be facing. Yet, with freedom being possible, maybe even probable, she stopped and turned at the sound of beeping behind her. She saw the service robot trying to brush the food off its body and away from its optical receivers, but struggling with its thick, three-pronged fingers. It might have been the high notes the beeping hit, but something told Lacy it sounded as if the robot was pleading for help.

She looked down the hallway in the direction she'd been running, then back to the robot. To the hallway, then to the robot, who was now slumped against the wall with its small arms hanging by its side in defeat.

"Dammit," Lacy said to herself and walked back to the robot.

Kneeling to the robot's level, Lacy unrolled her right sleeve and wiped the sloppy food off its eyes.

At the sight of Lacy, the robot jumped to attention and spun around to pick up the tray it had dropped. Almost all of the food had fallen off of it, but the robot held it in an offering to Lacy anyway.

"Thanks, but I'll find something else," she said, trying to show some kindness in her voice. *Maybe this little guy can be won over,* she told herself.

The robot looked at the tray, then back up at Lacy, shoving it slightly in her direction.

"No really, I'm all right. You brought a big breakfast." Or was that dinner?

The robot lowered its arms. Its head also tilted down, and it let out a low, sad "boooooooo."

"It's not that I didn't like it!" Lacy said, worried she'd hurt its feelings. "I'm sure this was very good too, but I'm not hungry. So why don't you run along back to where you came from?" She stood up and started to walk away, but the robot tottered around to get in her way, still holding the tray.

"I mean it! Go on!" She almost laughed at his insistence.

The robot said nothing but motioned the tray toward her room.

"Gonna tell on me if I don't go back?" she asked.

For a moment, the robot stayed silent, then out of nowhere, let out a deafening alarm.

"All right! All right! I'm going!" She said, and her

door opened like it had been listening to their exchange and was waiting for her command.

The robot silenced its alarm and offered the tray again.

Lacy swatted the tray with the little bits of food still clinging to it out of the robot's hands. "Fine. But don't run off. There isn't much to eat anyway. You can take it back in a sec." She walked into the room, and the robot followed behind her. "That wasn't an invitation, but fine. Make yourself comfortable."

The robot walked to the foot of her bed and waited for her to sit down.

"Got a spoon?" She asked the robot, who didn't answer.

Lacy told herself the food was meant to be eaten without utensils in this part of the universe and scooped it up in her fingers, then shot it back like an oyster. This time, the smell did nothing to save her from the bad taste. When her tray was cleared, she handed it back to the little robot waiting at her bedside, who took it happily.

The robot beeped twice, then raised an arm in a gesture like a salute toward Lacy.

Lacy, in return, looked at him curiously. "What's that?" She asked.

The robot dropped its arm and looked back at Lacy blankly.

"You got a name, little guy?" Lacy asked.

Again, the robot beeped twice.

"Well, I'm not calling you beep-beep."

The robot shook its body as a whole and waved its hands, unintentionally letting small bits of food fly off the plate. It then pointed to the top of its chest, where Lacy noticed three horizontal slits were clogged with the food she spilled onto him.

"Oh, golly!" She exclaimed and dropped to her knees to dig out the crud. "I'm sorry, is this your speaker?"

The robot gave a short beep in reply, which Lacy took as a yes.

"All right. There. Not perfect, but feeling any better?"

Instead of a reply, the robot stepped back a few inches, and a panel just below the speaker popped open. The gears and circuitry were all afuddle with gunks and bits of wet food.

Lacy knew where she was. She was captive on a transport ship of a more than likely, malicious empire, being taken to her death. She could trust no one on this ship and should take any chance she could to escape.

But... she thought, *this wasn't someone.*

This was a robot. Programmed to act a certain way. Maybe it could be reprogrammed. Back on Earth, robotics was only just starting to blossom into something not just exciting, but reliable. The technology of this world was all alien, literally, to Lacy. But at the end of the day, wasn't it just another computer? If she could tend to the *Silent Horizon*'s technological needs, she could tend to her new, soon-to-be companion, too.

"Okay, little guy, this might take a bit. I'm gonna shut you down, but I promise you'll be back to your old self in no time." Lacy held out a hand to shake.

The robot looked at her hand, processed what to do next, and went with its first guess. It handed her back the tray.

7. Creatures of the Nebula

Korr had laid out a fresh set of clothes for Dex on his bunk in the *Silent Horizon*. Beside them, folded up with the helmets on top, were the scarlet P.E.S.s. Dex would have felt more comfortable wearing either those or his own uniform, but reason told him if they were going out in public, it'd be safe to blend in.

Dex took a quick shower, shaved, then dressed himself in the loose-fitting, long-sleeved blue shirt and the black pants with a yellow strip down the side that Korr had left for him. He then tucked his pants into his new boots, also courtesy of Korr.

After getting dressed, Dex removed the belt and holster from his P.E.S. and wrapped them around himself. Then, for what he'd come back to the ship in the first place, he opened the storage container to grab his blaster. As he reached for the blaster, he noticed something else further back. Dex paused for a moment, then grabbed the bottle of wine he and Lacy had been saving to celebrate a successful mission. Amidst all the chaos of their crash landing on Prullen-1 and Korr's retrieval of the ship, the bottle remained completely undamaged.

For a moment, the world around him went silent. The bustle of robots working in the hangar outside his ship no longer existed to him.

Dex sat in the Captain's seat and stared at the label. He and Lacy had gone to the commissary together strictly as teammates the night before their flight out from "Grand Central" Space Station. Lacy wanted to go for the most expensive bottle they could find, given that they wouldn't have any other expenses for the foreseeable future, but Dex assured her that by the time they finally drank it, it wouldn't matter to them how expensive it was. When they got to the register, Dex gave a few quick glances around like he'd lost something.

"Everything okay, Captain?" Lacy asked.

"Yeah... hold on." Dex checked his pockets like he was looking for his wallet. "Hold on one second, I think I forgot something." Without letting Lacy get a word in, Dex jogged back into the aisles.

Lacy stood alone at the automated register in confusion, as the machine repeatedly asked her for payment.

In less than a minute, Dex had returned with a second bottle of wine. "Most expensive one on the shelf." He said with a smile and scanned it through the register.

"If you're this indecisive, sir, maybe they should have picked someone else to lead this mission." She said with a laugh.

Dex pulled out his military ID for the register to place the charge in his name. "You'd really want to kick me off the mission over a bottle of wine?" He asked playfully.

"Of course not! I was thinking more along the lines of swapping roles. I'll be the captain, and you take a demotion." Lacy said as they stepped out of the commissary, into the large concourse that circled the station.

Dex's eyes widened in feigned surprise.

"Only in responsibility, not pay," Lacy added teasingly. "Don't worry."

"Well, I'll have you know, this wasn't indecision at all. That first bottle is still for if we find a new world."

"When," Lacy corrected.

"Sure. When we find a new world. This bottle is for something else."

"Oh?" She stopped.

Dex's voice dropped the playful tone and shifted to sincere confidence. "At the risk of making this mission terribly uncomfortable... what are you doing tonight?"

Lacy lost her breath and almost dropped the cheap wine she was holding. "Golly, I mean, Dex... Captain!" She corrected herself quickly. "Don't you think... tomorrow being the mission..."

"I think," he cut her off, "tomorrow being the mission, why waste tonight?"

"Hmmm... maybe you're not my type."

He stepped in closer. "Maybe I am." He almost raised a hand under her chin, hoping to tilt her head up for a kiss, but she stepped back.

"I think, sir, this is not the time or place for this kind of behavior."

Along the inner wall, the station monorail pulled up and rang a bell to signal that the doors were opening.

At the sound of the bell, Lacy grabbed the expensive bottle of wine out of Dex's hand. "Thank you, Captain, but I should really be getting ready for tomorrow," she said and skipped over to the monorail.

"Wait a sec!" he called and followed her. "You can't just take my wine too."

She stepped into the car, and when Dex tried to follow, she blocked the entrance. "If you want it back... meet me tonight."

Dex took a moment to realize what she had meant, and the doors began to close.

Lacy rushed out the rest of her request. "Twenty hundred! Observati-" The doors cut off the rest, and the monorail rushed off to its next destination.

Dex stood alone, awestruck, and without a single bottle of wine in either hand. But he knew one thing. He had about three hours to get ready.

That night had been magical. Dex didn't know how formally he should have dressed. Although he tried calling Lacy to see what she was thinking, he got no reply and struggled between his formal military wear, decked out with half a decade's worth of awards and ribbons, or something more semi-formal. Or maybe she wouldn't dress formally at all. He ended up going semi-formal to be safe. It was the last time he'd have an opportunity to dress up until they returned home from the mission, and even if Lacy wasn't getting all done up, at least she would still appreciate the effort he put in.

When he arrived at the elevator to the observation deck, he was greeted by a security guard. "Sorry, sir. Deck's closed tonight."

"Oh? I was supposed to meet someone here." Dex looked around the hallway for Lacy. Perhaps he was early, and they'd have to make other plans. "Has anyone come by? A woman, maybe half a foot shorter than me?"

"What's your name, sir?" The guard had asked politely.

"Captain Dex Prullen."

The security guard stood aside, and the elevator door opened. "The room is yours. Like I told the lady, you have another..." he looked down at his watch, "Fifty-two minutes now."

"Thank you," Dex said as he stepped into the elevator.

"Make it count!" The guard offered as the doors closed.

The elevator shot up quickly to the observation deck, a large room that marked the highest point of the space station. Most of the station's residents called it the "park," as it was decorated with artificial trees, grass, ponds, walkways, and automaton birds and squirrels. The domed wall and ceilings doubled as both windows and screens, so the view could be changed to one resembling Earth on a summer day or night if the residents were feeling homesick. Tonight, as the elevator opened, Dex saw the windows were not just clear but zoomed in to enlarge the sun.

In front of the window, Lacy stood on a picnic blanket with a wine chiller. She was wearing a conservative, deep green dress that ended just below her knees and fell on the edge of her shoulders. Her hair, for once, was let down from the bun she had kept it in while on duty, and was now lightly curled, and resting just above her breast. Around her neck, she wore a small, silver magnifying glass necklace. But what caught him, as every time he saw her, was the blue of her eyes he'd wanted to fall into since he first met her.

From the moment Dex saw her standing by that window, he knew his life had changed forever. Dex Prullen was in love.

Dex strode toward Lacy, attempting to walk with a semblance of swagger. He hadn't been on a date since they were assigned to Grand Central to prepare for this mission, and even before that, none had stood out as exceptional nights. He'd almost forgotten how to carry himself and hoped that, even though Lacy probably only thought of this as a fun last hurrah before they left the comfort of their solar system, she'd see the sincerity in his heart.

As he approached her, Dex took her hand in his and politely kissed her fingers.

Lacy gave a small giggle.

"Too forward?" Dex asked.

"No," she laughed, "I promise I won't tell Major Haxley."

Dex smiled self-consciously, worried he'd looked like a fool. "You look lovely," he said.

Lacy put the picnic basket down at her side, then pinched the hem of her dress by her thighs and gave a little twirl. "You think? I figured, you know, last night and all... why not dress up a little? And *you... Captain..." she said nervously.*

"Dex," he politely corrected.

She smiled, "And you, Dex. You look very handsome."

"Thank you," he said with a light, very light, bow.

They both stood there for a moment awkwardly, giggling to try to relieve the tension, until Dex took the lead for the night and held Lacy's hand, walking closer to the window. "It's very lovely out there tonight," he said. "How'd you manage to reserve this place?"

"Oh, I have my ways," she said playfully. "Major Haxley. I spoke with him earlier. He doesn't hold a lot of sway with the station's command, but he knows people who know people."

"And he had it sorted out in just a few hours?"

Lacy pursed her lips and rolled her eyes. "Well... not exactly. We may have been waiting for you to ask for a few weeks now."

Dex gave a confused look.

"The Major and I have known each other since I was in college. He helped me get into this program. A very old friend."

"Huh." Dex's face shifted to suspicion. "I see."

He let his hand drop from Lacy's, then turned and stepped slowly along the window with his hands held behind his back, not so discreetly glancing back at her.

"You see what?"

"No, no. Don't worry, I understand everything now."

Lacy followed.

"Dex, what are you-"

"Captain." Dex corrected, but he couldn't hide from Lacy a smile poking through the facade as he said it.

She began to catch on to his game. "Okay, Captain. What are you now understanding?"

He stopped, and without turning his body, looked over his shoulder. "Can't say. It's classified." He then began pacing again.

Lacy scrunched her face in annoyance. She stomped after

him and pulled him by the shoulder to turn him around. "Captain Prullen, if we're supposed to be a team, I don't think you should be keeping secrets like this."

"Okay, Lieutenant. I see now why I was selected for this mission."

She crossed her arms. "Oh, you do?"

He paced now back toward the picnic blanket. "I'm just here for my good looks, aren't I?"

"Excuse me?" Lacy stopped in her tracks.

"You figured, 'Well if I'm gonna be stuck in space with someone for who knows how long, I might as well bring someone... irresistibly attractive.'"

"More like irritably."

"So you convinced Major Haxley to assign me to this mission because you just couldn't bear leaving me behind while you got stuck with some wet rag like... I don't know, Captain Deshaun."

She laughed. "A little off course there, sir."

"But only just a little. So I'm still slightly on, right?"

Lacy stepped closer. They were both brightly illuminated by the blazing sun just outside the window, but still, the brightest thing in the room to Dex was her eyes.

"Well, I can't say I picked you for the mission. But don't you think they didn't take our preferences into account?"

He stepped an inch closer. "So I am your type, then? And this isn't just a fun night before we sail into the unknown?"

She stepped in and tilted her head up. Airily, she said, "It doesn't have to be, Dex."

Dex held her cheek in his right hand and placed his left on her side. "Then I'll be sure not to waste it, Lacy."

At that moment, the universe filled with miraculous sights. The sun let out a solar flare, and an asteroid shot straight through its loop. Many people made a wish on that shooting star. On Earth, *a new robotic design was completed that would soon change the face of the planet. Deep in the furthest reaches of the universe, a star collapsed and formed into a black hole. But in the observation deck of the "Grand Central" Space Station, the only event that mattered in the whole universe to Dex and Lacy was that first kiss they shared.*

They sat for the rest of the night on the blanket, drinking their cheap wine and making predictions of what they would find beyond the stars. Dex made a promise that night, unspoken, that no matter what the mission demanded, nothing would ever happen to Lacy.

* * *

Dex sat alone at the console, with the (*now overpriced*, Dex told himself) bottle of wine he'd bought the night of their first, and only real, date. His face was red with heartbreak for Lacy and anger toward their captors. All he wanted to do was smash the bottle against the console and scream out all the hatred he felt toward the things that stole his wife away. But Lacy wouldn't want that. He knew if it were her in his position, she'd pull herself together and carry on. Whether that meant going after him or flying back to Earth to report what happened, she'd carry on.

Dex wiped a single tear away, the only one that managed to escape as his face strained with rage, and stood. He placed the bottle back in the cupboard where it belonged, grabbed his blaster, holstered it, and exited the ship.

When he stepped off, a junkyard bot approached him. "Korr would like to speak with you. It's safer on the bridge."

"Safer?" Dex asked. He assumed he'd have at least

a little while longer before the Empire caught up with them if they ever did at all.

He followed the robot out of the hangar, down a series of hallways, and up a short elevator to the bridge.

The room was large, about three hundred square feet, with rows of computers and empty seats along its walls. The front viewport, Dex could tell, wasn't a window at all, but a screen. Through it, he saw they were flying through dark clouds of green and purple. Asteroids floated by them, and every so often, lightning struck and boomed through the ship. And in the front of the room was a large, makeshift terminal, connected by wires taped to the floor and ceiling, leading to the computers surrounding the room. Korr Montori sat at the terminal, with his hands broken up into their cybernetic counterparts, speeding rapidly from one gear, lever, or keyboard to the next. Though Dex couldn't see from where he stood, Korr's eyes were rolled toward the back of his head, deep in concentration while he piloted the ship.

Dex's escort left the two of them alone, and as the door shut, Korr asked, "Like the work we did on your ship?"

Dex walked toward Korr. "I'm very much appreciative, Korr. I thought when I crashed I'd be spending the next week doing repairs."

"Well, repairs aren't all my boys did. Come on, take a seat."

Dex looked to the wall of computers and grabbed the first chair closest to him, dragging it over to Korr's terminal. When he sat, he asked, "What do you mean?"

"Remember I said your ship seemed a little outdated?"

Dex nodded. Lightning flashed and thunder boomed outside.

"We're still headed for Reechi, but we did what we could. Those patches on your hull are more durable than whatever it is you had before, and we had to completely rewire your antenna. So that should have a bit of a stronger signal too now."

"Wow... Thank you, Korr!" Dex felt he could almost hug the cyborg, but didn't want to interfere with his steering.

"There was one other thing. I'm not sure why, maybe it's just a cultural thing wherever you come from, but there wasn't any weaponry on your ship."

"Well, we weren't searching for a fight. We set out to find new, unexplored worlds. From our satellites and telescopes, we found nothing to suggest... well... *this!*"

Korr gave Dex a look to say, *Are you kidding me?* "Well, congrats, we installed what we could. It's not much, but if you've got someone tailing you, you'll at least have some defenses."

"And what if I'm the one tailing someone?"

"I wouldn't recommend going on the offense against the Zar-Meck starfighters. Especially in a ship like yours."

Dex sat back in his chair. He knew Korr was right, but was still annoyed. It was one more obstacle in the way of getting Lacy back. "If I can't attack them head-on, how am I supposed to get her back at all?"

"You want my advice?"

Dex nodded again.

"My advice is you don't. Turn tail and go home."

Dex's blood started to boil at the suggestion, but

he tried not to let it show.

"But I know that's not what you're going to do, so next best, I guess. Here's what I recommend. When we get to Reechi, I'll set you up with a guy I know who can get you a better engine. One capable of hitting just past hyper speed. I'll make you up some credentials before we get there to help you blend."

"What about my ship? If I'm going to the Empire's home world, won't they scan my ship? They'll shoot me on sight, or take me prisoner!"

"Most likely," Korr said plainly. As he did, the ship gave a jolt. Dex grabbed onto the terminal for stability. "Don't worry, probably just some baby jrahk-birds. Anyway, remember how I said I get by because this ship doesn't exist? You'll have to cloak your ship, which, you're welcome, taken care of."

"How's that?"

"You pretend you're someone else. Empire checks for clearance codes on every spacecraft. I have a team that scans Empire frequencies for working, low-profile codes. There aren't many, but we make it work. I'm sure I can spare one or two for you."

"Fair enough, thanks," Dex said. "Guessing I gotta work it out myself from there?"

Korr shrugged. The ship shook again, this time harder.

"You said that's a baby... whatever?" Dex asked, gripping tightly to the console. "What happens if we come in contact with a fully grown one?"

"We won't," Korr said matter-of-factly. "The older they get, the lazier. Children take care of the hunting, while the parents sleep in larger asteroids."

"What do they eat?"

"Mostly small organisms. This nebula is filled with plenty of little creatures. But ships they usually leave alone. I travel through here all the time. Never had any real problem with them. The trouble is, the nebula messes with the ship's internal computers. That's why I gotta be up here. Even my bots down there have a habit of going haywire sometimes." Another thud, again, tougher than the last. "Jeez, these guys are really annoying today."

Above them, they heard light thumping.

"Is that..." Dex began. "Yeah, it's climbing on the hull. Weird."

Dex sank into his seat. "Korr?" He asked.

"Yeah?"

The baby jrahk-bird began scratching at the hull.

"How often do you travel through here... with non-robot passengers?"

The realization slowly hit Korr Montori. After years of pirating, traveling through the nebula had become just another thing with no second thought. When he set the course for Reechi with Dex, he played it out like any other trip.

The scratching became more violent until the jrahk-bird began outright clawing away at the hull.

"All right, it's just a baby!" Korr told himself nervously. "Hold on, Dex, might knock into a few asteroids here!" Dex did as he was told, and Korr's mechanical thumb extended to hold down a button on the console. "Listen up, guys!" Korr's voice boomed through a speaker across the ship. "Secure yourselves, it's gonna get a little wild in here, and I don't want to have to scrap you later!" Korr lifted his finger off the bottom.

"Anything I can do, Korr?" Dex's voice shook with the turbulence of the transport ship. They had picked up speed and saw asteroids coming out of the clouds at a deadly rate. The sounds of asteroids bouncing off the hull rang through the ship.

"I don't think so, buddy. Don't worry, we'll be fine!"

As Korr spoke, a harsh scratching sound like claws on the world's largest chalkboard pierced their ears.

"On second thought, get on the guns!"

Dex shot his head around to all the surrounding computers.

"Upstairs!" Korr shouted through another screech. "Down the hallway, on the right, about thirty feet down. Climb up!"

Dex was on his feet and rushed out of the bridge without wasting a moment. He climbed the stairs Korr mentioned and found himself standing on the ship's hull, in a long, domed hallway that ran around the middle circumference of the ship. It was through the dome that he saw the jrahk-bird, clawing its way through the hull, throwing metal scraps out into the nebula.

Nothing about this creature said "baby." The jrahk-bird was massive, nearly forty feet from the end of its tail to its hawk-like beak. Out of its back were two sets of wings, the larger ones in front had a wingspan that tripled that of the creature's length. The second was half the size of the first, which branched off into another pair of clawed hands at its forearm.

It had no legs, but huge talons where the legs should have been, and the base of its tail was armed with a barbed stinger.

Dex paled and froze at the sight of the great beast.

Along the wall of the dome, about every fifteen feet were large turrets, with double-barrel heavy laser guns and muzzles sticking out just past the wall. Dex ran to the one closest to the creature, grabbed the trigger, and after firing once at the jrahk-bird, was thrown to the ground by the recoil.

The shot missed, but it was enough to get the bird's attention. It stopped clawing and looked at him, then began to climb.

Dex rushed back to the turret, fixed his footing, and aimed for the jrahk-bird's chest. With a loud blast, Dex was nearly thrown off his feet again, but managed to hold on and watch the impact of the twin blasters. They failed to penetrate the jrahk-bird's hide, but the damage was done. Dex saw the blast ripple and burn holes into the beast.

The jrahk-bird regained its grip on the ship and charged toward Dex.

Just then, the ship rotated hard to starboard. Dex held his ground, as best he could. He watched as an asteroid rolled across the hull into the jrahk-bird, crushing its larger left wing. The bird screeched in pain.

A weak spot, Dex thought. He rotated the turret to the injured wing and fired a third time.

The blaster bolts seared straight through the wings and sailed into the nebula, disappearing quickly into the gases.

"Yes!" Dex shouted in triumph. "Not gonna be on the menu today, you big dumb bird!"

The jrahk-bird gave Dex a discernible evil eye and pushed itself off the hull, flying into the nebula.

Over a speaker, Dex heard Korr's voice. "Nice shot!"

Dex looked around for a terminal to speak into.

"Don't worry about it," Korr's voice said. I can see and hear you through the camera feed. Listen, there's a strap just below the turret. These things are meant for the Zar-Mecks with a stronger footing. Straps should help a bit."

"But it's gone! I got it!"

Back by the ladder, some of the smaller junkyard bots began climbing up and arming themselves against the wall.

"I got it, didn't I?"

"You got that one, but mommy's gonna be pissed when her baby comes home with a busted wing."

Above them, a shadow nearly four times as big as the baby jrahk-bird flew past them. The small bots hanging on to the turrets did aimed upward as high as the cannons would go.

"Korr please tell me we're almost out of this damn nebula."

"Got a little ways to go still, Dex," Korr called back over the speakers.

Dex took a deep breath and said to himself, "Don't worry, Lacy, I'm still comin'."

The shadow passed over them again, this time headed toward the rear of the ship. The beast was stalking its prey.

Just then, the bird crashed down on the rear of the ship. Nearly all of the bots were thrown off their guns, and Dex was tossed up into the ceiling, and then crashed down hard on the floor. The wind was knocked out of him, and he struggled to regain his breath. From behind, one of the bots helped him to his feet, then placed Dex's hands on the laser cannon, before patting his arm in a "good luck" gesture.

Dex tried to turn the cannon, but the bird was too far down for him to get a good shot.

The bots down the line were all firing at rapid rates to get the bird off their ship. But they, like Dex, were not Zar-Mecks, and with every blast, when one bot was thrown off the cannon, another would take its place.

The jrahk-bird took the laser hits in stride, and with one swipe of its claw, demolished the rear of the gunner's line dome, as well as a good chunk of the hull.

"Dex!" Korr screamed over the speaker. "Dex, get down here!"

Seeing no other option with the gunner's line quickly being destroyed, Dex did as he was commanded. He ran back to the ladder and watched asteroids fly by, slamming into the jrahk-bird and bouncing off like rubber balls.

Climbing through the shaft, Dex heard the screeching of the creature as it tore its way through the bots.

Back on the bridge, Korr was doing all he could to avoid the asteroids in his massive ship and shake off the jrahk-bird.

Dex ran up behind him. "What else can we do? Your firepower is useless against that thing!"

"It's not useless!" Korr shouted back in frustration, more so at the situation than Dex. "I just don't have enough hands!" Korr dove the ship downwards, avoiding a large asteroid."

"Wait a sec..." Dex said quietly.

Korr rotated to port, and lightning flashed across

the screen.

"I have an idea!" Dex shouted and jogged back to the hallway. "Just give me cover! I'll distract it!"

"Dex! Dex, wait!" Korr shouted after him. But it was too late. Dex was running back down to the hangar.

From the moment Dex was in his old Captain's seat on the *Silent Horizon*, he felt like he'd never left. The ship powered up smoothly, and with the assistance of one of the junkyard bots guiding him, Dex flew out of the hangar.

The controls felt smoother in his hand than before. Though he'd been piloting it for over a year, he'd never flown in conditions like this, with such sharp turns needed at a moment's notice. He turned the ship upwards toward where the jrahk-bird was attacking, and when it was in his sights, he aimed for the beast's wing. It was raised to send another blow to the hull. Dex pushed the speed as hard as he could without losing steering and shot the *Silent Horizon* through the wing. It cut through like paper.

The jrahk-bird let out a howling screech and refocused its attention on the *Silent Horizon*. With a leap that shoved Korr's transport ship sharply downward toward an asteroid nearly as big as itself, the beast gave chase.

Korr radioed in to the *Silent Horizon*. "Dex! What are you doing?"

"It's me it wants, right?"

There was a pause.

"Right?" Dex asked again as he swerved his ship this way and that, always just barely missing a bite from the jrahk-bird's mighty beak.

"Dex, I can't let you sacrifice yourself! I spent all my troops on you to give you a chance!"

"You think this is a sacrifice?" Dex asked. He

didn't realize it, but he was smiling now. "I got a wife to get back to. To hell with dying!" Dex piloted the ship through a donut-shaped asteroid. The jrahk-bird crashed into it, trying to squeeze through, but it was too big. The beast screeched, then crawled around it, and continued its pursuit.

"Listen, Korr," Dex called over the radio. "I need you to try to get under me. When I say, pull up. And *hard!*"

"Okay, got it!"

Dex zipped from asteroid to asteroid, hoping the jrahk-bird wasn't as agile as his piloting, and it would crash into rocks, slowing it down or weakening it. But the beast was too strong and gained on him. When the jrahk-bird was right on top of him, Dex finally saw what he had been hoping for.

"See that asteroid up ahead?" Dex asked into the radio.

"Asteroid? Dex, that's a moon!"

"Okay, so you see what I'm talking about, good!" The *Silent Horizon* jolted forward. "Jeez, I just got this thing fixed!"

Knowing it might cost either him, Korr, or both of them their lives, Dex pushed the engine so hard he momentarily lost any maneuverability with the ship and forced whatever angle of descent he was stuck in.

"We're coming up!" The *Silent Horizon* took a small dive and just barely skimmed the surface of the asteroid, with the jrahk-bird following just meters behind.

"*Now!*" Dex shouted into the radio, "Do it now!"

Below the beast and the *Silent Horizon*, Korr pulled up hard and with a crunch that felt like it reverberated through the entire nebula, crushed the jrahk-bird between his ship and the asteroid. The jrahk-bird was ground up hard against its surface, leaving nothing behind but bits of mangled flesh, guts, and bones to drift through space.

Korr and Dex shouted out cheers through their radios. The bots left on the gunner's line gave no cheer. The six or so that hadn't been crushed simply returned to their posts.

8. New Friends

Lacy closed the panel on the small service robot's chest. She sat on her bed, waiting for any signs of life. It stood motionless for a moment before she heard its motors begin to hum again.

The robot looked up at her.

"So," she began, "let's try this again. You got a name, little guy?"

The robot stared through its small sensors, then looked down at the floor, and up again. "No." It said bluntly in a voice that teetered the line between robotic and organic.

Lacy was shocked at the realization that her efforts had been successful. "Ha! You can talk!"

The robot said nothing but continued to stare.

"Okay, well, you need to have a name. What do you think? What should we call you?"

The robot looked around the room, presumably for inspiration. After a moment, it gave up and shrugged its arms.

"Hmmmm. How about..." Lacy thought. "Flash?" She asked. All that came to her head was the conversation she'd had with the Analyst, but then a sci-fi film popped in that she'd reluctantly seen with her college friends years ago. "Or what about Gort? No, that's a silly name."

The robot started to lean to one side as if it were either bored or confused.

Lacy jumped. "I got it! Robbie!"

The robot perched itself straight upwards again.

"You like that one, Robbie?"

"It will do," replied Robbie, the robot.

"Great! Robbie, it's nice to meet you." She took his claw and gave it a shake. His arm flailed limply, as he didn't understand what she was doing, but didn't fight it either. "My name is Lacy. Lacy Prullen, and soon you'll meet my husband, Dex. Now, how about we get out of here?" She stood and began to walk to the door, only to be cut off by Robbie, who shooed her away with his arms up. "What's the matter?"

"You're not supposed to leave," Robbie said.

"I know I'm not supposed to, but I'm going to anyway. And you're coming with me!"

Robbie shook his whole body this time.

"Error. No. Wrong. My duty is in the ship's kitchen. Your duty is here."

Lacy put her hands on her hips. "My duty is not in here. My duty is with my own ship with my husband, Dex. Now are you coming along or not?"

Robbie raised his claw to his chin, imitating a pondering look.

Lacy looked down at him, tapping her foot to show her growing impatience.

"You gave me a name," Robbie said.

"What?" Lacy asked.

Robbie stepped a little closer. In his short existence, he had only ever been assigned to the transport ship, delivering meals. Before meeting Lacy, he hadn't even been a 'he.' He'd been an 'it.' His orders at all times were, "Bring this to so and so" or "Deliver this to room whatever." Not once in his memory bank could Robbie remember a "Would you please bring this to so and so," or "Do you have the time to deliver this to room whatever." It had never registered until now that Robbie had never been asked to choose for himself.

"You gave me a name," was all he said, as he reached out both claws and held Lacy's hand.

Lacy knelt to meet Robbie at his level. "Your call, buddy. Wanna tag along? I don't think I can find my way out of here alone."

Robbie stayed silent and stepped toward the dirty food tray that lay next to Lacy's bed and picked it up. His old programming told him to take the tray and return to the kitchen to wait for the next meal. The thing was, it wasn't pushing him anymore. He felt no drive to do as his programming told him.

With the tray in his hand, he shuffled over to Lacy. "Escape pods are three levels up."

Lacy beamed. "You're coming!" she shouted with excitement and hugged Robbie. Knowing he was her only chance to escape, she thanked him.

"We will have to ask permission from one of the bridge officers. I'll show you to the bridge." Robbie stepped into the hallway and took a sharp left, followed closely by Lacy.

"Hold on, Robbie. If we go to the bridge, they'll know we're trying to leave!"

"Correct. But, escape pod bays are locked unless there is an emergency, so we will need permission."

"Robbie, hold on."

Robbie stopped and turned around.

"Listen, these people can't know we're leaving. Got that? We're prisoners here, they don't want us to leave. So we gotta be real sneaky."

"If they won't allow us through, we cannot go. The bays will be locked."

Lacy looked around the curved white hallway they stood in, hoping for an idea to come to her. She was lucky to get a small robot to deliver her food, but if any of the Zar-Mecks had been around or seen her now, she'd be back to square one.

She asked him, "You said they open for emergencies, right?"

Robbie nodded.

"How extreme does it have to be?"

Robbie said nothing but tilted his head to the side.

Lacy sighed and knelt.

"If there's a fire in my room, would they open the escape pod bays?"

For his answer, Robbie's left claw over-extended outward, revealing tubing that, Lacy presumed, flowed up his arm. With the claws extended, a puff of CO_2 shot out.

"Great. I've got a mobile fire extinguisher."

At the remark, Robbie shifted the tray to his left hand and over-extended his right claw outwards to reveal the same-sized hole. This time, a flame shot out nearly four inches.

"Okay, that's not too bad. Any other tricks I should know about going forward?"

Robbie thought hard, wanting to live this first day of freedom to the fullest. For once, he could put his gadgets to good use, be creative, and try new things. He could explore tools he'd never tried before. This was his moment to show he could be his own robot. Robbie put the tray down gently and then shuffled a few inches back from Lacy. Slowly, he rested his claws on the floor and began shifting his weight toward them, more and more until...

"Wow..." Lacy said, unsure how she should react. "A handstand... neat." The confusion and lack of enthusiasm were clear in her voice.

Robbie lost his balance and fell to the ground with a loud crash reverberating through the empty hallway. "Was that a trick?"

She couldn't help herself. Lacy let out a small laugh at his eager question. "Yes, Robbie, I guess it's a very good trick. But I don't think it will help us very much."

Robbie re-oriented himself and let out a small, sad whine.

"At least not right now!" She saved herself from hurting his feelings. "But maybe later, you can show it off to everyone and they'll all really love it."

Robbie clasped his claw hands together in excitement. "I also have this!" He spread out his hands, and the once blocky claws extended out their tips into sharp inch-long knives. "Sometimes the cargo I am assigned to deliver food to gets aggressive."

Lacy's eyes were wide in surprise. "Well... glad you didn't think I was... aggressive."

The knives retracted. "You were. But I couldn't see."

Lacy stood up. "Uh huh... well, little guy-"

"Robbie," he corrected.

"Well, Robbie, I think I've got a plan to set off the

alarms. Do you think anyone would suspect anything if you went back to the kitchen now?"

"No," Robbie said bluntly.

"Okay great! Think you could head back there to grab me something quick?"

Robbie sat silent for three seconds, processing. "If it is small."

"Wonderful. Do you know what propane is?"

Robbie shook his body as if to say no.

"Damn. Okay, when they cook in there, they use gas to fuel the fire, yeah?"

Robbie nodded.

"What I need from you is a canister of that stuff, propane, as we call it. Bring it back here and we'll blow a hole in the hull."

Robbie grabbed his tray and stepped back quickly in shock. "I think we need permission for that, too," he said.

Lacy couldn't help but smile. "Robbie, no more asking permission. This is what we have to do. Don't worry, we'll be safe about it."

If Robbie had more than one eye, he would have raised one of his eyebrows to tell her how strange that sounded. But who was he to disagree? She had just granted him his freedom, and in his programming, he'd do what she asked. "Okay. I'll be back in a minute." Without any pleasantries, Robbie waddled away down the hall toward the kitchen. "But I think it's a strange idea!" He shouted back down to her.

With Robbie occupied, Lacy decided the best course of action would be to scope out the path they would take to get to the escape pod bay. Robbie had said it was three floors up, but that wasn't much to work with. Within the context of first seeing the transport, and how tall the rooms were on her floor, she assumed it couldn't be less than fifteen stories high. Twenty at most. But it was wider than it was tall. She knew she was in the lower half of the ship, and if it curved upwards toward the center, then three floors up would probably put the bays along the outer perimeter of the ship. And for all she knew, Robbie might only have referenced the closest ones. Based on what he said, she'd have plenty of ground to cover and try not to lose her bearings, without straying too far from her little friend.

She stepped off again the way Robbie had been leading her. After about thirty feet, nothing. She began to jog. Another forty or fifty feet, still nothing. She ran. She ran as fast as she could, but no matter how far she ran, she remained in the same empty white hallway.

Her heart began to race. She was trapped. *I can't get out. There's no way out!* Her thoughts screamed.

Just then, she heard a screeching down the opposite end of the hallway.

"Robbie?" She called.

The screeching continued, but it was muted by the sound of...

"Blasters," Lacy spoke the words out loud. She ran back to help Robbie. "I'm coming! I'm over here!"

The sounds of Robbie's tiny feet smacking against the ground and Zar-Meck blaster fire grew louder. When he rushed into view, Robbie came dragging a massive propane tank behind him that was scratching up the floor. Before she could say anything, a blaster bolt zoomed past Lacy's head. She dived to the ground, Robbie shooting past her, and saw three of the Zar-Mecks following behind.

"PRISONER! GO BACK TO YOUR ROOM!" Shouted one of the Zar-Mecks.

Lacy had spent too much time in captivity, especially being bossed around by those things. She jumped to her feet and dashed after her friend.

"Robbie!" She shouted.

"You wanted this!" Robbie shouted back without stopping. "I do not know what to do next! We passed your room!"

"Forget my room! Toss it in another!" Another bolt grazed her hair but continued past her.

As he waddle-ran, Robbie unscrewed the canister to let out a small hiss of gas. He then stopped at the first door that opened for him as Lacy ran past. The room was empty, and Robbie had no moral dilemma tossing it where it wouldn't hurt anyone. As soon as it was out of his hand, he raced to catch up with Lacy.

Lacy stopped and turned when she heard the metal clanging. "Light it!"

"Oh, right!" Robbie said and turned quickly to go back to the room. But it was too late, the Zar-Mecks were in his way.

"HALT SERVICE BOT."

Lacy stopped running at a point in the hallway where the curvature shielded her, and listened. At that moment, she believed her plan had been compromised.

Robbie did not feel the same way. This was still his first day with free will, and he did not want to give it up that easily. His left claw extended, and he sprayed out a thick cloud of CO_2, then dashed away before the Zar-Mecks knew what happened.

With the Zar-Mecks distracted, Robbie was able to make it back to the room, overextended his right claw, and set alight the gas that had leaked out. He then quickly shut the door and raced back toward Lacy.

Reaching her, he shoved Lacy as hard as he could through the door she didn't know she was leaning up against. As the door shut, he told her, "That was not fun."

Then the blast came.

The transport shook momentarily, but on the other side of the door, Lacy and Robbie could hear air rushing through the hallway, out into space.

"Think that's enough to open the bays?" Lacy asked.

"Only if we get there soon enough." Robbie put his claw up against the wall of the small room they were in, and a faint blue line rippled outwards. They began to ascend. Lacy thought about the three Zar-Mecks being sucked out into space. She knew it was unlikely, but she prayed to God that they were the same three that had captured her and Dex. As she prayed, the ship's alarms went off.

"HULL BREACH." A speaker boomed through the elevator, and presumably, the whole ship.

Lacy looked down at Robbie. "You ready for real freedom?" She asked.

Robbie clapped his claws together as he jumped up and down in excitement.

"Yeah, me too, buddy." She said softly.

The elevator doors opened on a similar hallway, but this time, the far wall was littered with windows facing out into space. This time looking out, she had lost all interest in what mysteries it held. She resented the possibilities that lay outside the window and wanted just for this mission to end. "Come on," she said to Robbie. "Let's get to those pod bays."

As she began to step off, Robbie held an arm out blocking her, then touched the wall to close the elevator door, and held his hand there.

"Hey, what the he-" she began, but Robbie cut her off.

"Shh," he said quietly.

Outside the elevator door, they heard footsteps drawing near, which stopped outside the elevator. Whomever it was began tapping vigorously on the wall outside, trying to call the elevator.

"Blast," an organic voice said. "Elevator must be busted. Try the next one!" The footsteps resumed, and whoever it was now ran away.

Lacy looked down at Robbie. A chill ran down her spine at the thought that they were about to be found, but Robbie was shaking hard.

"You okay, little buddy?" She asked.

"If they catch you, you go back to being a prisoner. If they catch me... I get shut down."

Lacy was silent. She gave the robot freedom but hadn't considered what it meant for him if she screwed up.

When the footsteps sounded far enough away, Robbie took his claw off the wall, and the elevator door opened. "This way," he said, and turned left. "They should be just overrrrr... here!" He stopped, and a door opened to a room littered with cylindrical pods hanging from the ceiling. "This is it!"

Robbie rushed to the first pod. It opened for him as he approached. Since it hung down to about a foot off the ground, Robbie struggled to pull himself up into it, but once in, quickly found himself comfortable in one of the escape pod's seats.

Lacy smiled at the little robot. She was ready to feel the same sense of freedom he'd had since coming into her life.

"Well done, Ms. Prullen." A cold voice sounded from behind one of the pods, and the Analyst stepped into view. "Please, by all means, step into the pod." He gestured toward the pod Robbie sat in.

Short-lived freedom.

Robbie jumped out of his seat and stood at the pod's portal to see what was going on.

"Robbie, burn him!" Lacy commanded.

Robbie's right claw opened up, but the Analyst calmly held out his hand. "There's no need. Robot," he directed his attention to Robbie. "Code 1-9-5-5."

Robbie's claw closed.

"You may have your escape." The analyst said to Lacy. "I won't stop you, but I'll tell you now, it won't last."

Lacy backed away toward the door, but it wouldn't open behind her.

"If a crew abandons its ship, there's only one destination programmed into the pods. So really, you'd just make a slower trip to the destination you're already headed to." The Analyst drew closer.

"You're wrong," Lacy said sternly. *I'll re-route it*, she thought to herself. "Nothing in the universe will bring me an inch closer to your Emperor!"

The Analyst chuckled as he closed the distance between them. "Let's just pretend you managed to divert course. Where would you go? Home? Back to your planet

Earth? You'd die of starvation before reaching it. Or! Maybe one of the empire's planets? They'd turn you in in a heartbeat. You have nowhere to run."

They were merely inches apart from each other, with Lacy up against the wall, looking up at the Analyst. "Dex will find me."

Without hesitation, the Analyst said smugly, "A dead man would have a hard time finding anyone."

Lacy wanted to scream and beat his face in, but she choked. She felt tears coming and held them back. "You lie!"

"I'd be happy to show you the security footage. His escape failed. His body splattered into a million pieces against the surface of our outpost. Now, do you think anyone will come? The choice is yours." The Analyst stepped aside and motioned toward the pod.

Lacy took a single step forward.

He can't be dead. I know he can't... but if he is.

Lacy was frozen. For a moment in time, she truly believed all was lost. If Dex was truly gone, why should she keep fighting? She could live without Earth. She could live without any form of civilization, for what it was worth. But she couldn't live without Dex. If he was gone, maybe it was time to give up. The thought came and went in a flash.

Dex wouldn't give up like that, he'd fight for me even if I'd died! Death couldn't stop him from coming for me.

She stepped off toward the pod, but a hand grabbed her wrist.

"As I thought. You seem to have some sense at least." The Analyst said. "We've really got a lot to learn about your species." Lacy tried to pull away, but the Analyst was too strong. She knew she'd be beaten and any moment now, if they weren't already, more of the Zar-Mecks would be closing in on her. If she couldn't have her freedom today, at least one person could. "Robbie, go!"

Robbie leaned out of the pod and reached for his friend, "But Lacy!"

"Just go! Be free!" Lacy yelled as she fought against the strength of the Analyst. With her free hand, she punched the Analyst square in the face.

His skin began to radiate yellow, but his grip on her held tight.

"Lacy! Come on!" Robbie yelled.

"Get out of here!" Lacy called after him. The door to the hallway opened, and Zar-Mecks began pouring in, surrounding Lacy and the analyst.

Robbie wanted to fight. Doing as he was told again made him feel like he was back to being just another soulless robot. But he knew the battle was lost. The defeat was taken harder than Lacy would have realized, but he closed the pod door and ejected into space.

As the Zar-Mecks closed in on her, Lacy watched Robbie's escape pod be sucked into the ceiling, then with a *pop*, sent into space. She stopped fighting and let herself be taken prisoner again. At least you've got your freedom, little buddy, she told herself for comfort.

9. Reechi

The rest of Dex and Korr's journey through the nebula continued without hindrance. While Korr's robots did repairs to the transport ship's hull, Dex slept in his bunk on the *Silent Horizon* in the hangar bay.

He dreamed of Lacy. He dreamed of them floating together in space. Lacy's head was tucked into his chest, his arms wrapped around her as he kissed her forehead. There were no sounds, just the beauty of space and the distant stars illuminating them. Lacy looked up into his eyes and spoke, but the words were incomprehensible. He knew she was speaking, but her mouth didn't match what his mind knew she was saying, and he could sense fear in her. Dex held her at a distance, trying to ask what she meant, but his voice couldn't escape his lips. A cold presence came over him, and they were both gripped by a large hand. Dex and Lacy were spun around, and his entire field of view was engulfed by flowing scarlet. No discernible features could be made out, but the being they stared at seemed to be constantly changing shape, staring at them with infinite eyes, probing them from all directions. No longer were they in space but in a vast, barren, murky brown and red world. A voice boomed and shattered his mind. Dex felt his soul escape him and flee toward the being. As it did, his insides were lit on fire. His eyes and brain melted. Dex screamed, but the cries were lost as he fell into a void with walls made of rotting bones that bled and laughed at his suffering.

Dex woke up with cold sweats. The voice of the being from the dream echoed in his mind, but he still couldn't make out any of the words.

The sound of his comms device snapped Dex to attention.

"Dex," Korr's voice spoke through the comm. "If you're awake, come on up to the bridge. We're almost out of the nebula. Wanna figure out a plan for Reechi."

Dex swung his legs off the bed, then was up and rubbed his eyes.

After a moment, Korr called again. "You there? All right, keep sleeping."

Dex stood up and walked over to the console to pick up his communicator. "Yeah, I'm up. Be there in a few. How long's it been?" He tossed the communicator on his bunk and started getting dressed.

"You've been out almost three hours. Everybody sleep that long where you're from?" Korr asked with humor in his voice.

Dex's eyes widened in surprise as his head popped out through his shirt collar. He grabbed the comm. "Korr, that ain't even half a night's rest where I'm from." He could almost hear Korr's shock from the silence over the comms. Dex laughed to himself. "I'm on my way now." He grabbed his belt with holstered blaster off the opposite bunk as he left his ship.

The bustle of the hangar bay was much calmer now than when he had first stepped into the hangar. Dex assumed Korr had his robots fully staffed on ship repairs.

When Dex arrived back on the bridge, the first thing he noticed was that the thickness of the nebula had decreased. Here and there were black spaces, and while there were still plenty of asteroids, they were able to see much further out. Even the sound of thunder was less frequent.

"Good sleep?" Korr asked from his control panel.

Dex walked toward Korr and pulled a seat up next to him. "It's nice to be back in my own bed. But I've felt better."

Korr gave him a look. "So, not a good one then?"

"Just some bad dreams."

Korr's fingers were broken up, messing with a dozen switches and buttons at once, but his attention was focused on Dex. "Tell me about them."

Dex rested his elbow on the console and rested his head in his hand. "I already lost it. Just some..." he paused and thought hard. "Red. All I can remember is red."

Korr eyed him hard. "Red? Just red?"

"Yeah, red. Maybe a bit darker, crimson or scarlet."

Korr sat back in his chair and looked out into the nebula. "Computer, think you can navigate from here?" An affirmative beep sounded from the console. Korr's mechanical fingers formed back into his normal-looking hands, then he turned to give Dex his full attention. "What you saw was a vision of the Emperor."

Dex looked confused. "H-... how do you know?"

"His empire has little religious imagery. But scarlet is His color. I don't know if you've noticed yet, but you won't be seeing the Emperor's colors anywhere."

Dex scoffed. "You can't just outlaw a color. That's ridiculous!" But he thought back to when he and Lacy were first taken prisoner. The Zar-Mecks had ordered him to remove his P.E.S. because 'none could wear the Emperor's colors.'

"When you're a god, I think you can outlaw whatever you please."

Dex calmed at the remark. "He may be a god here. But not one with a 'capital G'"

"What does that mean?" Korr asked.

"On my planet," Dex began, "we have many gods."

Korr nodded, "Yeah, I remember. You said they usually don't come down?"

"Yeah. Well, most of these gods, how do I put this? They don't do a whole lot. They kinda just exist in league with groups of other gods. They've got their own areas of expertise and report to higher-ups. Gods with a 'capital G,' or titans, they're sometimes called."

"And which ones come down to your people?"

Dex leaned back. "Well, none of those little G's have come down to my people. But there was one that most people accepted. Now that one's a God with a capital G. He runs the whole show. Doesn't report to anyone higher, and oversees all."

"So in your eyes, our Emperor is a god without a 'capital G?'" Korr asked.

"Buddy, I don't think your Emperor is either. As you said, evil is two sides of a coin. I think you've got a demon running your show."

"Not my show. I'm the only one who runs my own. But by the sound of that dream, he might be running yours soon."

"What do you mean?"

Korr spoke gently. "What I'm saying is, the

Emperor's looking for you. That dream, vision, whatever you want to call it, he's sending out his signals. If you're not already in his grip, he'll find a way to bring you in. You better keep tight security on that brain of yours, before he locks in."

"Then what happens?"

Korr breathed out deeply. "You'll have to let me know. Do you know how often I've met people like you? People who haven't turned heel at their first chance?" He stood up and walked toward the view screen.

Dex followed after him. "If you don't know, then half the stuff you just said could be nonsense. What are you, tryna scare me away from him? Scary superstitions aren't going to stop me from saving my wife."

Korr stayed facing the screen. "Dex, all I know is the Emperor always gets what he wants. He has a way of getting into our minds."

"What, are you talking about mind control?"

"He can't make me lift my finger or jump on one leg, but he has access. He can tap into my mind and take what he wants, or send visions directly back into it. On a massive scale, when that's all you know, when that's all *anyone* knows, what he tells you, it might as well be mind control."

Dex tried wrapping his brain around what he was hearing. "But... hold on," he almost reached for his blaster, feeling as if he'd fallen into a trap, but resisted, not sensing in Korr's body language any immediate hostility. "If he can look into your mind right now, why's he still looking for me?" Dex asked it as a challenge to see where Korr's loyalties - or lack thereof - truly lay, then followed it up with, "Why doesn't he look into your mind right now and see that I'm here in front of you?"

Dex prepared to jump out of sight based on Korr's next words.

Korr only shrugged. "Like I said, by all accounts, I'm a dead man. Why search me?"

It eased Dex the littlest bit. From his tone and body language, although Dex was no expert on the latter, something told him to believe his cyborg companion.

There was a moment of pause between the two men before Korr added, "Look, you can't change what's already happened. The Emperor knows about you, and he will search for you. I've done what I can for too many poor souls caught in the Emperor's grasp. They might be saved, but in the end, it just delays their planet's downfall. You may get out of this alive, but your planet's fate is sealed."

Dex put a hand on Korr's shoulder. "I understand."

Maybe Korr was just trying to scare him, or maybe he was telling the truth about the extent of the Emperor's power. One thing, though, was now certain to Dex. Korr had spoken from the heart and wanted to help his new friend.

"But I don't believe I've doomed my planet," he said. "Lacy was always the optimistic one, so maybe that's just her rubbing off on me. She wouldn't let our mistakes destroy our planet. She'd want me to make sure the Empire never found Earth. But I can't do that without Lacy by my side, and there's still a chance for her."

Korr looked at his friend. "I admire your spirit. Maybe one day I'll find a woman like your Lacy."

Dex patted him hard on the back and smiled. "I hope you do, Korr."

The skies cleared outside the view screen, and in

the distance, a small orb appeared.

Dex studied the orb. "Is that it?" He asked.

Korr nodded. "Reechi. Fifth planet of the Empire of the Void." He exhaled. "Guess we'd better start planning. We'll be there within the hour." Then, to the screen, he said, "Computer, zoom in on Reechi."

The screen did as it was commanded, and the image of the planet blew up so they could see it clearly. Dex's eyes widened in awe.

Reechi was a series of rings, one on top of the other in a more-or-less sphere shape, with a small star in the center. The planet was orbited by a purple moon, a quarter of the size of the planet.

"This can't be real..." Dex said in a hushed tone.

Korr laughed. "Oh, the wonders you'll see in these parts. If it weren't for the Emperor, I think you'd actually like this place."

"How about you send me postcards when Lacy and I get out of here?"

Korr shrugged. "Yeahhh... I don't know what that means."

With his hands on his hips, Dex dropped his head and shook it. He then laughed out a deep sigh. "Okay, how about we start planning? What do I need to know?"

"Let's discuss this over a drink." Korr turned to leave the bridge, heading back for the dining area they'd first talked in, and Dex followed. "First things first. This ship doesn't exist, and neither do I. At the first sign of trouble, I'm out. All I'm here for is to get your foot in the door."

They passed through the bridge door and walked through the hall. Dex asked, "And no one's going to question an Empire ship just... hanging out?"

Korr brushed the question away by waving his hand in the air. "I've got the proper codes. They're frauds, but unless we call attention to them, they should go unnoticed. Our biggest issue is you. You look enough like a taouron, but your eyes give it away."

"Taouron?" Dex asked.

Korr stopped, turned around, and gestured to himself. "My kind. You said you're called a human right?"

Dex nodded, and they continued walking.

"By the way, do you glow?" Korr asked.

"I... I don't even know what that's supposed to mean."

"We taouron glow when our emotions run high. So, try not to get too worked up at any point. It'll be suspicious."

"And my eyes? I feel like that's more of a giveaway. Do you have contacts I could borrow?"

"I wish. Honestly, the only option I can think of at the moment is a transplant, but we don't have time for it."

"How long would it take?"

Korr stopped again at the threshold of the kitchen. "Are you serious?" He eyed Dex hard.

Without an ounce of irony in his voice, Dex told him, "If it helps me get back to Lacy."

Korr rolled his eyes and entered the kitchen, walking toward the cabinets with the drinks. Dex took a seat at the table.

"Too long," Korr said. "By the time you were ready to see again, your girl would be long gone. For now, we'll just have to hope my guy doesn't pay you much mind. Just keep your head down and hopefully you'll be fine. But if they don't, we'll fly back up here and I'll bring you half the distance to the Heart of the Void." As he spoke, Korr warmed up their drinks and joined Dex at the table.

"What if things go south?" Dex asked. "I know, you're out. But how will you get back here?"

"I've been around the block plenty. I'll find a way out."

"And security forces? What am I up against?"

"The Emperor's army patrols every planet. We may run into the Zar-Meck on the ground. If you come into contact with them in flight, you'd better hope that new engine works."

Dex pursed his lips. "Fantastic."

After a moment of silence, Korr slapped Dex's shoulder and said, "Don't worry. I'm sure all will go well."

"You really think so?" Dex asked, unbelieving.

Without missing a beat, Korr said with a smile. "No. Not a chance in Maoul. But for as stupid as I think your goal is, I admire it, and I hope you succeed."

Dex gently nodded his head. "Well... let's not put this off any longer. Here's to Lacy." He raised his drink in a toast, and Korr joined him.

For the next thirty minutes or so, Dex and Korr prepared the *Silent Horizon*. Korr's bots had filled it with fuel, and Korr input the coordinates for the Heart of the Void. He also ordered his robots to stock up the ship with provisions and new tools to replace the ones lost at the outpost and a few new ones, including a jarrmin box and a small personal comm device. Dex checked his blaster's charge. Having never been used, the battery pack was full, and he had two spares.

Korr pointed out to him that he'd be arrested on

sight if he were seen with a blaster on his hip. Dex took off his jacket and converted the holster, along with a spare belt, into a gunner's strap on his left side, hanging from his shoulder. With his jacket on, the blaster was totally concealed.

"No open carry?" Dex asked with a smirk. "Your Emperor guy would hate America."

"Is that one of your planets?"

"No, it's on Earth, but a totally different world."

Korr also advised Dex to keep the scarlet P.E.S. and Zar-Meck suit hidden away, in case his ship is inspected at the port.

"Arrested on sight?" Dex asked.

Korr only nodded.

One of the smaller bots entered the *Silent Horizon*. "Sir," the robot said. "We are approaching the planet. Are you ready to descend?"

"We are," Korr replied.

"Good luck," the robot said, then turned to face Dex. "Don't die." It then promptly left the ship.

Dex took his seat in the captain's chair, and Korr sat in Lacy's. Dex thought it felt wrong, someone else sitting in her seat, but tried to brush it away. It wasn't as if he were replacing her.

The engines rumbled, and the two of them flew out of the hangar.

As Reechi came into their view, Dex was again taken aback with awe. Small ships flew all around the planet and through it. The surface of the planet's rings was a light brown and had lakes and oceans scattered throughout that sometimes fell off one layer, to the ring below it. Since the rings were constantly shifting, sometimes the water would flow directly into the sun.

Korr told Dex all planet life was maintained on the outside of the rings, while mining was done on the core side. Valuable minerals were Reechi's main export for trade, and though it was incredibly dangerous, the finds on the rings closest to the core made Reechi one of the richest planets in the empire.

Looking out toward the purple moon, Dex saw one of the Empire's ships orbiting it.

"The moon is the military's outpost," Korr told him. "That's a capital ship. Heavy with ground troops and starfighters."

"Is Reechi expecting war?"

Korr shook his head.

"I think they're just on the lookout." Korr gave Dex a look that filled in the rest.

Dex felt a chill run down his spine. They couldn't know where he was this soon, but he knew this mission just got harder.

Korr used the *Silent Horizon*'s radio to call in their arrival. "Moorak City Port Six, requesting landing."

The two men looked at each other as they listened to the radio feedback. Dex was clearly more nervous than his companion, and the looming capital ship did nothing to quell his fears.

After only a moment, a dry-toned voice responds to them. "This is Moorak City Port Control. We don't see any registration on your ship. Maintain your current course. Please identify and send over clearance codes."

"Port Control, I acknowledge. This is a private shuttle, two passengers. You'll find all you request through our clearance codes. Transmitting now." Then to Dex he asked, "Where do I send them from?"

Dex pushed buttons on the computer and turned it over to Korr. "Are the codes on a drive or something?"

Korr pulled out a small, inch-long gold stick with a small needle on the end. "Can your ship read this?"

"I... I have no idea what that is. Is this all you've got?"

From the computer, "Private shuttle, please send over your clearance codes. If you need assistance, we will send out a port security officer."

"Damn!" Korr slammed his hand down. "You should have said something!"

"Me? You're the one who had everything worked out! Try your robot... hand... thing!"

Korr looked at his hands and thought.

The port controller spoke again through the radio. "Private shuttle, we are sending someone to assist you."

This time, Dex was the one to jump into action. "Port control, that's not necessary, we are transmitting now." Dex eyed Korr hard to say, *get a move on!* "We just came out of the nebula and had an issue with a jrahk-bird. Messed with our system a bit."

Korr observed the ship's disc drive and worked to figure out a configuration his hand could take to transmit the data. As he did, Dex waited impatiently for a response from the port control.

The voice came back much warmer with a deep exhale. "I hear that," it said. "Buddy of mine was flying through two weeks ago, and they're still working out the kinks in his ship. We'll hold on the assist if you say you're all good. Hope y'all are doing okay."

Korr figured it out and, using himself as a converter,

uploaded the clearance codes onto the ship's computer.

"Oh yeah, we're just dandy," Dex said.

Korr shot Dex a confused and somewhat disgruntled look. He quietly shouted, "Dandy? What is that? Don't say your weird Earth words!"

"Transmitting the codes now," Dex said, then turned to Korr. "I don't know what is or isn't a word here, give me a break!"

They waited for a response. It felt like hours, and Dex could swear the capital ship was headed in their direction. He felt the dead stare from the Zar-Mecks on him. A nagging thought in the back of his mind told him the port control alerted the ship to Dex's presence, and any moment now they would be blown out of the sky. He looked over to his companion and saw that even Korr's fists were balled up tightly in fearful anticipation.

The radio sounded again.

"You are clear for landing. Set a course for Port Six, bay twelve. Glory be to the Emperor."

"Glory be," Korr said, and Dex repeated. They both let out a deep sigh and laughed once the radio signal was closed.

"Guess we should have planned a little better," Korr said through a laugh.

"Yeah, next time, I'll make the plan, and you just tell me how we can make it work," Dex said. "Why does the Empire even have these?"

"Interplanetary travel of private craft is highly restrictive unless you're on Empire business, or work for the military in some way. But even then, if it's Imperial business, might as well fly with the Empire. Good way to keep an eye on everything. You wanna see the universe?

Join the army or take public transport. Right now, I don't really recommend either."

"And us flying in a ship like this won't raise suspicion?" Dex pried. "This ship doesn't exactly look like one of their starfighters."

Korr bobbed his head from left to right. "Yeah, no, it doesn't. But I only said highly restrictive. Not impossible. Especially if you've got the cash for it."

Dex piloted to their destination, taking directions from Korr. Moorak City was large, covering a huge swath of land, but none of the buildings were very tall. The landscape on this ring was a bland brown, with little vegetation, and rivers broke up most of the city into smaller districts. The streets were packed with citizens, driving around in fancy hover-cars or cruising above the city in larger yachts. Far off, Dex watched a shuttle launch from the ground and fly off to another ring.

Dex told him, "That's how a lot of people get from one ring to another. It's the public transportation."

As they touched down in the port bay, the roof closed in over them, sealing them off from the brownish-green sky.

Dex looked over at Korr. He hadn't expected to be sealed in.

"You'll be fine. I'm sure," Korr tried to reassure him, but Dex understood what he meant. No more 'we' in Korr's words. He'd gotten Dex through and was one step closer to bailing. Dex said nothing in response.

Korr got out of his seat, but Dex stayed. "You coming or what?"

Dex replied, "If we're trying not to get me caught, I was thinking maybe I should stay with the ship."

"Not getting caught means not acting suspicious. Hiding on the ship and not checking in with the port officials is suspicious. Me hiring a guy to put a new engine in a ship that isn't mine is suspicious. Acting like you belong here isn't. Let's go."

Dex reluctantly stood and followed Korr.

"Let me take the lead," Korr instructed. "My guy is a few blocks from here, so don't-"

Dex interrupted. "Yeah, I know. Don't draw any attention."

They exited the ship and were greeted by a short being. He stood about four feet tall, with thick, hairy arms that reached nearly to the ground. His feet were round like suction cups and uncovered by shoes. The man had a round jaw and tiny blue eyes on his hugely protruding forehead. Instead of ears, there were two inch-deep holes on either side of his head, with small antennae lining the insides. Though the man looked like a small beast, he dressed as formally as Dex would expect any public servant to.

He spoke with a gruff but polite voice. "Welcome to Moorak City. Identification was transmitted with your codes, but due to policy, I still have to ask some security questions."

"Happy to oblige," Korr said with a smile.

"Great," the port official said and grabbed a tablet hanging from his belt. "Are you carrying any produce or liquids not approved by Empire customs?"

Korr shook his head.

The official typed onto the black tablet. Dex saw nothing on the screen but saw lights reflecting in the official's eyes.

"Are you transporting any unregistered firearms?"

Again, Korr shook his head.

The list carried on with the same questions Dex was asked at any customs checkpoint at an Earth airport. After a dozen or so, the official apologized for making them wait and let them proceed.

Dex and Korr left the hangar bay, and Dex was at a loss for the number of different species he was seeing.

Korr told him, "There are about two hundred intelligent species living on Reechi. That guy back there is one of the natives, a raestien."

"Interesting," Dex said to himself.

The cries of the city were loud. Hover-cars zoomed by at breakneck speed. The blocks were a mix of sturdy, well-maintained commercial buildings and ramshackle bazaars, with people shouting at each other to buy their wares or taste their foods. Strange scents floated everywhere and crept into Dex's nose. Some were appalling, and some were better than anything he'd ever smelled before. Even with the bad, he wanted to try it all and hoped that one day he'd be able to try these foods without being hunted by the Emperor's army.

As they walked through the streets, Dex took in all the strange sights while trying not to look out of place. He saw all the different types of species and made mental notes to ask Korr what each one was if they had time later. The most common species he saw were the raestiens, and by the look of it, they made up most of the working class. In most of the storefronts or restaurants they passed, it was the raestiens who did the serving.

The next largest group of species Dex noticed was the taouron. He couldn't tell if they were held in a higher societal tier than the raestiens, but the trend he saw was that their clothes were usually a little more formal than those of the other species. At least, they were by his Earth standard.

With each step, Dex paid less attention to trying to be inconspicuous and soon tripped on a sidewalk. Before he hit the ground, Korr reached out to grab him, but someone else stopped his fall, and his blaster fell to the ground.

"Watch where you are stepping, citizen." A voice said from behind Dex and pulled him back to his feet.

Dex's eyes widened in shock seeing his blaster fall from the holster, and he quickly grabbed it back up and slipped it into place. He then turned around to thank the person who saved his fall but went cold and pale at the sight of them.

"Are you feeling okay, sir? Do you need a doctor?" The Zar-Meck asked.

Korr began to back away.

Dex dropped his head a little and looked at the ground. "No, sir, I'm fine. Thank you."

The Zar-Meck gave him a once-over. "Mind your step now," he said, then carried on.

A bead of sweat formed on Dex's brow. When he turned to find Korr, he saw him standing more than five feet away. Even though he knew Korr was ready to ditch him, he still felt disappointed.

"Don't worry. I know not to give them your name." Dex continued walking without waiting for a response.

They carried on in silence the rest of the way to Korr's connection.

10. Tools from the Empire

Lacy sat in a comfortable armchair in the Analyst's office. He sat in an elegant chair behind the desk that separated them. It had been nearly thirty minutes of him reading from his tablet in silence, and her waiting for him to acknowledge her. She'd tried talking to him when she was escorted in, but no matter what she said, he never so much as looked at her.

At one point, a service robot came in carrying a mug of something that smelled to Lacy of cinnamon. Lacy perked up, thinking of Robbie, worried they retrieved him and changed back his programming, but swiftly resigned herself, knowing better.

The Analyst took the mug and shooed the robot out of the room with his hand.

Lacy saw this as a test, both the recognition of the robot and the lack of a drink offered to her, and decided not to give it. She felt confident in her decision when the Analyst eyed her, then returned to his tablet to type more.

Growing incredibly impatient, Lacy started patting the arms of the chair at a slow, steady pace. The Analyst didn't stir. After a few seconds, she upped the pace and looked around the room nonchalantly. She then noticed the Analyst's eyes twitch the slightest bit, like he was about to look at her, then changed his mind.

So I do have your attention? She thought to herself. Lacy slouched in her chair and began to quietly hum a melody of an old popular Earth song.

The Analyst didn't move.

Instead of a hum, Lacy began to whistle. *Who isn't annoyed by whistling?* She asked herself.

The Analyst moved again. This time, he didn't stop himself from looking at her. He studied Lacy for a moment.

Lacy stopped and met his gaze.

Their eyes were locked. Who would speak first?

Lacy didn't want to lose this battle of wills. Just because she was a prisoner on this ship didn't mean she had to be a prisoner to him, too.

His mouth began to open, but then... he returned to his tablet and smiled.

Frustrated and dropping care as to what would happen to her next, at least it would be something, Lacy stood up. She at least expected one of the Zar-Mecks to rush in and throw her back into the chair, but nothing happened. She walked around the office, a large room filled with antiques and murals she didn't understand. Lacy looked back at the Analyst and saw he was deep in thought with his tablet, so she began touching the antiques, waiting for a response.

Almost all of them, she quickly realized, were variations of the same figure. Ranging from crudely made clay figures that looked like they were made by a child to pieces of high art that even - she had to admit - belonged in a museum, depicting a scarlet figure with a golden head. Some of them were posed in menacing or aggressive ways, while others radiated with a sense of warmth and care.

The murals were the same. On one side of the room, in a style that reminded her of ancient Japanese art, the scarlet being appeared to be leading an army against strange, almost shapeless, oily black monstrosities. On the other side of the room, a mural showed people gathered around the being like he was Jesus Christ giving the Sermon on the Mount.

Lacy looked back at the one with the army and reached out to touch it. She extended her fingers to trace the scarlet figure on the canvas, but as her fingertips were just a centimeter away from making contact, the Analyst spoke up.

"That will be enough of that," he said.

Lacy jumped in surprise and looked back at him.

"Please, Mrs. Prullen, have a seat." The Analyst gestured toward the armchair.

Lacy hesitated a moment. "I'm glad I have your attention," she said.

The Analyst said nothing but motioned to the chair again.

She walked over to his desk and took her seat.

"Now, Mrs. Prullen-" the Analyst began, but was interrupted by Lacy.

"No."

The Analyst raised an eyebrow. "No... what, Mrs. Prullen?"

"You can address me as Lieutenant," she remarked sternly.

The Analyst cleared his throat. "As I recall, you stated yesterday that you wished to be called 'Mrs. Prullen.' Am I wrong?"

"That is my name. But until I know yours, you can

call me Lieutenant, and I'll address you by your rank as well."

The Analyst was silent again, and after a moment of staring, he returned to his tablet, tapped it a bit, then gave Lacy his attention. "I have no *rank*. My name is Jaskek Dreed."

Lacy hadn't expected such a complacent response. She nodded her head in an 'okay then... ' gesture. "So you're not military then?"

"Our military has officers and the Zar-Meck. In terms of rank, Mrs. Prullen, we don't have any. There is the Emperor and his people."

Lacy nodded again.

"It seems your people take a different approach to this," Jaskek said with a bit of condescension in his voice, if Lacy was interpreting it accurately. "If I understand correctly, your husband holds command over you?"

Lacy pushed her tongue against the inside of her lower gums in annoyance. "Only on paper. Don't you guys have marriage here?"

Jaskek studied his tablet. "But it says he's a Captain, which, according to your ship, means he is in charge of you."

"Have you listened to our logs too?" Lacy asked.
"Yes."

"Then you should know that our rank only determines how much we're paid."

"I disagree. Listening to your husband's logs, as you have very few, it appears to me that he is the one giving orders."

"We have different roles. He flies, and I keep the ship in the air. He comes up with ideas, and I tell him how we can make it work. It's fifty-fifty, like a healthy marriage should be."

"Hmm." Jaskek typed more on his tablet. "I guess that brings us to why I called you here. You, like your ship's records, are very inconsistent. I can't imagine your mission going smoothly if you weren't respecting the foundations your people set for you."

Lacy shifted her posture. "Our mission was perfect until you showed up."

"Was it not you who landed on *our* outpost?" Jaskek replied sharply.

Lacy didn't say anything.

Jaskek scrolled through his tablet. "Last time we spoke like this, we discussed your ship's historical documents. Specifically, their lack of consistency. Tell me about them."

She knew if she wanted a way out of there, she'd have to work with him. Just enough, though, to keep him hooked. Lacy knew Jaskek would release her to her impending doom once there was nothing left to learn. She thought hard about her next move, and Jaskek did his best to hide his impatience.

"Don't you have legends around here?"

Jaskek raised an eyebrow.

"You know," Lacy began. "Myths? Fables? Stories of heroes that fought off evil or scary stories to spook little kids?"

"Of course," Jaskek said. "It's a core foundation of the Emperor's teachings to pass on his history to the next generations. As you have just studied over on that mural, our Glorious Emperor has cast out evil across the universe for us."

Lacy fixed her posture and sat up, leaning slightly toward the Analyst.

"I'm not talking about history. Don't you ever make stuff up? Golly, don't you people ever have any fun?"

"Why would we seek to confuse our youth? Is it not important on your planet to educate your children?"

Lacy sighed deeply in annoyance. "Of course we do! We also let our people be creative!"

Jaskek exhaled and typed something onto his table with his eyebrows raised. "This seems like it would lead many people astray from the truth. But... your world hasn't been educated. Once the Emperor's forces find your planet, we will remedy this."

Lacy rushed to find something to say, but was cut short in her thoughts.

"In our talk," Jaskek spoke up again, "you called these stories 'fiction.' Fabrications or alterations of reality, it sounds like. Your ship's database was absolutely filled with..."

"Movies," Lacy interjected. "And books."

"Yes, books I know, and we have plenty of those. And 'movies,' you call them, we have similar mediums of visual storytelling, although the term you use is strange. So... simple-minded."

Lacy shrugged off the condescension. "It works, doesn't it?"

"Hm. Regardless, you claim your people are encouraged to be creative, and that's the best you come up with. Movies."

He's looking for a reaction, Lacy thought.

They eyed each other for a moment, patient to see who would break the silence. But while Lacy thought she was making the officer's job harder, every move, and lack of, was just more information Jaskek was happy to work with.

"These characters and stories are made up," Jaskek began again. "They never existed, yet from what we could find, the volume of 'fiction' in your database strongly outweighs the... let's call it 'non-fiction.'"

Lacy nodded sarcastically with a smile. "Creative."

Jaskek pursed his lips and carried on as if not being criticized. "This tells me that earthlings value their own fabrications more than dealing with reality. Tell me, is your world dying?"

"Excuse me?"

"The only logical explanation for this is that life on your world is so terrible, your people are trying to escape it. Which would make sense for why you and your partner were attempting to flee this 'Earth.'"

"No, it's not like-"

"Were your people dying?"

"No!"

"Famine? Plague?"

Lacy opened her mouth but was quickly interrupted.

"Was it war?"

"No, we-" Lacy became flushed with annoyance.

"I found in a scan of these stories a strong uptick in the use of the word 'war' in the last decade. Upon further research, I found that many of these stories are all referencing the same event. It's strange, all of these fictional stories share nothing in common except for one major event. Explain this to me."

"See, there was a war. There were a few. But even when it was over, some people couldn't escape it." Lacy thought about what Dex had told her about his father, how, after the war, he would be plagued by nightmares and claimed he was back on the front lines. Even by the time the *Silent Horizon* began its voyage, no one knew how to help him.

Jaskek relaxed a bit. Lacy was sitting straight up, stuck in her thoughts.

"These stories were sometimes the only help some people had to get by. When Dex and I left Earth, things were getting better. In fact, life was the greatest we'd probably ever known as a race. But whenever things were bad, we would watch these movies and see these heroes who had the same struggles as us. They would overcome, and for a little while, it gave us all hope for something better.

"But they didn't accomplish anything. They weren't real." Jaskek was blunt and demeaning in his response. "Were there not enough *real* stories to inspire the people of Earth? Truly," he scoffed again, "You Earth does sound quite sad."

"It didn't matter if it wasn't real to the people watching these movies. I can't really explain it better than that. Film wasn't really my thing-"

Jaskek cut her off. "So, what you're saying is you don't know what you're talking about?"

"No! That's not at all what I meant! It's like... It's like music! You have music here, at least, right?"

Jaskek's continued monotonous tone was irritating Lacy to the point where she could kill him just for hearing another bland word. "Yes, of course we have music." Then, with pride in his voice and a slight glow in his skin, "We have the grandest operas in the known universe!"

"About your Emperor, I suppose?"

Returning to the monotonous tone, "Well, naturally."

Lacy huffed. "Well, I'd bet our music is a little more interesting."

The tone of Jaskek's voice shifted again. "And why would you say that?"

The shift was not in pride but in... *curiosity?* Lacy thought to herself. Jaskek, for the first time in their appointment, put down the tablet. By the way he did so, Lacy guessed it was an unconscious gesture. She thought, *he's not asking for his report anymore. I've got him.*

"Sometimes," Lacy began, "people connect more to things that aren't just a story. Sometimes, it's an emotion itself that people need to connect with. If you've done your research on our ship, have you listened to 'Rhapsody in Blue?'"

Jaskek tilted his head to the side quizzically.

Lacy harumphed, then reached across the desk between them, grabbing Jaskek's tablet before he could react. "How does this thing work?" Lacy asked.

Jaskek calmly stood up and held out his hand. "Safety measures," he said. "You can't. That tablet is assigned to me, and me alone." He tapped his temple with his free hand. "Special lenses. Only I can read what's on there."

Lacy pursed her lips and handed the tablet back. They both took their seats.

"Now," Jaskek began. "What was the name of that song?"

"Rhapsody in Blue."

"Hm. Strange." Jaskek's words were blunt again. He tapped on the screen, then looked as if he were scrolling.

Lacy saw the lights flicker in her eyes. "Here we are." He laid the tablet down on the desk, and the music began.

An oboe hit its notes rapidly for the first few measures, then crescendoed high and fell.

Lacy kept her focus on Jaskek. His eyes wouldn't stray from the tablet, and he showed no sign of emotion.

The strings assisted the melody, and the trumpets made their introduction. The volume remained low for a few moments.

Jaskek leaned in and stroked his jaw in concentration. "What is going on in this? What's the-"

Lacy shushed him.

Jaskek gave her a look of annoyance, then went back to the music.

At a minute in, the piano entered. The music briefly swelled, then exploded into a symphony!

Unprepared, Jaskek gave a slight jump. He tried to hide it and conceal his face from giving anything away, but Lacy saw all she needed. His skin, though incredibly faint, glowed.

The music continued, flowing between moments of the powerful orchestra blasting into a party, and low moments of the piano stealing the show in softer, rapid solos.

Lacy tried to keep her concentration on Jaskek's subtle shifts in his expression, the intensity of his glowing skin, but soon enough, even she was swept up in the music. It was because of this that she knew she'd picked the right song.

Two and a half minutes into the song, the piano player's fingers danced rapidly across the keys. Jaskek's skin was illuminating more, but still lightly, and pulsing almost in sync with the music. Two minutes and fifty seconds, the music's tempo increased. Lacy could see in his eyes that Jaskek was enthralled by the music. The tempo slowed down momentarily at three minutes in, and then another explosion of the brass instruments!

Lacy's own heart was racing. Partially for Jaskek's reaction, but mostly for her own love of the piece. But it was cut short.

Jaskek shot out his hand and turned the music off, then tapped another unknown button on the tablet.

Lacy sprang to her feet in a mixture of annoyance and mild anger. "What was that for?"

The illumination of Jaskek's skin dulled but didn't entirely fade. "That's enough of that. You'll be escorted back to your room now."

The door in the rear of the room opened, and a Zar-Meck entered. It walked briskly to Lacy's side and grabbed her by the arm. In its other hand, it held a baton at the ready.

"I will send for you when we arrive at our destination."

The Zar-Meck began to pull Lacy away.

"You liked it!" She shouted over her shoulder, trying to pull herself away from the Zar-Meck. "Admit it! You loved that music!"

Jaskek stayed seated and refused to look up from his tablet or say a word as Lacy was removed from his office.

* * *

Hours later, Jaskek stood in his small quarters,

looking out toward the Heart of the Void. Ahead of him was his Emperor, his God. He hadn't expected to return so soon after receiving his first assignment.

Jaskek could feel his heart beating heavily. Since his appointment with Lacy, the melody she'd played for him was stuck in his head.

Stepping away from the window, he walked over to the door to his quarters and looked into the hallway. It was empty, but he still made sure that when he closed his door, it was locked. Until they reached the Heart, Jaskek would not be disturbed.

From the small desk next to his cot, Jaskek picked up his tablet. He scrolled through his schedule and ensured there was nowhere he had to be for the next hour. *All clear*, he told himself.

Finally at peace, Jaskek navigated the *Silent Horizon*'s logs.

"Rhapsody in Blue" played on the imperial transport ship one more time.

11. Trouble on Reechi

The mechanic's shop took up nearly the entire length of the block, yet was the shortest one on it. The front of the building was mostly open garage doors, with a sign overhead written in a language Dex didn't understand. He assumed it was just the name of the shop.

Dex and Korr walked into the shop, where species of all kinds, though mostly raestiens, were tuning up speeders and hover-cars; smaller-scale craft.

Korr tapped on one of the worker's shoulders, a small, blue-furred creature with bug eyes. "Is Hwaq around?"

The bug-eyed creature spoke in an alien tongue that came out in rapid, nasally bursts. Waving at them to follow with mechanical arms serving as extensions to its naturally stubby arms, the mechanic led them through the shop.

They made their way into a cluttered office, where an overweight raestien sat behind a desk. He was reclining with his feet up on the desk, and his eyes closed. It smelled to Dex of car exhaust. He struggled to hold back a cough, but still felt a surprising sense of nostalgia for Earth.

The bug-eyed creature walked around the desk and shook the overweight raestien awake.

"What! What is it?" Hwaq shouted in a gruff voice

and sat upright in his chair. He looked around and saw Korr. "Ah! Korr Montori! Good to see you!" Hwaq leaned forward and reached across the overcrowded desk. Dex assumed he was going to shake Korr's hand, but instead, Korr wrapped both his hands around Hwaq's fist and bowed his head.

"Glory be to the Emperor," Korr said with reverence.

Hwaq pulled his hand away and slumped back in his chair. "Glory be," he said. "Go on now, have a seat." Hwaq then turned to the bug-eyed creature. "Don't you be havin' a job to get to?"

The bug-eyed creature threw up its stubby arms, muttered something in its species' tongue, and left. As it did, Korr took a seat across the desk from Hwaq. There were no other chairs, so Dex stood in the corner, where a shadow just barely covered his face.

"Those bohtith, biggest slackers in the known universe. I've had that guy on my payroll for nearly fifteen years. Would've fired him years back if it weren't for their darn union."

Korr feigned agreement. "I hear ya, Hwaq. Used to have one of them on my crew. Thank the Emperor I don't have to tolerate unions on my ship."

They both laughed. Dex stood where he was with his arms crossed, not making a sound, trying to stay unnoticed.

Hwaq wiped away a tear from his laughter that hung on his over-extended forehead. "So Korr, what can I do for ya?"

Korr flashed the mechanic a dashing smile, "Straight to the money with you, as always."

"Well. If you stopped by my place once in a while, said 'hi' to my family, or stayed for dinner, it'd be different. But this is my shop."

Korr threw up his hands in defeat. "Fair's fair," he said. "Maybe next time I'm in town, you can make me some authentic Reechian food. How is Laqqa by the way?"

"Good, my friend. She just delivered our seventeenth kid."

Dex barely held in his surprise, but Korr acted like it was just another thing. He said, "Congrats, my friend. The Emperor has definitely bestowed his blessings on you."

"And I'm grateful for it every day."

"Good... good," Korr began. "Well, I guess as a little bonus to help out with the newborn, I've got a high-paying job for you."

Hwaq fixed his posture in the chair.

Korr gestured, without turning, to Dex. It was an intentional move; address the real customer but keep the conversation between himself and Hwaq so that he wouldn't have time to notice what was off about Dex. "My friend here needs a new engine for his ship. Hyperdrive."

Hwaq raised an inquisitive eyebrow. "Mighty tall order. What do you need one of those for?" He stared down Dex.

So much for that move, Korr thought to himself.

Dex looked down at Korr.

Korr looked back at Dex and gave a slight nod of the head toward Hwaq.

"My wife," Dex said bluntly. "An anniversary present."

"Uh-huh... she must be high maintenance, taking a

hyperdrive to impress her!" He laughed.

"She's worth it, I can assure you," Dex said calmly.

Korr turned back to Hwaq and began to speak, trying to get the mechanic's eyes back on himself, but was cut off by Hwaq.

"You do know these hyperdrives don't come cheap?"

"I can manage." The cool never faltered in Dex's voice.

Hwaq pursed his lips. "It'll take some time to get ahold of one."

Without hesitation, Dex told him, "Give me the price."

Hwaq looked over at Korr. "I'm not liking your friend's attitude. Not the most polite guy, is he?"

Korr shot a warning glare back at Dex, then returned to Hwaq with a polite smile. In a low voice, he said, "Look, the guy's under stress. It's a last-minute thing, marriage is falling apart, and her dad hates his guts."

"Wonder why," Hwaq retorted with his eyes on Dex.

"Listen, it's a one-time thing, then we'll be out of your hair." He looked up at Hwaq's bald head. "Office, at least. Just do it for me? I'll even bring some apps to dinner."

They both leaned back in their chairs. Hwaq considered for a moment the cost of the operation. He then clucked his tongue and offered Dex his price. "50,000 credits. I can get it installed in three days."

Dex had no sense of the value of anything on Reechi, or anywhere in the Empire for that matter, but acted like it was just another thing. "80,000."

Hwaq was shocked and confused.

Korr couldn't believe what he'd heard.

Dex continued. "80,000, get it installed today."

"Listen, taouron, we ain't got hyperdrives just lyin' around. If you want it done today, it'll be closer to 100,000."

"85."

A smirk appeared on the raestien's face. "98."

Dex dropped his arms and pushed off the wall, standing a little taller. The shadow cut a line across his lips. "85. I've seen your garage. There are plenty of your guys just hanging around. I'm sure one of them can spare some time to find a hyperdrive."

Hwaq glanced at Korr as if to ask for advice. Korr just shrugged. Looking back at Dex, Hwaq offered, "95."

Dex stepped a little closer, the shadow ending just above his nose. "Work with me a little. 87."

"You want a hyperdrive today, someone's either gonna get scammed or paid off. 93."

Dex stood his ground. "88. My girl's dad has a nice fleet of yachts that could use an upgrade. I wouldn't mind referring you." Dex gave a smirk.

Hwaq liked the sound of rich clients. And with seventeen kids to feed... "89 and it's a deal."

With true joy, Dex let the smile loose and stepped out of the shadow, holding out his hand to shake on the deal. "Knew you'd come around."

Hwaq looked at Dex and his outstretched hand in confusion.

Korr hid his rising fear.

Immediately realizing what he'd done, Dex curled his fist. "Pardon, got excited."

Hwaq maintained his confused look but wrapped his hands around Dex's fist. "Glory... be... to the Emperor..." he said slowly, then released his hand.

Dex cleared his throat and stepped back. "Glory be."

There was a terrifying moment of silence for Dex and Korr as Hwaq sat in his chair, staring Dex down.

Dex and Korr straightened themselves.

"You're an odd fellow," Hwaq said, pointing at Dex. He stood. "But I like the size of your pocketbook. Let me see what my boys can do." Hwaq shuffled his way around the desk and out of his office, closing the door behind himself.

As soon as they were sure no one would hear them, Korr jumped to his feet. "What in Maoul is wrong with you?"

Dex stood his ground. "I'm in a rush. I don't exactly have time for courtesy."

"We're walking a thin line as it is, Dex. You're lucky he didn't notice something was up when you reached for him with... whatever that was."

"It's a handshake. Like your weird fist-grip thing."

"Whatever it is. You're sticking out too much. If he said one hundred, you should have stuck with that! You're already costing me a fortune, what's a few thousand credits more?" Korr dropped his hands on his waist and paced the small office, facing away from Dex.

"At least you're only risking money."

Korr turned sharply. "What was that?"

Dex said nothing as the office door opened and Hwaq walked back in. Under his breath, Dex told Korr, "I'll pay you back somehow, don't worry."

Hwaq didn't hear them. "All right," he said. "Looks like we'll be able to get your ship's engine installed today. I just happened to get an offer from an old friend for a decently priced hyperdrive."

"How long do you think it'll take?" Dex asked.

"What, is the party tonight?"

Without hesitation, Dex said yes.

"All right, give me four hours or so. Where's the ship?"

An hour later, the three of them were riding in a hover-truck back to the spaceport. A hyperdrive was secured in a trailer attached to the rear. How Hwaq obtained it, Dex didn't want to ask. He knew he'd been pestering him enough, and how lucky he was to still be on a good track to get to Lacy.

It must have been the haggling, but during the brief drive back to the port, Hwaq lightened up a bit to Dex. "You from Wiccar too?"

Not wanting to engage too much, and not wanting to be rude, Dex looked out the side window as he talked. "Born and bred."

"Nice, I've always wanted to take a trip out there," Hwaq began. "I've seen photos of their oceanside cliffs. Abso-lutely gorgeous. Been thinking about taking my wife there for a second honeymoon. First was on the third moon of Areeno. I tell ya, for a desert planet, some of its moons are incredibly beautiful. You been out that way?"

Dex tried to give a sense of interest in his voice. He appreciated all Hwaq was doing and the fact that he was probably being genuine right now. It made Dex feel even worse about avoiding eye contact so hard. "Not yet. Not a fan of the desert. Gonna try to avoid it as long as I can."

Hwaq scoffed. "Well, I tell ya, if you don't check out its moons, you're missing out."

As they talked, Dex kept mental notes of how many Zar-Mecks they passed on the street. By the time they arrived at the port, he'd seen six. It wasn't many, and he thought he could make an escape from just six, but he knew better. That had only been one small section of a single street. If something happened, there would be dozens of Zar-Mecks all over him.

When they arrived at the spaceport, a taouron security guard waved them through.

"I do plenty of jobs here," Hwaq said. "At this rate, I should just be contracted with the port. They could at least refer me or sumthin', I don't know." They rode around the open bays slowly, avoiding docked ships and port workers. Many of them waved to Hwaq or jokingly cursed him for his driving.

"All right, where's yours?" Hwaq asked.

Dex scanned the bay. "That one, just past the yellow junker."

Only when they approached the *Silent Horizon* did Dex realize that it might be too different from the style of all the other ships in the port. He hadn't seen anything that resembled it and was sure Hwaq had seen nearly every kind of spaceship ever made.

"Well, would you look at that..." Hwaq said quietly to himself as the three of them exited the hover-truck.

Dex and Korr shot him a look.

"Where'd you get this beaut?" Hwaq asked Dex without taking his eyes off the *Silent Horizon*.

Dex looked at Korr, who mouthed something that Dex couldn't understand. "Uh... a friend. Custom build."

Hwaq looked at Dex quizzically. "Come on... I gotta know. I haven't seen a ship like this since I was a kid!" He walked under the ship and ran his fingers along the hull. "It's just like the prototype at the universal fair, what was it, thirty years ago! Sleek futuristic design and everything."

Dex thought of a response quickly. "Where do you think I got the idea for the make? My girl's dad is a collector. Remember the yachts I'm sending your way?" He knew he was getting too close for comfort, but figured if he cozied up to him, talked his language, he'd put himself at better odds. Dex walked alongside Hwaq and smacked him on the back. "Get this job done in decent time, and maybe I'll let ya take a spin."

Before Hwaq could turn to look Dex in the eye, Dex had turned away, walking back in Korr's direction.

"Nah, nah, now don't be messin' with me now, kid."

"Get started and we'll see!" Dex waved a dismissive hand in the air, then addressed Korr quietly. "How'm I doing?"

"I won't lie, buddy, you've got me on the edge of my seat. But..." he looked past Dex to Hwaq, who was now unfastening the trailer from the hover-truck. "Under other circumstances, I'd say you'd fit in just fine on my ship."

Dex smiled. "Maybe one of these days. If life ever calms down."

"Hope it does. But where would the fun be in that?"

They both laughed. "Korr, you and I have very different ideas of fun."

Hwaq pulled the hovering trailer around to the

airlock of the *Silent Horizon*. Dex jumped ahead of him to open the door.

"Thanks, kid," Hwaq said.

Looking at the size of Hwaq compared to the engine he lugged in and the one he'd be taking out, Dex was amazed at the strength raestiens must be capable of.

After Hwaq was through, Dex called over to Korr. "Why don't you take a walk? Get yourself a drink or something. Can't be fun being cooped up in that ship all day."

"Yeah, you'd know, huh?" Korr shouted back.

Dex said nothing but just smiled with a nod, then followed Hwaq in.

* * *

Korr walked around Morak City looking for a bar. He wasn't thirsty, just needed somewhere to get in on all the latest rumors.

Through his first three drinks, nothing stuck out to him. Conversations ranged from the affairs of the miners on the flip side of the planet's rings to a new world being inducted into the empire. At first, that caught his attention, but it quickly became apparent to him that the conversation he overheard was not about Dex's Earth, but a jungle planet three times the distance from the Heart of the Void as Polminar.

Even if Korr didn't hear anything about Dex and Lacy, he could at least keep his ears open for potential jobs.

Korr watched Zar-Mecks patrolling the streets. He was waiting for a sign that they were alert to Dex's presence. Eventually, he told himself it was just paranoia.

For as strange as Dex had acted, it wasn't enough to tip anyone off.

When almost an hour had passed, he paid his tab and headed for one of the local bazaars. If rumors weren't being shared at the bar, Korr was sure he could find some there.

* * *

While Hwaq worked on the engine, Dex read up on the preliminary report the *Silent Horizon* created for Reechi. He studied the ringed-planet system, how they rotated within each other, and the moon outpost that orbited it.

The readouts weren't incredibly detailed. It let him know the general size and density of the masses, as well as levels of organic life. What he got told him that Reechi's entire surface was heavily populated, save for a handful of lakes.

Using what he had, Dex made new files on the ship's computer for all the things he'd seen in this part of the universe. He updated the *Silent Horizon*'s map to include Reechi (with Morak City and the places they'd stopped), the Nebula, and the outpost. Though he hoped he'd never have to return to any of these places, Dex knew it'd be best to have them documented and memorized. After inputting those planets, he gave Korr a quick call through their comms devices and asked for the coordinates of the Heart of the Void, just in case. He also made detailed records of the new species he'd encountered. The officer in him said if he and Lacy ever made it back to Earth, they'd want humanity to be prepared for what could one day knock at their door. Personally, though, he knew he couldn't risk the same ignorance on other civilized planets as he had on Reechi. If he showed up at the Heart of the Void without gaining a basic understanding of how this culture worked, as well as what kinds of creatures operated in it, both he and Lacy would be doomed.

Working silently, Dex hoped Hwaq had forgotten about his presence.

From the moment Hwaq started his work, he hadn't spoken to Dex. Though Dex wasn't paying Hwaq much mind, every so often he heard Hwaq questioning the parts of the *Silent Horizon*'s engine. They were small things like, "What the hell is this?" spoken in a disgruntled murmur.

One of Dex's worries was that the hyperdrive wouldn't be compatible with his ship, but thus far, Hwaq gave him no bad news.

After the first two hours, Dex decided he needed some fresh air. As he walked down the hallway to the airlock, Hwaq called out to him. "Heyya, Dex, right?"

Dex stopped and looked into the engine room. Tools and engine parts were everywhere, but the new hyperdrive looked to be fitting in just fine. "Yeah?" He asked.

Hwaq rose to his feet and wiped his hands on his pants. "Said this was a custom build, right?"

"Mhmm." Dex nodded.

"Huh, never really seen a make like this before. Anywhere." Hwaq looked around the room once, then back at Dex. When their eyes locked, Dex quickly dropped his head and rubbed his eye.

"You all right there?" Hwaq stepped a little closer.

"Yeah, just uh... got something in my eye."

"Ah, that's annoying, lemme get a look," Hwaq quickly jumped over to Dex.

Dex threw up a hand between them and began speed walking out to the airlock. "No, don't worry, got it!" He said as the door opened. "You just finish up, and I'll get your payment!"

As the airlock shut behind him, Hwaq began to shout back, but his voice was cut off.

Once a few yards away from the *Silent Horizon*, Dex pulled the comm device off his waistline and called Korr. "Korr, this is Dex. You copy?"

After a moment, he heard. Back, "Yeah, I hear ya. I'm still here, what's up?"

Dex glanced back at the ship and saw Hwaq unloading the old engine down the ramp. "Might wanna start heading back. Looks like your friend is finishing up, and I am more than ready to get out of here."

Through the comm, Korr asked, "You think he's onto you?"

Dex turned again, away from his ship. "Not yet, but I think he's getting suspicious." As he said this, Dex heard a ship zooming by overhead. He looked and saw a small saucer that looked like a miniature version of the Zar-Mecks' capital ship. "How we looking on Empire presence out there?"

In a hushed tone so Dex had to raise the comm close to his ear, Korr said, "If I had to guess, Empire forces around here are on the lookout. There's more patrols out walking than when we got here, but I wouldn't say they know you're here. I'll start heading back, though."

"Copy. See ya soon." Dex slipped the device back onto his waistline.

Another saucer passed overhead, and Dex looked up.

Without Dex noticing, Hwaq had appeared by his side. He, too, was looking up at the sky. "Don't usually see their starfighters coming down like that. Wonder what's up?"

"I try not to think too hard about it," Dex told Hwaq. "Sometimes it's just not my place to get involved. Engine done?"

Hwaq turned his head to Dex. "Just about. Wanna start up your ship for me? Make sure it's connected all proper?"

"Sure thing." Dex walked briskly back and into his ship. His heart began to race. So far, no trouble, and they were almost clear. Before entering, Dex noticed Hwaq wasn't beside him. He looked back and saw the small raestien mechanic shuffling around one of his pockets and pulling out a comm device similar to the one Korr had given him. Dex entered the *Silent Horizon* but didn't let the airlock close. Instead, he listened to Hwaq's conversation.

"Laqqa, you hear me?"

A pause.

"Laqqa... Laqqa, I'm in the port, I can't hear ya too well."

Another pause, this one longer.

"Can't be!" Hwaq grunted into his comm. "Yeah, thanks for the warning, I'll be on the lookout, don't worry... No, don't mention it to the kids, they'll just get worked up... Don't worry, I'll be fine! I'll see you in a bit." Hwaq put his comm device away. It was a few seconds before Dex heard any footsteps, then quickly raced to the ship's console.

Dex rushed to start the ship's engine, hoping,

praying that Hwaq had everything right.

The *Silent Horizon* gave a familiar whirr and hum as the computer systems booted up.

Hwaq's voice from behind asked, "Everything running okay?"

Dex shot his head around and gave Hwaq a quick nod. "Yeah!" A bead of sweat began to form next to his temple, and he added, "Yeah, just uhmmm, gotta give the ship's computer a moment. Then we'll try the engine."

Hwaq was standing on the threshold of the hallway. His huge arms hung low next to him. Dex could see slight twitching in his fingers.

Trying to ensure the situation remained calm, Dex added, "I'm impressed with your turnaround time. Sorry for hassling you earlier."

Hwaq stepped a little closer, walking slowly. "I understand, don't worry. We've all got places to be. 'Specially with all the Zar-Mecks around."

Dex did his best to suppress his nerves, but it felt like his whole body was shaking. "Can't mind them too much if you haven't done anything wrong, right?"

Hwaq was almost at Dex's feet.

They heard another saucer zoom overhead, this one sounded louder. Closer.

"Ah!" Hwaq exclaimed, pointing out the *Silent Horizon*'s window. "Look at that, they're act'lly landing."

Dex turned quickly and saw one of the saucers landing in the bay next to them. The sweat was coming more intensely.

Before he had time to turn back around, Hwaq's bulky hand grabbed him by the jaw and spun him around. "Knew something was off 'bout ya!"

Their eyes were locked, and Dex couldn't turn away. Hwaq stared at his human eyes. "This honor will be better than anything you could've paid me."

The jig was up. Dex attempted to push Hwaq's arm off, but the raestien was too strong. Instead, Hwaq pushed him deeper into the seat and covered Dex's mouth with his spare hand. "If ya know what's good and right, you'll just come with me to the port security. This don't have to be a problem." He talked as if trying to console Dex.

But Dex hadn't come this far to give in now. He tried desperately to fight back, but Hwaq was too strong, and his grip was getting tighter. Dex's jaw felt like it was about to snap. He started kicking out his legs, hoping to hit something, anything! Hwaq stood his ground and shouted at him to stop fighting with him until Dex realized...

I have a gun.

Dex reached into his coat, pulled out his blaster, and fired.

Hwaq stumbled back, letting go of Dex. He clutched the instantly cauterized wound on his left side. It missed any bones or vital organs, but seared flesh and fat.

They were both in shock.

Dex had never fired the blaster outside of the range before and had prayed he'd never have to use it. Even now, after he'd fired the blaster and knew the stakes, he wanted to toss it aside. He wanted to apologize, but then saw the rage in Hwaq's deep blue eyes.

Hwaq screamed and charged Dex.

Dex threw himself out of the chair and onto the floor, keeping his blaster pointed at Hwaq.

Missing his target, Hwaq's fists came down hard on the ship's console, mashing the buttons. More parts of the ship activated, and in the back room, the engine began running.

From the floor, Dex backed up to the wall and aimed at Hwaq's chest. "Just go home, Hwaq! Go back to your family, you don't have to be a hero!"

Hwaq was in a frenzy. He swung again laterally at Dex, attempting to knock the blaster away.

Dex fired another shot, and Hwaq's massive hand swung into him. The blast lodged itself in Hwaq's right shoulder, but that only angered him more.

The blaster went flying across the room, landing on the port-side bunk.

Without a weapon, Dex was momentarily lost for what to do, and that single moment was all the time Hwaq needed. He grabbed Dex by his jacket and swung him in a full arch overhead, smacking him back on the ground.

Dex couldn't breathe. Before he knew it, Hwaq's hands were coming down again. This time onto his chest. Dex rolled to the left and was up against the bunk, blaster only a few feet away. He tried to get to his feet and make a break for the blaster, but as soon as he was up, Hwaq had him by the ankle and yanked. Dex fell, smacking his face into the *Silent Horizon*'s hard floor.

Hwaq held him by both legs now and stepped to the left, swinging Dex like a bat, at full force into the framing of the starboard-side bunk. The frame made contact across his core. Whatever wind he had managed to take back in was quickly knocked out.

Dex wheezed.

Hwaq dropped Dex's legs. "Ready to turn yourself in?"

Dex fell to the floor, wanting the fall to continue

into unconsciousness. He coughed, and small flecks of blood hit the floor. Dex took a deep breath in and let it out slowly.

"I didn't want to do this," Hwaq said. "I don't want my kids to worry if their dad's gonna come home tonight."

Dex attempted to rise to his feet. They wobbled, and he collapsed, but he tried again, holding onto the bunk's frame.

"I have a duty," Hwaq continued, watching Dex's feeble attempt to stand. "I serve the Empire to protect my kids. To protect my wife."

Dex was on his feet, leaning against the bunk. "Then you should understand-" he took another deep breath. "...why I can't let you take me. Wouldn't you choose your family over the Empire?"

Hwaq was shocked at the question. Without hesitation, he said, "It's because of the Empire that my family prospers. I owe everything to the Emperor, no matter what that means. Now come with me. You can't win this one."

"I'm sorry, Hwaq. I really am." Holding on to the top frame of the bunk, Dex jumped and swung his feet up four feet in the air, kicking Hwaq hard in the face with his heels.

Hwaq tumbled back onto the floor, hitting his head on the console. His mind went blank for a moment, brain hemorrhaging, and when he opened his eyes about five seconds later, Dex was on the opposite side of the room with the blaster in his hand.

"I won't kill you, Hwaq. You'll still get your pay. Somehow, I promise I'll send it." He looked out the window and saw two Zar-Mecks patrolling the bay with batons. "Just get off my ship! Go back to your wife and kids!" Dex's face had gone red. He was desperate. Looking outside the window again, he saw the Zar-Mecks looking at his ship and gesturing something. Others appeared further back. Even worse, they heard the airlock open and heavy footsteps walking toward them.

Hwaq rose to his feet. "I would die before I abandon the Emperor!"

Dex knew what he had to do. He dropped his hand slightly and fired twice.

Hwaq collapsed and gripped his knees, screaming in agony.

Worried the Zar-Mecks heard, Dex crouched down and rushed to Hwaq, grabbing him under the arm and dragging him. "Just go home! You fought well, and you're no less honorable. Now just let me be!"

Not wanting to give up, Hwaq bit Dex's arm.

Dex gritted his teeth through the pain and continued to drag. "Do that again and I'll blow your teeth out!"

Just outside the ship, Dex heard the voices of two of the patrolling Zar-Mecks. One of them said, "This looks like the one from the alert."

Dex dropped Hwaq, still gripping his knees in pain, in the ship's hallway. "Screw it. You're either off my ship now, or you get sucked out the airlock."

An artificial Zar-Meck voice called to him, "Identify yourself!"

Dex slowly turned his head. The two Zar-Mecks were standing on the ramp just outside the still-open airlock. Dex cursed to himself.

The Zar-Meck closer to Dex spoke next, "That's

the one." He raised his baton. "By order of the Emperor, you are under arrest."

Dex knew he could be bested by just one Zar-Meck in terms of speed and agility. It'd be pointless to try to draw his blaster on them. If only he had...

Way past the Zar-Mecks, standing in the shadows up against the bay's walls, Dex saw Korr.

A smile almost found its way onto Dex's face at the sight of an ally, but then Korr was gone. He'd disappeared into the shadows at the first sign of trouble as he said he would.

Dex's heart sank. This might be it. At least one way or another, I'll probably be closer to Lacy.

"Step slowly," the Zar-Meck commanded him. "Just exit the spacecraft and don't try anything."

From the ground, Hwaq cried out, "Thank you! Oh, thank you, glory be to the Emperor!" Hwaq propped himself up on his elongated hands and attempted to crawl toward the Zar-Mecks.

They commanded him, "Stay where you are, citizen!"

But Hwaq didn't listen, he was too overjoyed at being rescued from the evil alien. "I knew you'd get him! He tried to kill me!"

The Zar-Meck's attention was focused on Hwaq, and Dex seized the opportunity he saw. He walked slowly behind the injured raestien, feigning surrender, and just before crossing the threshold, slammed the emergency airlock button. The door slid down fast on Hwaq's feet. Dex heard the screams of the mechanic and felt pity, but knew it had been his only option short of killing him. The Zar-Mecks stepped over Hwaq and banged on the door, demanding that Dex open it.

Not wanting to waste any more time on Reechi, Dex ran to his seat and took control of the ship. It took only a moment to get the *Silent Horizon* off the ground. Dex had no way of knowing but prayed Hwaq's feet had been unstuck before they took to the air. For the Zar-Mecks, though, he couldn't care less how far they fell from.

Blaster fire began shooting past his ship from Zar-Mecks on the ground.

Dex reached across to where Lacy should have been sitting and smacked a series of buttons. The computer screen pulled up a window showing a rear view from the back of the ship. Dex saw the port shrinking in size and blaster bolts coming his way. The aim was close, but the Zar-Mecks failed to hit any part of the ship that would do serious damage.

The ground forces weren't his only obstacle, though. Flying into view from his front and back were numerous Zar-Meck starfighters.

Dex banked hard to port, flying level along the planet's ring.

The Zar-Meck starfighters adjusted course and began firing. Laser blasts zoomed past the *Silent Horizon*. Dex pushed the ship as hard as he could to outrun the starfighters, while zipping up, down, left, and right to avoid their blasts.

While struggling to stay in the air, Dex tried calling Korr on his comm. "Korr!" he shouted. "Korr, where'd you go!"

But there was no answer.

Coming up fast, another of the planet's rings was making its rotation straight through Dex's trajectory. Dex angled the *Silent Horizon* downward to avoid the land mass and flew across the lower crust.

The starfighters stuck to him but fired with more intent, and less often. Glancing up at the crust, Dex saw miners watching the action play out. Not wanting to put them in harm's way, he revolved the ship around the crust and skimmed the side of the mass before angling back up toward space.

Dex knew he wouldn't be able to shake the Zar-Mecks until he could activate the hyperdrive, but with the number closing in on him, he couldn't focus enough attention on getting it ready. He had to find a way to cut them down!

As if he were just a player in a sick game by the universe, the Zar-Meck capital ship slid into view directly ahead of him. Dozens of Zar-Meck ships flooded out of it in his direction.

A million ideas raced through his head. None of them made any sense. There was no way one man could fight off a whole fleet! He glanced back down at the rear-view screen, and an idea came to him.

Rotating the ship in a hard 180 degrees, Dex shot the *Silent Horizon* back down to the surface. Blasts from the six or seven starfighters that were now in front of him hit the ship's hull, but Dex was already cutting through their ranks.

The Zar-Mecks made a quick turnaround and were joined by the dozens that came out of the capital ship.

Facing the planet's core, Dex saw exactly what he'd hoped for. The closer they got to the core, the smaller the rings were. They rotated more slowly, but the gaps between them were much narrower. Dex didn't have the firepower to fight the Zar-Mecks but had enough flight experience to stand a chance in these conditions.

His heart raced faster than ever as he committed to the new plan.

As the battle ensued overhead, civilians watched and cheered on the Imperial forces. They cursed the ship that stood against the mighty Zar-Mecks and cried in sadness when the first starfighter crashed into an oncoming planetary ring.

"One down!" Dex cheered to himself.

He was rapidly coming up on the planet's inner rings. Dex intentionally flew as close to, and in and out of, as many rings as possible.

One by one, the Zar-Meck starfighters backed off. They wouldn't risk jamming themselves up or bottlenecking in the tighter spaces. While most still followed closely and blasted away at Dex, some of the ships in the rear broke off and flew around longer paths to try to cut him off.

One of the starfighters was successful and came up on Dex's starboard side fast.

Dex gritted his teeth and jerked the ship hard to starboard, crashing against the oncoming starfighter, sending it careering onto a ring's surface.

As Dex flew past the planet's core, he was nearly blinded by its intensity. He had to squint his eyes, but held his hands steady on the controls, maintaining a path he hoped would lead him to safety. To make matters worse, the blaster fire was once again intense. For now, the Zar-Mecks didn't have to worry about firing on civilians, though Dex believed they would have taken it as an honor to be killed in the crossfire if it was to catch the Emperor's prisoner.

The *Silent Horizon*'s computer rang in alarm. The

hull had taken serious damage. If Dex was ever going to make his escape, it would have to be now.

In a leap of faith, Dex ignored the blaster fire raining down on him and activated the hyperdrive. He heard the engine whirring louder in the back. Not knowing when or if it would actually be ready, he watched the skies until all the rings were out of his way. He quickly input the coordinates for the Heart of the Void.

An opening finally came. Before he could think twice, Dex slammed down on the console to activate the new engine to full power. Light warped around the *Silent Horizon*. The planet stopped rotating, and the blaster bolts from the starfighters were frozen around the ship. Dex couldn't tell if a few seconds or a minute passed. Then, with a loud bang and a flash of intense and beautiful swirling colors, the *Silent Horizon* jumped to hyper-speed away from Reechi.

12. An Audience with the Emperor

The transport ship began its descent to the surface of the Heart of the Void. Lacy saw as she was being escorted out of her room by a pair of Zar-Mecks armed with blasters, a massive golden hand next to the planet, and could only wonder what it was.

Minutes later, she knew they were close to the exit by the noises echoing down the hallway, and the stronger presence of Zar-Mecks and officers walking around intently.

As they approached the exit ramp of the ship, Lacy was amazed at what she was seeing. In front of her, past the tarmac the transport was stationed on, was a grand skyline of magnificent gold and brown pyramidal skyscrapers. Reaching well over three thousand feet into the air, they were elegantly swirled, and many had bridges that connected to other pyramids. Beautiful vegetation grew off of and cascaded down the structures.

It looked to Lacy like she had just stepped into El Dorado on a massive scale. But what grabbed her attention more than anything else on this new planet was the castle in the sky. From where they stood, Lacy assumed its base must have been at least a square mile. Because of its distance and height, she couldn't discern what the structure looked like, but she knew it was the Emperor's palace. This idea was solidified by what was behind the planet. She understood now what the golden hand she saw was.

The Heart of the Void was held in the hands of the Emperor. A massive statue of the Emperor in his scarlet robes floated in space. The spikes of its golden head grew out and over the floating castle like rays of the sun. The Emperor truly created a godly image for himself above these people.

At the moment, there was only one thing missing. Lacy looked around for someone. She and her Zar-Meck escorts stopped at the bottom of the ramp as if they were waiting for further instructions.

Not wanting to talk to the Zar-Mecks, Lacy waited for a real person to walk by. Presently, an older gentleman with a similar uniform to Jaskek walked down the ramp and past her. "Hey, you!" She called after him.

The Zar-Meck to her right smacked the butt of its blaster into Lacy's side. "Silence, prisoner!" It commanded.

Lacy nearly keeled over, but the officer intervened. "That won't be necessary," he said with an uppity voice. To Lacy, he asked, "What is it you want?"

Lacy looked up at the officer. "Where's Jaskek? He's been in charge of me."

"Hm." The officer grunted and pulled out a tablet. "Making friends, are we? I wouldn't get too fond of anyone." He stopped scrolling on his tablet, and he scoffed. "Excuse me," he said and promptly returned up the ramp.

Lacy turned to watch him almost speed-walk toward another officer. She couldn't tell what he was saying, but knew something was very wrong by the way the uptight officer was gesturing as he spoke.

The Zar-Meck to her left spoke next. "Look forward," it said bluntly.

She did as she was told and turned to face back toward the city, taking in its incredible beauty. Behind her, she continued hearing the muffled but agitated voice of the officer, then footsteps walking down toward her.

After a moment, the officer returned to her and let out a deep, annoyed sigh. "You will be coming with me."

"Is Jaskek not coming?" Lacy asked.

The Zar-Meck to her right tensed its arms to strike her again, but the officer raised his hand to ward it off. "Officer Dreed is indisposed. In light of that, I have been informed you will be under my supervision. Now, if you will, this way." He turned from her and tapped something on his tablet.

The Zar-Mecks nudged her forward. A few seconds later, a small topless shuttle landed in front of them.

The four of them boarded. There was no pilot on the shuttle, instead, the officer tapped another button on his tablet, and they took flight toward the floating castle.

Though the wind was loud as they flew through it, Lacy still called to the officer. "You got a name?"

He didn't hear her.

Lacy began to stand, but the Zar-Mecks extended their arms over her legs.

"Where do you think I'm gonna go?" She asked, and they brought their arms back in. Lacy stepped forward two rows to be behind the officer.

She called, "Hey!"

He turned and shot her a look. "What are you doing?"

"What's your name?"

He scoffed. "That's none of your concern," the officer said, then turned away from her to face ahead.

Lacy tapped him on the shoulder.

"I'm Lacy."

Without turning his head all the way, the officer said. "I don't care."

With the palace-city looming ahead of them and the cold presence of the three Empire cronies around her, Lacy began to realize she was genuinely missing Jaskek. Not in a way that she wanted to hug him if she saw him again, but at least he was someone to talk to. Even if it was just for his own gain.

She sat the rest of the trip out in silence, gazing down at the city below. She watched the citizens and vehicles going about their business, oblivious to what was going on above their heads.

As far as Lacy knew, she was the first human being to step on a civilized world outside of the Earth's solar system, yet no one on Earth would ever know, and no one below her would ever care. Though the realization was crippling, she fought to keep her head high, and her being dignified.

Lacy could now see the palace-city's design. The architecture was reminiscent of the Hanging Gardens of Babylon, continuing the theme of blocky, but regal, with many grand parapets that hovered above the main structure. Everything about the palace-city proclaimed majesty to all who gazed upon it, but to Lacy, it only proclaimed her doom.

The shuttle pulled up along the edge of the palace-city base to a courtyard, where they were met by a tall, elegantly dressed, purple alien.

Lacy didn't have to be told to get off the shuttle and helped herself. The Zar-Mecks followed behind her. The officer began to stand but was stopped by the purple alien.

"You will not be needed here," the purple alien said in a deep, wisened voice.

The officer nodded his head and silently tapped on his tablet, sending the shuttle off to their next destination.

The purple alien stood at least eight feet tall. He had a long, flat face, with a chin that curled upwards with a horn adorned with rings and engravings. Its eyes were long and angled upwards, giving them a naturally intimidating look. His hair grew out of just the very top of his head. It was very long and ornately braided with gold strings wrapped in it. He wore an ornate green robe that hung loosely with an open chest and trailed off behind him. The only decoration on his clothing was a pin similar to the one Jaskek wore on his uniform.

"I suppose it's time for your Emperor to meet me." Lacy's phrasing didn't go unnoticed by the tall alien.

"From here, you will only speak when the Emperor commands you." The alien scowled. "It will be less painful that way. Now, follow." He turned slowly, and the Zar-Mecks shoved her into motion.

Walking through the palace-city, Lacy couldn't help but admire the architecture and decor. Other members of the purple alien's species populated the palace. Lacy observed them tending the hanging gardens, wiping windows, and cleaning the walkways. Everything was so pristine, to the point where it looked like the aliens lived only to clean and manufacture the place. She also noticed that as her party walked near one of the gardeners, they tried to hide how they cowered from Lacy's escort.

While it was technically one building, many of the rooms had open walls and ceilings, and hallways were bridges from one room to the next. Some were small, while others were nearly fifty feet long. Lacy could look over the railing of one of the bridges and stare down at the city below. That is, if her guards let her stop to stare.

After a few minutes of walking, they reached the center of the palace-city. Across the largest bridge yet, like crossing over a river, she gazed upon a beautiful golden pyramid, with rays shooting out of its peak, just as the statue that wrapped around the planet. Beyond the bridge, the Emperor waited for her.

* * *

On the Heart of the Void's surface, officers and Zar-Mecks were preparing the newly arrived transport ship for its return to the Royal Void Outpost. On the way, they would be delivering supplies to other outposts on their route and disseminating updates about the new "human" species that had found its way into their Empire, via the notes of one of the Empire's analysts.

With all the bustle going on to prepare for their next voyage, no one paid much mind to a memo that came through to the hangar supervisor about a Zar-Meck starfighter that had been stamped for decommissioning. The ship in question would promptly be removed from the hangar and left for ground control to deal with.

The starfighter was shuttled across the tarmac to a new hangar where it would be dismantled, and salvageable parts would be shipped to the factories on Gallach.

In the new hangar, before a crew could begin their job of dismantling the starfighter, an officer from the Emperor's Army called their attention.

"Is this one the starfighter from RVO-19?" Jaskek asked the crew chief.

A taourun civilian responded, standing at attention, appropriate for addressing an officer. "Yes, sir. Just got brought over."

Jaskek walked slowly down the length of the circular starfighter.

"Is there an issue, sir?"

Jaskek stopped and slowly did an about-face to look back at the crew chief. "From whom did you receive the order to dismantle this ship?" He slowly walked back toward the crew.

The crew chief looked curiously from Jaskek to his crew, then back to Jaskek. "I uh... I should have the memo here." He snapped at one of his crew members, who promptly ran off out of sight and returned with a tablet. The crew member handed it to Jaskek, who scrolled through.

Jaskek said nothing and expressed no emotion. Half a minute passed before he stopped scrolling. Lights danced in his eyes.

"Everything all right, sir?"

Jaskek shot a glare at the crew chief. "Don't touch this starfighter. By order of the Emperor." He started walking toward the hangar's exit when the crew chief stopped him.

"Excuse me, sir!" The chief called. "I don't mean to pry, but our order was to dismantle this ship."

Looking over his shoulder, Jaskek replied plainly,

"You're welcome to carry out your tasking if only you don't wish to ever meet the Emperor's grace." Without another word, Jaskek left the hangar.

The starfighter wasn't touched again by the crew, nor were any reports sent back to the transport ship. All anyone knew was that they did exactly as they were told.

* * *

As the great doors of the pyramid opened, the tall alien waved the Zar-Meck guards away. They did as commanded without a word.

Lacy watched them leave, wondering if she would be able to make her escape.

"They will not be far," the tall alien said as if reading her mind. "Come. He has waited long enough for you."

Lacy turned her attention back to what lay beyond the doors. The hallway she stared into was lit by floating torches, but they failed to give off enough light for her to see how deep the hall went.

The tall alien walked in.

Lacy was hesitant. The Zar-Mecks would no longer force her, but she had nowhere to go. She knew her doom lay down the hall, but after all this time... a nagging feeling told her she had to at least see the Emperor, the man or beast that enthralled nearly the entire known universe to his will.

She looked back one more time and saw one of the servants across the bridge looking at her. Faintly, she could have sworn she saw the alien shake its head.

Lacy took a deep breath and decided it was time. If she were to meet her fate, she'd do it head-on.

The doors closed behind her as she entered the pyramid.

Lacy quickly caught up to the tall alien. As they walked, the torches floated alongside them, lighting the way.

"Budget doesn't cover any more lights?" Lacy asked, knowing she probably wouldn't get an answer.

This was proven correct by a few moments of silence. "I mean you'd think, Emperor of the universe and all that, he'd keep the place a little more... modern."

Still nothing.

"So how'd you get this job? Good references or... nepotism?"

The tall alien remained cold and stone-faced, but said, "You will not have such tongue when you gaze upon his glory."

After what felt like minutes of walking, the hallway ended, and Lacy found herself in a massive empty room. The tall alien held out a hand to tell her to stop walking.

The floating torches that followed them were still the only sources of light in the room, and Lacy began to feel a punishing, cold emptiness consume her. She'd never been afraid of the dark, but something about this room made her soul freeze.

In a hushed tone, the tall alien said to her, "You are about to experience a great honor. Treasure this moment." He then called into the darkness, "My Lord! I humbly bring you the Earth woman!"

When she looked up at him, he'd already disappeared back down the hallway like a ghost.

Lacy was now truly alone.

Then, from the darkest corners of the room, a

million individual voices came together as one called to her with doom. "I have waited eternities for a being such as yourself," the voices thundered.

Lacy shrank at the voice. In the depths of her soul, she was terrified but refused to let it surface.

I will not fear him, she told herself.

Whether Dex would come after her or not, she had to be strong. If not to survive long enough for him to come, then for his memory. With the strength the thought of Dex gave her, Lacy spoke back to the voice. "I am truly sorry for the length of the wait, and applaud your patience. If I had known of your greatness sooner, I would have flown slower."

Suddenly, the room lit up. Lacy's eyes took a moment to adjust, and when they did, she almost thought blindness would have been preferred. The room was even larger than she could have imagined from the look of the outside of the pyramid. She stood on a ledge that wrapped in a perfect circle around an impossibly deep, black pit, black as her most horrible nightmares. Pillars of fire were spread along the ledge, illuminating the surrounding walls constructed of brown rotting bones of millions of different alien races. The ground she stood on was a deep, sandy maroon. Out of the pit, a platform rose. When it reached a level plane with Lacy, something began to take shape.

Lacy watched as red and gold colors swirled together, and formed a scarlet robe, arms, golden hands, and a golden head with rays that shout out like a sun. The Emperor stood before her on the platform, over fifty feet tall. There was no face, yet Lacy could feel eyes piercing her.

"Wh... who... what are you?" Lacy's voice shook. It was the same image of the shrine she'd seen before, but her mind saw something her eyes couldn't, and she had never known fear like this before.

"My children call me Emperor Armourus, yet I have no name that mortals can truly comprehend. From eons beyond when time was conceived, I am the hand that will grasp all infinities!"

Lacy was speechless. The thundering voices echoed in her mind. Behind the solid golden facelessness, she wanted to believe she saw movement. The gold ebbed and flowed like oil under the scarlet robe, and shone brighter with the columns of fire reflecting off of him.

"From the very first moment of creation, I felt your presence and needed you," the Emperor continued. "Now that you are here, I must savor this moment."

In the pit far below, a secondary platform began to rise up to the ledge.

"Come forward," the Emperor commanded.

Without a thought, Lacy began to step forward, but then caught herself and stopped. Her guard had been down, and she felt the mysterious powers of the Emperor trying to work within her. Looking from the platform to the Emperor, she took a defiant step back. "With respect, I did not travel here just to be ordered around by a tyrant!"

The flame column burned brighter and cooked the room as the Emperor's voice boomed louder through her head. "Come forward, insolent creature!"

Lacy felt as if a hook was stuck in her chest, pulling her toward the platform. She wanted to grab ahold of it and rip it out. Mustering her resolve, she fought against her body's urging and fell to a knee, refusing to walk.

The flames calmed down to their original state. "You have true strength in you," the Emperor said calmly. "Is this why you were sent to my Empire?"

Lacy raised her head to stare down the giant. She breathed heavily, feeling like she'd run a marathon trying to fight off his control of her. "I... I was sent here..." She fought to control her breathing. "I was sent here to tell you to go to hell!"

The Emperor paused for a moment as Lacy rose to her feet again. "I will enjoy consuming you."

"I should let you know, I won't go down easy," Lacy told the Emperor bluntly.

"We shall see. You will be prepared for my feast. Your sacrifice will mark the beginning of a new age for my Empire, and the birth of a greater universe."

While the Emperor's voice boomed through the room, vestiges of terrifying creatures began to float along the sides of the room, looking down on Lacy. Two were the faintest bit recognizable, horrible skeletal caricatures of the taouron and the race of purple aliens she'd seen working around the palace city. They were all dressed like royalty in magnificent gowns. The common physical trait they shared was skullcaps that burst violently outward in terrible, sharp, and barbed horns, and dark eyes filled with malice and misery. It was only now, Lacy saw, that the Emperor's robes weren't just a deep scarlet. They weren't even blood-red robes. It was itself... blood. Flowing and wet, dripping into the pit below, blood.

His voices echoed again, "You will serve in my world as an emissary of your race. My army will find your planet and subject your people to my reign, and through you, their sacrifice will strengthen my Empire a thousandfold."

The tall alien reappeared behind Lacy and placed a long three-fingered hand on her shoulder.

Lacy didn't even flinch. She couldn't fully comprehend what the Emperor had threatened her with. Lacy only knew it was terrifying, but she refused to let her fear show. "If you find my planet, you will also find an end of your empire. My people are stronger in spirit, it seems, than any other race in this universe. We will not fall easily."

The Emperor ignored Lacy and spoke next to the tall alien. "Tarnascus, my loyal servant, prepare for a feast and gather up worthy offerings."

Tarnascus the servant fell slowly to his knees, then clasped his hands together above his head in a salute. "I will do as you command. Glory be to you, my Emperor."

The Emperor said nothing but waved them away with his huge golden hand.

Tarnascus rose and turned Lacy to walk back down the hall.

Lacy looked back over her shoulder at the Emperor and the court of phantasms as the flames started to dissipate. Though losing his illumination, the Emperor remained a haunting image.

13. Dex Arrives

The *Silent Horizon* pulled out of hyperspace in an empty sector of space.

Dex wiped the sweat across his brow and thanked God he was still alive. Before moving on to the next task, Dex gave himself a moment to just relax in his chair and compose himself.

After a few moments, he let himself laugh, then opened a new log on the ship's computer.

"Day... what is it... Four eighteen? Seventeen? Jeez, I don't know. If anyone back on Earth ever hears this... You won't believe what I've just been through. Word of advice: if you head in the direction of the coordinates attached to this log, bring lots of guns. I recently escaped a planet called Reechi..." Dex recounted the story for the log, having fallen into his natural Captain-y rhythm. He gave a brief synopsis of the people he met on Reechi, the different aliens he saw, the Zar-Meck attack, and Korr...

"Korr..." Dex whispered the name. "Korr, you bastard." Without a proper closing, Dex ended the log and turned to the ship's radio.

"Korr! Come in, Korr! Do you hear me!" Dex waited a moment for a response, then double-checked to make sure he used the right signal Korr had given him.

A minute passed, and Dex received no response.

"Korr, I know this signal works, now answer me, you coward!"

Dex waited another minute and was momentarily relieved to receive a response until the words came through. "You knew what was coming, don't start playing dumb now."

"Don't you think it was a little late to back out, Korr?" Dex asked angrily. "Hwaq saw you with me, think he's gonna keep quiet?"

Almost instantly, Korr responded. "I don't think he's gonna say anything to anyone. Ever."

It took Dex a moment to realize what Korr meant. "You didn't..."

"I laid out my cards plainly, Dex." Dex stood and paced alongside the console, leaving the radio signal open.

Korr continued to speak. "I truly am sorry it came to this." There was a hint of sincerity in his voice. "Hwaq was a good friend of mi-" Dex shouted into the radio, filled with anger.

"So you murder your friends now?"

Korr's voice came back over the radio, stern but composed. "Would you rather it be you?"

Dex stopped pacing and dropped his hands onto the console. "And why wasn't it? He had kids! You just met me!"

Korr let out a deep breath that Dex heard faintly through the radio. "I've known Hwaq for a long time. But his loyalty to me is beat out a hundred times greater by his loyalty to the Emperor. Maybe under enough suffering, you'd turn me in, but even now..."

Dex stared at the speaker, waiting for a response.

Korr sounded exhausted when he spoke again.

"Don't ask me for more help, Dex. You've got your hyperdrive, just go home. There's still time. Forget your girl. It's not worth the suffering the Emperor will put you through. Even if you did get her back, the two of you will never truly be free of him, but at least you'd have time."

Dex took a moment to compose himself. His heart beat rapidly at Korr's words. He looked around the cabin at the empty bunks. The one that hadn't been used for over a year, and the one Lacy should have still been in. Dex turned back to the radio and said, "I'll suffer through anything the Emperor throws at me. I'll spend eternity running from or fighting the Empire. They can shatter my bones again, and a million times over, and rip my soul from my body. But I will save Lacy. Even if the Emperor takes me, I will save her."

"Dex, please-"

"Korr, I'm going to face him." Dex began to input the coordinates for the Heart of the Void into the navigation systems and let the computer map a course. "I might die, but you could at least give me a fighting chance. If you truly believe the Emperor is as evil as you say, at least we'll go down doing something good for the universe."

Dex waited for a response, but Korr wouldn't give any. After a moment, he smacked a hand on the console. "Come on, you son of a bitch! If you're doing nothing with your life, do you really wanna live forever?"

Still, Korr wouldn't answer.

Dex fell into his chair and realized he wouldn't win Korr over. "If you change your mind... just don't keep me waiting too long." Without waiting for a response, Dex closed the line.

As he prepared for the launch to hyperspace, Dex

ran through the ship's computer looking for any problems the new engine may have caused. So far, everything looked fine. No alarms had gone off. The only thing that stuck out to him was the *Silent Horizon*'s fuel level. The initial journey out into Empire territory had cost them little fuel, having only used it to accelerate them to cruising speed. Powering the rest of the ship took minimal effort from the engine. Looking at it now, based on how much fuel he had spent from the jump out of Reechi, Dex guessed he would only have enough fuel for two or three more jumps.

As long as it's enough to get back to Earth, he thought. Even as the thought came out, he knew he didn't believe it.

"As long as I can get Lacy back," he corrected himself out loud.

Everything was now set. The *Silent Horizon* plotted a course for the Heart of the Void, and the engine was ready. Time slowed as light wrapped around the ship.

As the fabric of the universe was pulled open in front of Dex, a voice called out to him by name. It was incomprehensible and had a tone of calm questioning, like Dex's presence was uninvited but not unwelcome. In an infinitesimal moment that lasted an eternity, an image shot into Dex's mind of a vast green landscape, sliced into tiny elevated islands by thin rivers, and just before that, a valley.

Before he could study the scene, the vision was gone. Dex could no longer hear the voice. He was back flying through hyperspace, watching the colors of the stars swirl together as he zoomed past them.

The computer estimated the trip would take just under two hours. Dex thought this was plenty of time to formulate a plan. The biggest problem, though, was that Dex had no idea what he'd be going up against.

He assumed that if this was the Empire's home world, defenses would be incredibly high. If he went in guns blazing, he surely wouldn't get remotely close to the planet's upper atmosphere. Even if he tried to go in stealthily, he wasn't sure if his clearance codes would still work.

Regardless of how he would initially approach the Heart of the Void, Dex knew that he would eventually find himself fighting again. This thought scared him, too. He'd been up against the Zar-Mecks twice already. On the ground, he wasn't fast or strong enough to face them without help.

Dex then realized, *I may not have the speed, but I think I can get the strength!*

Rummaging through the storage above the starboard side bunk, Dex found the black cube of Zar-Meck armor.

As if reading his mind, the cube didn't move until Dex knew he was ready to let it cover him again. The warm and relaxing feeling took over Dex. His vision was covered only for a moment before the purple visor appeared over his eyes.

Dex looked around the *Silent Horizon*'s cabin, getting a feel for the suit. The purple tint felt off-putting to Dex, and again, the suit read his mind. The visor's tint shifted to a transparent white.

So, it can recognize what I want it to do! Dex thought to himself.

He spoke aloud, "All right, give me a gun!" Dex shot his hand up like he was drawing a blaster, but nothing appeared.

"Come on!" He re-drew his hand similar to the way

the Zar-Mecks swapped out their weapons. "Just give me a weapon!" As the word was spoken, a screen appeared on the visor's heads-up display. A list of weapons and images of them popped up. He saw the familiar blasters and batons the Zar-Mecks carried, as well as others such as small grenades, short swords, and daggers.

Dex locked the image of the blaster in his head, then quick-drew the weapon out of his armor's thigh as he'd seen the Zar-Mecks do. It clicked for him that the suit needed specifics for what it could conjure up.

On the right side of the heads-up display, he saw an outline of his body, with a note to the side labeled "Armor capacity." It was currently at 93%.

Did those bots give me a busted suit?

Dex let the blaster assimilate back into the suit, and he saw the armor capacity rise to 95%.

"Of course," Dex told himself. "Suit can't be perfect."

Dex tested out the other weapons, seeing how much they took away from the suit and how they felt in his hands. The closest he'd ever come before this to sword fighting was playing knights with his cousins as a kid. Dex knew fighting with bladed weapons would be the last resort.

Recognizing that the suit was fluid, he wondered if he could focus on where the armor should cover more heavily, or if he could retract parts of it. Dex mentally commanded the suit helmet to retract, but was disappointed when nothing happened. The suit was capable of only so much, but it gave him a leg up he hadn't expected.

Dex made a mental note to try to get one for Lacy, too, if they had time during their escape.

With the suit explored, the only thing left for Dex to do was figure out a plan of attack.

* * *

After leaving the hangar, Jaskek put in a call for a shuttle through his tablet. But before he could complete the request, a different shuttle arrived with an Imperial Officer sitting in the front.

"Officer Dreed, what are you doing out here?" The officer inquired.

"Classified, Officer Orbek," Jaskek replied without hesitation. "Regards the prisoner."

Orbek stepped up and out of the shuttle. "Is the prisoner over here, Dreed?" His tone was hard.

"No, sir, I-"

Orbek interrupted, "No! She's already up in the palace because I had to bring her. Now, I'll ask again, what are you doing out here?"

Jaskek remained calm, standing tall with his hands clasped behind him. "As I said, sir. Classified."

Orbek harrumphed and stepped closer. "If you're looking for reassignment to Mascoadon, I'd be more than happy to file the request."

"Officer Orbek, how much time have you spent with Lieutenant Prullen?"

"What's that, Dreed? Lieutenant Prullen?"

"As I thought." Jaskek stepped closer and hardened his face. He towered over Officer Orbek, with his flesh beginning to illuminate. "You know nothing of the prisoner. You have no idea what her kind is capable of. No one does, except me! I have witnessed what they can do.

The chaos they can create! What I'm doing here is greater than anything you could possibly dream of sacrificing for the Emperor. Compared to what I have to do, you'd look at Mascoadon as a pleasure trip! Now, stand aside, Orbek."

Orbek watched madness dance in the young officer's eyes. He stepped back closer to the shuttle. "I think, Officer Dreed, you need to return to your training. It seems your first duty station was a bit more than you can handle."

Jaskek closed the distance again and let himself calm down, so the glow left his skin before he spoke. "Or you are too old to see a bigger picture."

Orbek was pressed against the shuttle door, standing in Jaskek's shadow. "The only order for the prisoner was to bring her to the Emperor. There is no danger, Officer Dreed. Now come with me back to the ship. We'll sort everything out there." Orbek opened the short shuttle door and stepped through, never taking his eyes off Jaskek.

There was a pause between the two officers. They eyed each other intensely until Jaskek stepped aboard.

"Good," Orbek said. "Now sit."

Jaskek did as he was ordered, taking a seat in front of Orbek.

As the shuttle took off for the short trip to the transport ship, both taouron felt the tension in the air. Orbek felt grateful to be sitting behind Jaskek, not wanting the analyst to see that his skin was now glowing faintly.

In the row ahead, Jaskek was looking around, studying the ground below them as if searching for something. Orbek was growing more and more unnerved at his behavior. Jaskek then looked up to the palace-city floating above. A small fleet of shuttles was flying toward it.

Orbek spoke, attempting to add levity to the tense feeling he had. "The Emperor surely isn't wasting a moment with this prisoner. Those must be the offerings for the sacrifice."

"Reroute the shuttle, Officer Orbek."

"What was that?" Orbek shouted to overpower the wind blowing past them.

"Reroute the shuttle. Take me up to the palace."

"Officer Dreed, right now your duty is-"

Before another word escaped him, Jaskek had jumped back, riding the wind to give him a boost into the row of seats behind Orbek. With lightning speed, Jaskek placed his hands around Orbek's head and snapped his neck.

The officer's lifeless body fell to the floor of the shuttle.

Jaskek knew this was the moment his fate was sealed.

Taking out his tablet, Jaskek rerouted the shuttle to the Emperor's palace-city.

* * *

After deciding on a "plan," Dex took to practicing his swordsmanship. He played back clips of Errol Flynn films, studying his footwork and how he held his sword, knowing that it was by no means the best training, but with the limited time he had, Flynn's movies were the only thing he could come up with. Between clips, he would practice against the one P.E.S. suit Korr and his army had managed to retrieve, which he had propped up against the back wall. Giving no resistance, it was still one of the toughest enemies he'd ever fought.

Half an hour later, he sheathed the Zar-Meck sword back into the suit and told himself matter-of-factly, "Yeah, I'm gonna die."

The proximity alarm rang through the ship, signaling that the Heart of the Void was approaching. Dex pulled the *Silent Horizon* out of hyperspace.

The sight of the Empire's home world left him in awe. Dex gazed upon the Heart of the Void. He was amazed by the magnitude of the statue that looked to be holding the planet quite literally in its grasp. Equidistant from the planet and statue were three massive black holes, constantly pulling at the world, maintaining a perfect balance of its place in the universe. Dex felt that if there were a center of the universe, this place must be it.

Time for taking in beauty was cut short. Rapidly approaching on the *Silent Horizon*'s radar was a small object.

Dex pulled up imaging on the ship's computer and saw a small pod hurtling toward him.

Angling the ship so the rear blaster Korr installed could be properly aimed at the pod, Dex waited for a prime opportunity to fire. But as it got closer, he knew something was off. The pod looked nothing like the Zar-Meck starfighters and was making no attempt to hail him or fire. Furthermore, the computer read no signs of life coming from the pod. Dex kept his guard up, sensing it could be a ploy. At this distance, he would have already been spotted by the pod, so Dex decided to be the one to make the first move.

"Unidentified craft, identify yourself or I will fire

on you," Dex called into his radio.

After only a moment, as if expecting the call, he heard back a very plainly stated, "Robbie."

Dex was taken aback. Firstly, he expected more of a fight before anyone gave themselves away, and also, what are the odds of someone being named 'Robbie' out here?

"Sorry..."Confusion held heavy in Dex's voice. "Say again?"

Again, "Robbie," very politely and plainly was all that came through.

Dex looked at the radar screen. The pod was still coming in fast in a course that would soon fly past him. "Okay... Robbie, I need you to slow down your ship, or I will be forced to fire on you."

"Please don't."

"Excuse me, what?"

"Please do not fire."

Dex didn't know what to say. The pod wasn't arming up or slowing down. It just continued to cruise.

"I do not know what I'm doing."

Dex was at a complete loss.

"Robbie, are you from Earth? How did you get out here?" Seeing the pod wasn't slowing down, and not wanting to let it reach the Heart of the Void, Dex flew into the ship's path. He planned to stay in the ship's path, ready to blow it out of the sky at any moment.

"My friend put me in this pod. I don't know where she is. I think the officers got her."

This guy just sounds like a scared kid, Dex thought, and then it clicked. An Earth name and his friend was a woman. "Okay, Robbie, who was your friend? What was her name?"

"Lacy Prullen."

Dex laughed. A tear of joy welled in his eye. He shouted her name into the comms, "Lacy? Where is she now?"

There was a moment's hesitation before Robbie responded. "I am unaware of her location. She only instructed me," Then in a recording of Lacy's voice, Robbie played back over the radio, "Just go! Be Free!"

Dex's heart leaped at the sound of Lacy's voice. He tried to speak, but his voice was lost in shock. Dex wanted to sit and treasure the moment for as long as he could, but the *Silent Horizon* and Robbie's pod were still on a direct course for the Heart of the Void.

"Uh-Okay-Robbie... Robbie, listen, you have to slow down your ship."

"I am unable to pilot this craft."

"Well, you have to try Robbie. Is there a control panel in there?"

Robbie took a few seconds to respond. "Yes."

Of course, there is. He's talking to me somehow, Dex thought to himself. "All right, great, look around for something labeled thrusters. See 'em?"

Another few seconds passed. "No."

"Damn." Dex ran his hands through his hair in frustration. "All right, here's what I'll do. I'm going to try to manually slow down your pod. From my reading, it doesn't look like your thrusters are on. Say a prayer for us, buddy!"

As Dex prepared his maneuver, Robbie called back again. "A prayer."

Dex didn't understand what Robbie meant, or if he heard him right, but he brushed Robbie's words aside.

Lined up perfectly with the pod, the *Silent Horizon*

began to slow, closing the distance between them. Dex hoped that if he slowly added resistance to the pod, he could slow them both down without damaging either ship. Once they came to a halt, Dex would use the spacewalk suit to retrieve Robbie. The hardest part would be bringing Robbie back onto the *Silent Horizon* if he didn't have a suit of his own. Realizing this, Dex called the pod to ask if he had a suit, but was cut off too quickly.

"I will come to you. It will be easier."

"Wait, Robbie, what?"

Instead of receiving an answer, Dex saw through the rearview camera feed the pod of Robbie's shuttle open. Air rushed out, and along with it, a small ash-black box.

Dex shouted into the radio, "Robbie! Robbie, are you okay?"

No response came.

"Robbie!" Dex threw himself out of his seat and rushed to get dressed in the spacewalk suit. He was dressed and ready in under thirty seconds and trudged along in the heavy suit down the hall of the *Silent Horizon* to the airlock. Passing through the first door, Dex hooked up the oxygen line, and as he initiated the depressurizing, he could have sworn he heard a knock at the door.

Dex brushed the ridiculous thought from his mind and waited impatiently for the depressurization to finish. The moment the hissing sound left the room, Dex heard the knocking again.

"Hello?" Dex asked toward the door. "Robbie, is that you?"

He waited for a response that wouldn't come.

Dex reached out to open the door, realizing only too late that he didn't have his blaster accessible.

The door opened, and holding on to the left side of the door with a tiny claw hand, dangled Robbie, the small ash-black robot.

"Robbie? You're a... a robot?"

"May I come in?" Robbie asked, sounding like a scared child.

"Y-... Yeah, I mean yes! Come on!" Dex reached out and grabbed the robot.

Dex closed the door behind Robbie, then re-pressurized the airlock. "How did you get over here? I saw you fly away!"

Robbie didn't speak, but instead sprayed a bit of his extinguisher from his left claw as he'd demonstrated for Lacy before.

"Good to know," said Dex, taking off his suit helmet. "Well, Robbie, it's nice to meet you." He grabbed Robbie's claw to shake it, and the small robot's arm flailed about.

"I do not understand your kind. You must be Dex. Lacy's partner."

Dex let go of Robbie's claw and began to escort him back to the main cabin. "I'm her husband, yeah. And I need to get back to her. I think she's down on that planet."

"She is. I think she is dead now." Robbie spoke so matter-of-factly, but Dex had come too far to believe the robot.

"She's not dead. Not yet." He began to undress from the suit.

"How do you know? Have you seen her?" Robbie began to shuffle around the room, inspecting the alien craft.

"No, not yet, but I believe she is."

"But you are not certain."

Dex, now sitting on the ground, pulled a foot out of one of the pant legs and threw the suit on the ground. "I am certain. I refuse to believe she's lost."

Robbie dropped his attention from the contents of the scarlet P.E.S. he'd been studying and looked back at Dex. "You're very strange, Dex Prullen."

"You're the one to talk."

Robbie stepped closer to Dex. "You and Lacy are both very strange."

Dex finished undressing and laughed lightly as he hung the suit back up. "Yeah, she's a weird one. One of a kind. There's no one like her in the whole universe, and that's why I know she's still alive."

"I highly doubt there is no one like her."

Dex walked back toward the front console but didn't take his eyes off the robot following him. "Have you ever met someone like her?"

Robbie stopped in his tracks. He thought of Lacy helping him pick out a name. It was the first time any living being or intelligent machine had asked for his thoughts on something. "No. Never."

"I thought not." Dex took his seat and regained control of the ship's navigation. "So, do you believe me?"

Robbie pulled up next to Dex. "No. She is most likely dead."

Dex glanced down at Robbie and gave the robot a hard look.

Robbie shrank away half a foot. "But... there is clearly no convincing you. In her memory, I will help you go die, too."

"Whatever. Come on up here, little guy." Dex

picked the robot up and placed him in Lacy's co-pilot seat. "We're not gonna die, though."

"If you say so. What is your plan?"

Dex breathed out deeply. "Well... I'll admit it's not great. I'm assuming she's on her way to, or with, the Emperor now. So I'll look for a palace or castle or whatever, fly in hard and fast, hop off the ship, grab her, hop back on the ship, and fly off, hoping and praying the whole time we don't get blasted to smithereens."

Robbie stared blankly at Dex, then out into space toward the Heart of the Void. "We are going to die."

"I'm all ears if you've got any ideas."

The robot looked back and forth between Dex and the Heart of the Void, then shook his head. "I have no plans. All I know is where Lacy would be."

Dex beamed. "Why didn't you say so?"

Robbie didn't know what to say, he only shrugged.

"Well, where is she?"

"All sacrifices are brought to his palace. It floats high above the planet's surface, in the northern hemisphere, under the crown of the Emperor."

"You mean that huge statue surrounding the planet? That's the Emperor?"

"Some cultures in the Empire believe that to be the Emperor himself."

"And is it?"

Robbie and Dex both stared ahead at the great statue holding the planet. "It is possible," Robbie said. "The first peoples of the Empire believe it is."

"Great," Dex said plainly. "At least he doesn't look like he'll bother us too much on the surface. Think you can navigate the ship to the palace?"

"I am not programmed for flying."

"That's fine, I just... wait. Of course! Robbie, I need you to fly this thing!" Dex looked half mad with excitement.

Robbie shot a glance at Dex. "What? Dex, I said I am not program-"

Dex waved his words away. "I don't care what you're programmed for. I need you to fly. Look, all you need to know for now is this: right here controls movements up and down. Next to it, here, is left and right. Push this one in to go faster, pull it out to slow down. I don't need you pulling any crazy stunts, just keep this baby in the air for as long as possible, okay?" Dex's heart was now beating heavily with excitement. With a co-pilot - even one that had never flown before - his odds increased greatly. If things went well, the *Silent Horizon*'s flight assistant should work wonders for Robbie.

"I cannot fly."

Dex's smile began to fade.

"But I will try before I die."

Dex clapped his hands in triumph. "Yes! Okay! Awesome, thank God. Here we come, Lacy."

"Strange person," Robbie said to himself.

Dex accelerated the ship faster toward the planet. "All right, I have some old clearance codes on the computer. I'll submit those when we get close to the planet. Should be good enough to at least get us through."

Robbie said nothing, but Dex could feel him wanting to be negative about their chances.

"What do I do if the Emperor's Zar-Mecks get on the ship?"

"I think you'll be fine, Robbie."

"Should I have a blaster?"

"Robbie, it doesn't even look like you have fingers. How would you pull a trigger?"

Robbie looked at his claws, then dropped his arms, letting his body fall back against the seat in defeat. A mechanical groan escaped his speakers, as if he had not been aware of his bodily condition.

"Just try to shake them off, okay?"

"Okay," Robbie said quietly.

"You are so weird," Dex said to himself.

As the *Silent Horizon* drew close to the planet, the ship was hailed just as Dex had expected. A port officer requested their clearance codes, and this time, Dex didn't hesitate to send them.

The response from the port officer took much longer than it had on Reechi, but after about two minutes, they were granted permission to land and instructed where to go.

"All right, when we get closer to the ground, I need you to point me in the direction of the palace," Dex instructed. "Once we're on top of it, you take over the steering. If we can land, great. If not... I'll figure something out."

The view of the main city came upon them, but Dex wouldn't let himself pay it any mind. He had to stay focused on the mission.

"Over there," Robbie pointed out toward the palace-city, hovering far off in the distance.

Dex jerked the *Silent Horizon* off their course and flew fast toward the palace-city.

Over the radio, the feminine voice of the port officer called to them. "Remain on your course or you will be taken out of the air. This is your only warning."

Robbie reached out to grab Dex's arm. "Dex, I am having second thoughts about this."

"Too late!"

The palace-city was approaching rapidly.

Over the radio, the port officer called them again. "Dex Prullen, whatever you are planning, you will not succeed."

Dex and Robbie stared at each other in disbelief.

Nearly on top of the palace-city now, Dex saw a squad of Zar-Mecks waiting for them with blasters ready.

"All right, Robbie, your turn to fly. Take us in low."

"What? Dex, I cannot fly!"

But Dex was already on his feet and slammed down on the flight assist button before running to the port side bunk to grab the cube of Zar-Meck armor, which encased his body the moment his fingers made contact. Dex wrapped his rigger belt around his waist, then prepped two grenades. "You ready, little guy?"

"No!"

Dex was already headed for the airlock as Robbie shouted at him. "Remember, keep me low! I have a comm to the ship, just stay alert!" The door slid shut behind Dex as he entered the hallway and rushed to the airlock.

Already, he could hear blasts from the Zar-Mecks ricocheting off the *Silent Horizon*'s hull and felt the ship shake more under the control of Robbie's piloting.

The airlock opened as they passed over the squad, and without hesitation, Dex dropped both grenades out to the platform below.

The Zar-Meck squad was thrown by the blast in every direction. One had even been knocked off the platform entirely, falling down to the planet's surface.

"Robbie, you hear me?" Dex called over the comm.

"I hear you," he heard back.

"I need you to make another round. And get lower!"

The *Silent Horizon* turned for another pass and dropped another thirty feet.

Dex mentally prepared himself as the platform approached. They were still a good twenty feet up, but the Zar-Mecks were getting back up.

Blaster ready in one hand, and a grenade ready in the other, Dex jumped down to the palace-city.

14. One Heart to the Next

Lacy stood with feet locked into place on a hovering platform, facing a mirror in a large, domed dressing chamber at the peak of a large tower. Vines and flowers decorated the pillars holding up the roof. From her vantage point, she could see nearly all of the palace-city below her, but refused to give its beauty any attention or praise.

Lacy was being dressed in a magnificently detailed scarlet gown, embedded with beautiful gems along its long sleeves and the trim of the even longer train. One of the tall purple aliens who referred to themselves not as a species, but as the Children of the Void, a thin woman named Rassmenda, had helped her dress and covered any exposed skin on her hands, chest, neck, and face with thick crimson paint that emphasized her bone structure while embellishing with elaborate detailing, and flowed naturally into the design of the dress. Rassmenda took her time in every aspect of the dressing and painting, ensuring the fabric fell just right in just the right places, shining the gems, and fixing the jewelry that hung around Lacy's neck, off her ears, and out of her hair. The final piece was a haunting, yet simultaneously magnificent, skeletal crown.

Rassmenda carried it delicately by the two largest of the many thick horns that protruded from the sides.

From its furthest point side to side, the crown was three feet wide and extended nearly that length in height. A hundred gold strings dangled from piercings in the crown.

Lacy kept her eyes forward, looking back at herself. She maintained a strong, sturdy expression. For all the admittedly beautiful and impressive work Rassmenda put into preparing her, Lacy refused to express any recognition.

The crown was gently placed on Lacy's head, and she noticed the paint on her face blended seamlessly with the coloring of the horned bone crown. Rassmenda pulled the jewelry in Lacy's hair through open slits of the crown and placed them strategically to hang down along the sides and back of her head.

"You are about to receive a great honor," Rassmenda said gently. It was the first thing she had said since Tarnascus passed Lacy off to her. "You will stand high in the Emperor's court for all eternity. A queen and mother, delivering your children into the world beyond, of our Emperor."

Lacy studied the crown, thinking of the similarity it had to the headdresses of the ghostly figures she saw in the Emperor's hall. The Emperor's words were mysterious, but she gathered that she would be converted into some kind of deity, trapped in a terrible undead existence. Now with the crown and body paint, she feared a physical transformation, too.

If it went through, would it be painful? she thought. *Is there any turning back? If not... how will I be able to keep fighting him?*

Her heart beat heavily at the thoughts.

Rassmenda took a step back and assessed her work. "You are ready. The Emperor will rejoice at having you in his court."

Lacy attempted to calm her heart. "I will rejoice when the Emperor dies."

Rassmenda dropped her head, fearful of Lacy's words. "You should not speak as such," she said quietly. "You are a gift unto the universe, serving a greater purpose than you could have ever wished. Only one of each race will ever be accepted into the Emperor's court. You will have power over all your peoples."

Lacy turned her head slowly to face Rassmenda, focusing on balancing the crown. "But the Emperor will still have total control over me. Won't he?"

"There is no one greater than the Emperor. He has wonderful control over all of us. You have the gift of being close with him on a level our simple minds cannot begin to comprehend."

"No tyrant has ever been a great person," Lacy snapped at the woman.

Rassmenda jumped back in shock, and for a moment, Lacy felt a twinge of guilt. This life was all the alien had probably ever known. Lacy wouldn't have been surprised if Rassmenda had never even stepped foot on the city below.

Lacy turned back to the mirror. "I hope one day you leave this planet. I hope you see the universe. You'll see there is so much more than this box you live- *hey!*"

She had moved so silently and quickly, draping a cover hanging from either side of the crown to hang in front of Lacy's jaw. Though it didn't cling to her face, it absorbed all sound escaping her mouth. Lacy couldn't pull it off, no matter how she tried. Even when it was pulled up to reveal her mouth, it still absorbed her words. The cover emitted a short-range field that blocked any sound from passing around it.

"You will blaspheme the Emperor no more. Come, it is time for the feast." Rassmenda left the room, walking to a staircase that wrapped around the tower. The platform Lacy was stuck to followed after, staying to the side of the staircase.

Off in the distant skies, something passed through the clouds. Lacy saw it briefly, hoping it was Dex, but knew it was nothing more than a bird.

At the bottom of the tower, two lines of mixed alien races wearing matching scarlet togas. At the head of the procession stood Tarnascus, wielding a large golden staff, and another Child of the Void to his left. This one looked similar to Rassmenda and kept her head hung low. She wore a white gown that matched the styling of Tarnascus' robes.

Lacy's hover platform fell in place between Tarnascus and the lines of sacrifices. Rassmenda took her place to Tarnascus' right.

"Mermorrum," Tarnascus said to the woman to his left. "You may begin."

Without hesitation, Mermorrum's head shot up, eyes focused on the Emperor's Pyramid ahead, and bellowed deep, alien words. Lacy had no idea what they meant, but they were repeated by the people behind her in perfect unison.

Tarnascus stepped off toward the Emperor's Pyramid. The ritual had begun.

Mermorrum let out another cry, followed by another repeat by the alien sacrifices.

It sounds like a prayer, Lacy thought.

As Mermorrum began her next chant, an explosion roared in the distance. Tarnascus and the two women next to him didn't react, but Lacy and the rest of the sacrifices turned to try and see what was going on.

Dex! Lacy told herself, beaming as the thought passed through her mind. *It has to be Dex!*

There, above the rooftops by the edge of the palace-city, Lacy saw the *Silent Horizon* being hit by blaster fire. She couldn't help but glow with excitement. Turning back to Tarnascus, she yelled, "You hear that? Didn't I say he'd come!" forgetting entirely that she was muted by the face cover.

The Emperor's Pyramid drew closer. Lacy turned back once again, attempting to catch another look at the *Silent Horizon.*

* * *

Dex landed on the solid ground of the palace-city. The three remaining Zar-Mecks were back on their feet, firing at the *Silent Horizon* as it passed overhead. Before the Zar-Mecks could notice him, Dex threw the grenade he'd dropped down with. The moment it hit the ground, it detonated, tearing chunks of the Zar-Meck's armor away. Dex raced over to the downed Zar-Mecks and blasted one in an area of exposed flesh.

The others were too fast. They were up on their feet, blasters ready.

With his free hand, Dex picked up the body of the dead Zar-Meck, using it as a shield. The suit he wore helped a little, increasing his speed and strength, giving him just enough of an edge on these guys.

Dex sidestepped to the right, blasting the nearest Zar-Meck so rapidly and intensely, one would have thought he carried a machine gun.

With the second one down, Dex threw his Zar-Meck shield at the remaining enemy, then charged, knocking him down. Dex took three precise shots to break the armor covering the Zar-Meck's chest, then a fourth to end its life.

With all of them defeated, Dex stepped back and gave himself a moment to catch his breath. A flash on his heads-up display told him he had taken damage. The suit's power was now down to 78%.

Dex pulled his comm device off his belt and called to Robbie. "You all good up there, little guy?"

"NOOO!" Robbie shouted back immediately. "I THINK THAT THIS IS FEAR I FEEL!"

"Are you going down?" Dex called back, trying to suppress the mounting panic in his voice.

"No! I do not like flying!"

"Okay, you'll be fine, Robbie. Just keep that ship in the air, I won't take too long." Dex clipped the comm back onto his belt and scanned the roads around him.

There were no identifying marks or directions. Using one of the vines hanging from the top of a nearby building, Dex climbed to the roof to get a better view.

Off in the distance, he spotted the Emperor's Pyramid. "Robbie! That pyramid, is that the Emperor?"

"Yes!" Robbie called again through the comm device. "Lacy will be there!"

Dex didn't waste time responding. He was running across the roof, jumping from one building to the next, trying to avoid slipping through alleys that would send him falling to his death below.

Five rooftops later, a blaster bolt shot through the air, slamming into Dex's leg as he jumped from one roof to another. The impact slowed his momentum, and he was able to just barely grab onto a vine that hung on the side of the building.

"He fell!" A Zar-Meck voice shouted!

A second voice responded. "Go confirm! If he's dead, he's dead. But if he's alive, orders are to bring him to the Emperor."

Dex tried to pull himself up but stopped when he heard heavy footsteps racing toward him. He looked around for other options and saw a footpath about fifteen feet to his right. If he could swing over to the path, Dex figured he'd be able to lose the Zar-Mecks within the city and would have greater cover.

Using the vine to swing, Dex ran across the wall and jumped when he couldn't swing any further.

Dex landed in the center of the narrow footpath and dashed through a narrow hall with a vegetated trellis roof.

"It looks like he fell!" The Zar-Meck called.

"No! He's down here!" Another shouted, and blaster bolts ripped through the greenery.

Dex took cover against a wall and prepped two more grenades.

Blasts shot down sporadically throughout the crammed hall. There was no one point the Zar-Mecks were firing from. Dex could tell he was completely surrounded.

In a bid for more time, Dex tossed the grenades through sections of the roof that had been completely obliterated. When the explosion rocked the hall and surrounding buildings, the Zar-Meck firing halted briefly, and Dex took off.

As he approached the end of the hall, opening up to a beautiful garden and pool area, Dex found himself trapped again.

A Zar-Meck was waiting for him, sword drawn.

Dex raised his blaster to fire, but the Zar-Meck caught the bolt with his blade.

Right, Dex thought, *I don't have time for this.*

A thought passed to use another grenade, but they had been depleting his suit's power level quickly, and he'd need it as a shield more than anything. But what would one more hurt? Dex drew a grenade and tossed it in the Zar-Meck's direction. Without hesitation, the Zar-Meck grabbed the grenade and tossed it back with incredible speed.

Dex tried to flee, but the grenade blew up, knocking him off his feet.

Before Dex knew it, the Zar-Meck was on top of him, bringing down his sword. Dex drew his blade and blocked the attack.

A second blow came down swiftly, with much more force behind it. Dex dodged to the left and rushed to his feet. A follow-through came that slashed across Dex's back. The suit took most of the damage, but Dex still felt the force behind the swing and was pushed up against the wall.

Dex turned quickly, seeing the Zar-Meck coming at him in a lunge. Dodging the slightest bit to the right, the blade missed. The Zar-Meck crashed into Dex, who sliced the villain's hands with his own blade. The Zar-Meck dropped the sword and jumped back, avoiding Dex's upward slash. Blasts from the far end of the hall shot toward them. Dex refused to let the Zar-Meck swordsman retreat or retake any advantage. He swung madly as the Zar-Meck drew a new sword from his suit, then beat down continuously, keeping the Zar-Meck pinned against the wall. Dex's body was tired, and each swing came with a heavy breath, but the adrenaline pumping through him kept Dex going until a blow came down so hard and fast that it sliced off the Zar-Meck's sword hand. Without a second thought, he stabbed the Zar-Meck in the chest.

With the blasts flying too close for comfort, Dex escaped down the hall into the garden. The tip of the pyramid began to peak over the buildings. Dex got his bearings and ran at full speed toward Lacy, shooting at Zar-Mecks as they neared him. When passing a bridge, Dex dropped a grenade behind himself to destroy it, hoping to slow down his pursuers.

Now, even with the sounds of blaster bolts zipping through the air and explosions going off left and right, Dex heard chanting coming from the Emperor's hall.

"I'm almost there, Lacy," he said to himself.

The closer Dex came to the pyramid, the more enemies came down on Dex. Constantly switching between his blaster for enemies on rooftops and at distances, and sword for up-close combat, Dex was quickly adapting to the suit's mental command system, but his power level dropped steadily.

After passing a number of towers and courtyards, dodging the onslaught of Zar-Meck blasters and grenades, as well as one that looked oddly out of place, not paying attention to the rest of the action, Dex came to one of the wide bridges that met the pyramid on the other side.

Surrounding the pyramid was the entire population of Children of the Void that resided in the palace-city. There were hundreds, all kneeling with their hands clasped in reverence above their heads. Dex heard a low mumbling coming from the crowd.

The ritual procession was entering the Emperor's Pyramid, still chanting their prayer to the Emperor. Standing tall on her platform above the rest of the sacrifices, Lacy was in clear view of Dex.

"Lacy!" Dex called.

Lacy turned at the shout and saw Dex across the bridge. "Dex! Dex, I'm here!"

Rejoiced and motivated at the sound of her voice, Dex took a step onto the bridge, but as he did so, half a dozen grenades were thrown to the ground ahead of him from Zar-Mecks on the rooftops behind. A moment of shock took over. Dex froze and was then thrown backward by the force of the explosion. He was momentarily in a daze; ears popped and head spinning. When he came to, Dex saw the bridge completely destroyed and the large doors of the Emperor's Pyramid shut.

Dex tried getting to his feet. Suddenly, someone grabbed his arm and pulled him hurriedly into a nearby building.

"Listen, Captain Prullen, we don't have much time."

* * *

Jaskek's shuttle pulled up under the palace-city. The echoes of the battle above told him he wasn't far from the action, but still at a safe distance for the time being. He hadn't expected Dex to make it to the planet, but no one else would be causing that much chaos.

Using a low-hanging vine, Jaskek pulled himself up onto a walkway, then sent the shuttle away with his tablet.

If the Zar-Mecks' attention is on Dex, I should have no problem intercepting the ritual procession, Jaskek thought.

He still walked quietly, checking every corner for Zar-Mecks to be safe.

Knowing how the rituals worked, though never seeing one in person, Jaskek wasn't worried about running into the Children of the Void. All he had to worry about was not getting caught in the crossfire.

With every building he passed, the sounds of blaster fire and grenades drew closer. Even when he ran away from the battlefield, the threat of getting stuck in it would catch up to him.

Jaskek's luck ran out when he took a wrong turn and came upon a Zar-Meck hiding in a corner, waiting to ambush Dex.

The Zar-Meck turned, hearing Jaskek's footsteps. It raised its blaster and aimed at Jaskek's head. In a powerful voice, the Zar-Meck commanded, "Officer Dreed, you are not permitted to be in this area. Return to your post!"

Jaskek stiffened himself. "Stand down, soldier. And lower your weapon when speaking to an officer."

The Zar-Meck's voice amplified, and it took a step closer. "RETURN TO YOUR PO-"

Its words were cut short. Dex had run past behind it, seeing a Zar-Meck and not wasting an easy hit.

The Zar-Meck fell forward toward Jaskek, then spun to catch the already-gone human.

With his attention diverted, Jaskek rushed up

behind the Zar-Meck, grabbed its blaster, and aimed it under the Zar-Meck's chin. The Zar-Meck fought hard, trying to pull and shake Jaskek off.

Maintaining his hold on the Zar-Meck, Jaskek pulled the trigger repeatedly until the armor cracked and a blaster bolt shot into its head.

The lifeless body fell to the ground, and Jaskek felt no remorse. He only grabbed the blaster, then peeked around the alley corner to see if Dex or any other Zar-Mecks were there.

A group of footsteps quickly approached. Jaskek fell back against the wall, hidden as Zar-Mecks passed, giving orders through comm devices for where to cut Dex off.

"The human cannot get to the palace. Destroy the bridge if need be."

Jaskek doubled back to find an alternate route to the Emperor's Pyramid, until he too found himself looking upon the wide bridges. It was only a moment after he'd come out into the open that a bridge a hundred feet or so to his left was destroyed.

Jaskek watched Dex's body fly backward. He looked toward the bridge to his right but saw a pair of Zar-Mecks attempting to hide on a rooftop, ready to shoot anyone who got close to them. He ultimately realized that his best chances to get out of there alive were with Dex.

Ignoring the blaster fire that was sure to come his way, Jaskek dashed over to Dex's momentarily incapacitated body, using the smoke and dust from the bridge explosion for cover, and dragged him into the nearest building, a huge spiraled tower. Blaster bolts struck the ground all around them, and once in the building, Jaskek shut and barricaded the door.

Kneeling over Dex, Jaskek said hurriedly, "Listen, Captain Prullen, we don't have much time."

The palace-city then ruptured as if there had been a small earthquake. Jaskek had no idea where it came from. Grenades couldn't have made such an impact.

Dex looked into Jaskek's taouron eyes. "Korr? Is that you?" He asked in a daze.

"I'm a friend of your wife, Lieutenant Prullen. We can still save her, but you have to do as I say. Can you stand?"

The world began to clear again, and Dex rose slowly to his feet.

"Yeah," Dex said. "I..." The realization hit that he didn't know the man who dragged him. His heads-up display identified Jaskek as an officer in the Emperor's army. Dex quickly drew his blaster. Jaskek swiped it aside. In a flash, Dex adapted, conjuring a sword from the suit in his left hand and bringing it up to Jaskek's neck.

"Calm down, Captain Prullen," Jaskek spoke boldly, not giving away a hint of fear for the blade at his throat. "I am the only way you will get your wife back."

"Oh yeah? How do I know I can trust you? You said you're a friend of hers?"

Jaskek pursed his lips. Although he had just said that, it had merely been a way to bring ease to the situation. "Chances are she'll kill me once we find her."

"Then why would you help her?"

Jaskek took a moment to think, knowing the wrong word would bring him death too quickly. "Because whether for her own good or out of pure kindness, she helped me, even though I was sending her to her death."

Dex lowered his blade slightly and considered. "You stay in front of me. I still don't trust you, so the moment you make the wrong move, I won't hesitate to kill you."

"I could have left you to die by that bridge."

"You could also be escorting me to my death for your own glory."

"Do you really wish to waste more time arguing?"

"Fine. What's your plan?" Dex dropped his sword to his side.

Jaskek looked around the room for inspiration and glanced at the staircase that rose to the top of the tower. He then rushed to the window and opened the shutters the littlest bit. "Come here," he commanded Dex. "How far do you think that gap is?"

Dex looked through the window. "Sixty feet. Seventy with the distance from this building." He looked at Jaskek and tapped his suit's helmet. "Lotta cool gadgets up here."

Jaskek backed up toward the stairs. "So I've heard."

A squad of Zar-Mecks crossed in front of the window and began banging on the barricaded door.

Jaskek commanded Dex again, "Quick, drop some grenades on the floor here. But do NOT detonate them, then come to the top of the tower."

Dex didn't question Jaskek. He summoned six grenades from the suit and carefully but quickly laid them down on the ground, then raced up the stairs behind Jaskek.

At the top of the tower, Dex asked, "What's the grand plan?"

Jaskek was lying on the floor, but quickly got up to grab Dex and pulled him to the ground. "Stay low! The

Zar-Mecks have got those bridges covered. We'll never get across going over them. So we'll have to make our own."

"What?"

"Get ready to jump. We'll detonate those grenades and ride the tower. It's tall enough to cross the gap."

"You're insane! What about the people down there?"

"The ones praying your wife has a good death?"

Dex paused, then, "You're right. I'm sure they'll move. All right, let's do this." He summoned two more grenades and watched in his heads-up display the power level drop down to 8%. The suit was no longer covering his whole body.

The first grenade he dropped down the tower steps. "Let's pray this works," he told Jaskek.

Jaskek said nothing, only harrumphed.

It took a few moments, but as the Zar-Mecks inevitably broke through the barricade, the grenades waiting to meet them detonated.

Jaskek and Dex felt the tower rumble and begin to fall. At the first hint of sway, Dex primed and rolled the second grenade off the ledge in the direction away from the pyramid.

"What are you doing?" Jaskek asked nervously.

"Fixing your plan."

The grenade detonated halfway down the side of the tower. The blast was strong enough to shift the tilt of the falling tower in the direction of the pyramid.

Zar-Mecks on other rooftops began shooting in their direction, hoping a stray bolt would find a target.

On the pyramid side of the bridge, the Children of the Void could no longer ignore the sounds of battle.

Many turned to see what the latest explosion had been and ran when they saw the heavy bricks of the tower falling toward them.

Dex thanked God for their fleeing. Even in his anger toward the Empire, he'd wanted to avoid death where he could, save for the soulless Zar-Mecks. They could burn for eternity for all he cared.

"Get on the roof!" Dex shouted at Jaskek as the tower came closer to the ground.

Before Jaskek could struggle to get up, fighting against the speed of his fall, Dex had grabbed onto the ledge of the far side window and was pulling himself onto the outer wall. Jaskek climbed through just in time, and they both jumped off onto the solid ground of the palace-city as the tower crashed down and tore away a piece of the Emperor's Pyramid.

Dex rolled away from the crash. Bits of what was left of the Zar-Meck suit tore away as they scraped across the ground. All that remained of the suit was the blaster.

Children of the Void were fleeing to the far side of the pyramid and trying their best to keep the prayer chant alive.

"Hey! Jason! Or whatever your name is! You okay?" Dex called through the cloud of dust and rubble that rose around and above the ruined tower.

"It's *Jaskek*! I'm fine! Legs are killing me, though."

Dex coughed up some of the dust. "Welcome to the Airborne."

"What?"

"Nothing, army joke, doesn't matter. How do we get in?"

Jaskek began climbing over the tower to get to

Dex. It's just over here."

The two of them raced toward the great doors of the pyramid. The Children of the Void watched them, mumbling their prayer, trying to figure out if they should intervene.

"The Emperor is in danger!" Jaskek announced to them. "Open this door so we can save him!"

Without hesitation, the crowd of aliens rushed to the heavy doors and pulled them open.

"Thank you! You shall be well rewarded!" Jaskek said, and the two of them ran into the hall. He then said in a hushed tone to Dex, "Dumb aliens."

* * *

Lacy's heart raced, but she tried to maintain a stoic expression.

I will not fear him, she told herself repeatedly.

The chanting had only grown louder since entering the pyramid and continued down the dimly lit hallway that felt like it went on for miles.

Up in front of the procession, over the sound of the chanting, Tarnascus began his own prayer to the Emperor.

"Great Lord of all worlds and beings, we bring to you these sacrifices! Your devoted followers who give their souls willingly, so that we may live closer with you, and in your spirit."

The procession began spilling out of the hallway, into the Emperor's great hall. The pillars of fire were already lit, illuminating the horrific walls of dusty, rotted bone. The Phantasms of the Emperor's court began to materialize. One grotesque horror show for every species of alien that offered itself to the Emperor and a reminder of what Lacy suspected was waiting for her.

I will not fear him, Lacy told herself again. *I will not let him take me.*

She tried to listen without turning her head for any sounds of battle outside the pyramid, but the walls were so thick, nothing came through.

Tarnascus continued with his prayer. "Great Lord of all worlds and beings, we bring to you this woman!"

The three Children of the Void - Tarnascus, Rassmenda, and Mermorrum - approached the edge of the bottomless pit and knelt, then raised their arms in a salute.

Towering above the pit, with his robes of blood and crowned head that shone as the sun, the Emperor beckoned his sacrifices closer.

"This woman is brought before you," Tarnascus continued his prayer, "so that your reach may grow, and other peoples may know your embrace."

Mermorrum ceased her prayer and sliced her left hand upward to signal the others to cease as well.

There was a moment of silence in the Emperor's Pyramid.

Lacy looked around and saw that she was the only one without her head down. The Emperor took notice of this.

"Why do you not honor me, Earth woman?" His thousand voices boomed through the great hall. The Children of the Void and all sacrifices shivered in fear and worship.

Tarnascus approached her and removed the cover

over Lacy's mouth that was silencing her. He then quickly returned to his place along the edge of the pit.

Lacy felt a shiver too, but only of fear, and repressed it. The eyes of the phantasms cast their glares down on her.

No, not hatred, she thought, *that looks like... anger? No... disappointment.*

The only look she could relate it to was her father, giving her the "I'm not mad, just disappointed" speech. But why? The weight of the crown bore down on her.

"SPEAK WOMAN!" The voices of the Emperor again threatened to rupture her ears.

The others in the room looked like they wanted to shield their ears and antenna, but would never block out something as holy as the voice of their god.

"I..." Lacy started, stifling the tremble in her voice, wanting to speak boldly. *I will not fear him.* "I honor no one... who feeds off the suffering of others! I will not give in to a tyrant who only lives to kill! I know what you are. You are all that is wrong and evil in this universe! You are not a god, you're the devil!"

Everyone kept their heads down.

"If you will not honor me, then you WILL fear me!" The sound of his voice shook the entire palace-city.

The aliens in the room struggled not to fall flat on the ground, and Mermorrum nearly fell into the pit. But Lacy, locked onto the hovering platform, was unmoved and stood tall.

Proudly, she declared, "I do not fear you!"

"We shall see." The Emperor's voice returned to a bearable tone. "Tarnascus, I am ready to accept your offerings."

Tarnascus stood slowly, "As you command, my Lord." He turned to the group of sacrifices, now helping themselves to their feet.

As he turned, a platform rose from the pit to the ledge.

Tarnascus welcomed the sacrifices forward. "There is nothing nobler, nothing greater any of you could do with your lives than to serve your Emperor in this way. The children you leave behind will be proud of you, and one day, you may look back through the eyes of the Emperor, and watch them do the same."

The sacrifices walked to their deaths.

Lacy refused to give up hope. Dex was only just outside, and she knew it. *He's probably running down the hallway now*, she told herself. But there were no footsteps behind her.

The platform looked like a large dinner plate. The sacrifices were all raising their hands toward the Emperor, like small children wanting to be lifted into their parents' arms.

The pillars of fire now burned brighter. The Emperor grew larger and raised his arms out toward the people on the platform as if to receive them.

"I thank you for your sacrifice," he told them. "You shall all receive my greatest gift."

The sacrifices began to cry out in their alien tongue. They praised the Emperor and reached out, hoping to touch his massive golden hands. Some were even climbing over each other in an attempt to get closer.

"Be still! Now is the time to join me!"

The platform hummed. Instantly, the people calmed. They felt the Emperor's power move into and through them. The Children of the Void were silent, their eyes locked on the Emperor.

Lacy watched, worried as to what would happen next.

In a low hum, Tarnascus, Rassmenda, and Mermorrum began to pray.

Lacy heard the cries begin again, but this time... something was off. It was subtle, but it no longer sounded like cries of worship.

No... these people were in pain.

The cries quickly became screams of terror! The phantasms watching the sacrifice were taking a more solid, but still slightly transparent form. Their dark eyes were rolled to the backs of their heads. And though the Emperor had no facial features, there was a surely defined look of pleasure emanating from the emptiness that should have been his face.

For once, Lacy had to shield her eyes from the horrors she was witnessing. The screams of terror ate away at her heart.

Throughout the suffering, the prayers from the three Children only grew louder, as if competing with the alien's screams.

For half a moment, the building shook again lightly. It was the only moment, Lacy saw, that Rassmenda and Mermorrum flinched throughout the ceremony. Lacy couldn't tell if something was wrong or if the power coming from the Emperor was affecting them too.

When the screams stopped, there was a terrible silence in the room. Lacy held her tear-soaked hands over her eyes. She felt a coldness wash over everything.

Slowly, she pulled her hands away from her face.

The sacrificial platform descended, and Lacy only caught a glimpse of a horrific mass of mangled bodies. Tarnascus stood before her with his hand out to escort her toward the pit.

"It is time," he said in a soft, but still firm voice.

The locks on her feet released. Lacy looked back toward the hallway one last time. Still no sign of Dex. She turned back and met the Emperor's eyeless gaze.

"If you take my soul, I swear to you, you will not have me as a prisoner. You will have me as an enemy, fighting you for eternity." Lacy extended her hand and allowed Tarnascus to lead her to a new, smaller platform that rose out of the pit.

The Emperor welcomed Lacy to her doom with his arms wide.

"It will be an interesting eternity spent together, then," was the Emperor's only reply before the next part of the ritual began.

Tarnascus began a new prayer. After every verse, Rassmenda and Mermorrum would repeat him. Every verse was louder than the last.

The platform Lacy stood on began to glow, and she felt a strange energy flow into her.

Her heart raced.

I am not afraid.

Her eyes were locked onto the Emperor's face.

The body paint on Lacy's hands and face began to radiate with heat. She could feel it molding into the dress, crown, and her flesh, accentuating the features it had created. The energy force she had felt was now shifting to pain. Lacy gritted her teeth and clenched her fists. She even let a tear escape her eye, but she would not scream for mercy or look away from the Emperor.

Tarnascus' prayer echoed around the hall but was drowned out in Lacy's ears by her internal screams of pain.

Suddenly, the prayer was cut short.

Mermorrum let out a gasp of shock and fell into the pit.

Lacy felt relief from the pain. She broke contact with the Emperor and turned. Tarnascus' tall frame concealed her vision of the hall, but two blaster sounds rang out. He fell to his knees, writhing in pain.

Walking boldly toward the pit were Dex and Jaskek.

"Lacy!" Dex called to her.

Lacy's voice was stuck in her throat. She was overjoyed at the sight of him and let the tears flow. "D-Dex!" Without wasting a moment, she leapt from the platform to the ledge of the pit.

Dex ran to her, reaching out for her arm as Lacy's foot slipped on a loose rock.

"Don't worry, I've got you!" Dex comforted her as he helped Lacy to her feet.

Behind them, Jaskek had Rassmenda stuck up. "Don't make any moves," he warned her.

"WHO ENTERS MY HALL!" The voices of the Emperor roared.

Jaskek fell into shock at the realization he was in the presence of the Emperor. His skin illuminated brightly.

Dex held Lacy in his arms as he looked up at the Emperor, trying to avoid being stabbed by her hulking crown. "Lacy, we have to get out of here! We're running out of time."

They started shuffling back to the hallway, hand in hand.

"Jas! Come on, let's go!" Dex smacked Jaskek's shoulder as they ran past him.

"Rassmenda, my servant, stop them!"

Rassmenda was frozen, unsure of what was happening. She thought, *how could anything like this happen in the Emperor's presence? How could someone do this to god?* But she was not one to keep the Emperor waiting. Putting the Emperor's word before her ineptitude, Rassmenda ran after the trio and grabbed Lacy's arm.

"Please!" She cried, "You don't know what you're doing! It is a gift! A gift he's giving you!" Tears streamed down her face as she pleaded with Lacy. For how thin her frame was, she had incredible strength and dragged Lacy and Dex back to the pit. "It is a gift!" she cried again.

"Let me go!" Lacy demanded.

Dex aimed his blaster at her with his free hand. "Let her go!"

Rassmenda, unconcerned with the blaster, only cried and pleaded, terrified of disappointing the Emperor.

Dex fired a blast into Rassmenda's leg. She fell to the ground and quickly helped herself back up, continuing to drag Lacy, as if it was no more than a slight inconvenience. A trip over a rock, almost.

Jaskek was yelling at Dex to take care of Rassmenda.

Dex was yelling at Rassmenda to let Lacy go. He didn't want to have to kill her.

Rassmenda was yelling at Lacy to come with her.

Lacy was sick of the yelling, and especially of being dragged this way and that across the universe by this god-awful Emperor. With a sudden burst of adrenaline, she pulled herself in toward Rassmenda, tilted her head down, and plunged the crown through the woman's stomach.

Rassmenda's eyes widened in shock. Blood flew from her mouth. She let go of Lacy's arm, taking the crown with her.

Lacy's hair fell down her shoulders and back, gold hair pieces dangling with it. She said tensely to Dex, "I... cannot begin to tell you... how much I hate that damn woman."

Dex and Jaskek didn't know what to say.

"Are we going or what?" Lacy asked and picked up her dress.

Dex began to speak, but Jaskek interjected. "Yes, right now. I have a ship that can pick us up." He began tapping on his tablet for the Zar-Meck ship he'd docked in the hangar to fly to his location.

The three of them started running again down the hall.

"Wait, no, we have a ship!" Dex said. "Hopefully it's still in the air!" He pulled the comm device off his belt and called to the *Silent Horizon*. "Robbie! Robbie, you there?"

"Robbie?" Lacy thought Dex showing up had already made her as happy as possible, but this was a great surprise.

"Yeah, I'll explain it later!"

The door was just ahead, and thankfully still open. Jaskek ran through first. The Children of the Void were still waiting patiently outside.

"Not to worry," Jaskek assured them. "The Emperor is fine!"

The Children of the Void gave a communal sigh of relief.

"Now if you'll please step aside-" Jaskek cut himself short when a grenade landed at his feet. "Back!"

He ordered Dex and Lacy.

The three of them fled behind the great pyramid doors for cover from the grenade. When it blew, the Zar-Mecks couldn't care less for the Children of the Void they had slaughtered. They had their orders.

"Lacy, take this." Dex handed off the Zar-Meck blaster to Lacy and drew his own from his holster.

"Dex, you know I'm terrible with these."

"Yeah, well, maybe the range was just an off day."

For the second time since being taken prisoner on Prullen-1, Lacy let herself laugh. Even after almost being turned into a demonic being, and now being under fire by soulless embodiments of evil, she was with Dex again. If this were the end, it would be a good one because they were together. She pulled him in for a kiss.

Dex was caught off guard, his head still in the battle, but he let himself enjoy the moment. He wrapped an arm around her and placed his other hand on her cheek, pulling her in close.

The kiss washed away all the pain they had endured since parting. All things wrong in the universe were temporarily set right as they embraced.

When the kiss ended, Dex looked into Lacy's eyes. Something was different.

"Lacy... your eyes..."

Lacy's eyes were still primarily blue, but looked like they were dotted with tiny stars and galaxies. They shone in magnificent, tiny dots of color as never before. Dex gazed into her new eyes that were a sea of space.

"No time, you two," Jaskek interrupted. "My ship's almost here."

Dex came to and turned to Jaskek, "Hold on, how

well can you control your ship from here?"

"What do you mean?" Jaskek peeked out the door, and a blaster bolt shot past his head. He quickly returned to cover.

"Can you target the Zar-Mecks with that thing?" He pointed to the tablet. "If you can take out the Zar-Mecks, we can make an easy getaway to our ship."

Jaskek thought about this plan. "It's worth a try. But we'll only have a minute before the Zar-Mecks figure out what's going on."

"Great! That's enough." Then, into his comm, Dex asked, "Robbie? Come in, buddy. What's your status?"

Static for a moment, then "THERE IS A FIRE. WHERE HAVE YOU BEEN?"

Dex sighed in relief. "We're ready for exfil." To Jaskek, "Where should I tell him to meet us?"

"West side landing pad. We'll have to be fast."

"I'm planning on it," Lacy said. "Anything to get out of this dress."

Dex called Robbie again. "Listen, pal, we're gonna meet you at the WEST. SIDE. Landing pad. You got that?"

"I TOLD YOU I CAN'T FLY! I DON'T KNOW WHY I HAVEN'T CRASHED AND THE SHIP IS ON FIRE!" Robbie sounded hysterical.

"You're fine, Robbie." Dex tried to calm him down.

"I AM NOT!"

Lacy took the comm. "Robbie, it's me, Lacy!"

Immediately, his tone changed. "Lacy? It's you? Really? Hello friend! I told Dex you were dead! I am glad I am wrong, for now!"

"That's great. Listen, I believe in you, okay? You can land the ship."

"I will do my best," Robbie said with sincerity, not wanting to let Lacy down.

"You both ready?" Jaskek asked.

Dex and Lacy raised their blasters to give an affirmative.

"Good," he peeked out past the door again. "Because it looks like my ship's here."

A Zar-Meck starfighter flew across the rooftops and began blasting any living thing it saw.

"Let's go!" Jaskek shouted and rushed out the door.

Lacy followed after him, but Dex held her back. He puffed up his cheeks, and she did the same, and they blew out together as their lips met.

"Guppie kisses," they whispered together.

"I love you," Dex said.

"I love you, too," Lacy replied.

"*Come on!*" Jaskek shouted.

Dex and Lacy rushed out the pyramid doors, blasting anything that resembled a Zar-Meck.

The starfighter gave them adequate cover. Enough at least for them to cross the bridge without it blowing up, and once they were running through the halls and alleyways of the palace-city, all they had to do was keep up their speed. Jaskek was in the lead, followed by Lacy and Dex in the rear.

Zar-Mecks continued to blast at them from rooftops, and some were waiting to ambush them from behind corners.

A swordsman jumped out from behind the trio as they stepped onto a long but narrow bridge. He lunged at Dex, who instinctively dodged out of the way. Lacy dodged too as the swordsman's blade charged toward her, and together, she and Dex shoved the man off the bridge.

In pushing the swordsman, Lacy nearly pushed herself off the narrow bridge. Dex grabbed her and pulled her in. "You okay?" He asked.

Lacy nodded quickly, heart racing.

"Look out!" Jaskek called to him from the far end of the bridge.

The couple looked up and saw two Zar-Mecks about to fire. They jumped back to solid ground, avoiding the blasts that came down so heavily it destroyed the bridge.

Dex and Lacy took cover.

"Lacy, you take the left, I take the right."

"Got it."

"Ready, now!" They poked out of their cover and began blasting at the Zar-Mecks.

The Zar-Mecks ducked, and under cover fire, Jaskek climbed to the roof.

Seeing Jaskek on his target, Dex shifted fire to the Zar-Meck on the left.

Jaskek, sneaking up on the enemy, rushed the Zar-Meck and threw it off the roof.

Dex and Lacy hit their mark simultaneously. Two blaster bolts, one to the chest and one to the head, sent the remaining Zar-Meck flying back with its helmet shattered.

"It's clear," Jaskek called to them.

Lacy eyed the distance of the chasm between them. "It's too far! We won't make it!"

Behind them, in the direction of the Emperor's Pyramid, more Zar-Mecks were running toward them and opened fire.

The *Silent Horizon* flew overhead.

Dex looked around for new routes, knowing there

was absolutely no time to spare.

"I think I have an idea. Hold on!" He wrapped an arm around Lacy and grabbed a nearby vine. "Always wanted to do this," he said, almost to himself.

Lacy didn't question him. She only held on for dear life as he swung the two of them across the chasm. Blaster fire raced past them, and Lacy did her best to fire back with the arm wrapped around Dex's front.

He let go when they made it to the other side and tumbled to the ground. Jaskek was already back down in the hall, giving them cover fire as they got to their feet.

"Landing platform is just over there," Jaskek said.

Dex and Lacy ran together hand in hand, with Jaskek firing back at the Zar-Mecks.

When they approached the landing pad, the *Silent Horizon* was touching down. It was in terrible shape, scarred by blaster burns all over the hull. The airlock was still open from before, and smoke was escaping from it.

"Jesus, he wasn't kidding," Dex said.

Lacy was the first one onto the ship. Dex swapped roles with Jaskek, laying down covering fire while he boarded. Dex boarded last and sealed the airlock.

His eyes burned from the smoke in the cabin, and all three of them were coughing.

"Are you all on?" Robbie's electronic voice called to them.

"Yes!" Lacy coughed twice. "Yes, we're here! Let's go!"

Robbie pulled away from the platform and zoomed into the upper atmosphere.

Lacy rushed to her co-pilot seat and brushed Robbie to the side. "Thanks, Robbie. I'll take it from here."

Robbie hopped down from the chair and attended to the fire burning from the starboard side bunk with his reserve extinguisher.

"What happened, Robbie?" Dex gestured to the flame as he walked through the cabin to his seat at the main console.

"You did not close the door. A stray blast got in as I flew away."

Dex shook his head as he took a seat. "All right, party's over. Prime the engine. This heading." He pointed to a random spot on the map.

Jaskek was looking over his shoulder. "That's not where Earth is."

Lacy glanced over at Dex. "He's right. Why aren't we going to Earth?"

Dex kept his focus on the console. "We need to throw them off. If we take a straight shot to Earth, they'll follow our trajectory. We'll be dooming the whole planet. Plus, we can drop your friend off somewhere safe." He thumbed Jaskek, whom he'd felt hovering too closely over his shoulder.

"What?" Lacy asked with a bit of revulsion. "He just helped us escape!"

Something exploded outside the ship.

Dex toggled through the computer's displays and brought up the rear-view feed. They had company.

"Lacy, a rear turret is installed. I need you on that."

She slid into officer mode for a moment and manned the turret. "Roger, Captain." Then, back out of the officer's tone, "But we can't just leave him now!"

"I agree," Jaskek said. "I won't be able to show my face in the Empire again until I've brought back something to prove myself."

Dex caught him without either of them noticing. *Until.* The word Dex had been expecting to hear.

"Baby," Dex said to Lacy, "change of plans. I need you piloting."

Lacy's gaze rushed back across the console in confusion. "Wait! Wait, Dex, what?"

Before anyone knew what was going on, Dex was on his feet and socked Jaskek in the face.

Jaskek fell back and hit his head on the floor.

"Dex, what are you doing?" Lacy screamed, then rolled the *Silent Horizon* to the left as a Zar-Meck straighter careened toward them, firing repeatedly.

"He's not here to save us. He just wants to be the first to the prize." Dex kicked Jaskek while he was down.

"Dex, stop!" Lacy cried, but couldn't pull herself away from the controls. The Zar-Mecks were hammering down on them hard. She could barely dodge their attacks.

"Wait!" Jaskek coughed up blood. "Okay! I'll admit..." another cough as he got to his feet, propped up by the port side bunk. His skin began to glow again, flickering like a beating heart. "It's true. When I first found you, that was my plan. But things changed!"

"See!" Lacy insisted.

Dex looked at his wife, still unsure.

"I can see now," Jaskek continued. "I don't need both of you." He had feigned the level of pain he'd felt, grabbed Dex's blaster, and drew his own, aiming at both of the earthlings. "Just need one of you to operate this ship."

"Lacy, don't try anything," Dex told her, with his arms raised.

"Now, for all the work we put in to save her, I think

it's only fair that Lacy is the one who gets to come with me."

A voice in the back of the room asked politely. "Can I come too?"

The three of them all turned their heads to see Robbie in the back, swaying back and forth lightly, holding his claws like a child asking for dessert.

With Jaskek's head turned, Dex threw his fist into the man's gut.

Jaskek dropped the blasters and staggered back. A moment later, he lunged at Dex, shoving him up against the console, with his hands around Dex's neck.

Dex countered, knocking Jaskek's elbow down to break the contact, then punching up into his jaw.

Jaskek's glow beat more intensely. He intercepted Dex's next blow, threw a punch into his gut, then twisted his arm, throwing him to the ground.

"Robbie, help him!" Lacy called to the robot, who sat unsure in the corner.

Robbie perked up at hearing his name but was unsure of the right action to take. On one claw, he wanted to help his new friends, and on the other was an officer in the Army he had served for his entire existence. His programming told him one thing, but deep down under all the circuitry, another voice told him something else. The voice that won was his own.

I have a choice now.

Robbie rushed to assist Dex. His right claw was overextended, ready to flame Jaskek.

Seeing the robot rushing, Jaskek only had to give a light kick to knock Robbie onto his back.

Robbie flailed his arms trying to get himself back

on his stubby feet.

"I have spent too long being a bystander of history," Jaskek said. "Earth will fall to the Emperor. But I will at least have a taste of your world before handing it over to him."

Dex was on his feet, arms raised, ready to throw down. "You think you'll be welcomed back after what we just pulled?"

"The Emperor cares for worlds, not individual, replaceable lives. In time, I will prepare your world for his arrival and be welcomed back as a hero! My debt paid off! I will be honor-"

Dex cut him off with a jab to the face.

The retaliation was swift. Jaskek rushed Dex, grabbing him by the neck and throwing him to the ground.

The *Silent Horizon* rattled under more blaster fire as Dex's head hit the ground. He couldn't breathe; it felt like his lungs collapsed.

Every moment Lacy tried to turn her attention from the battle she was facing against the starfighters to help Dex, another one came in, pinning her to her duty. Instead of leaving her post, Lacy barrel-rolled the ship hard to the left. Dex and Jaskek rolled around the cabin with the contents of the overhead storage.

Dex was hit in the head by something small, and when Lacy leveled out, Jaskek was back on top of him, ready to choke Dex out.

"Should have taken me back with you!" Jaskek spat through his clenched teeth.

Then, over the radio, a voice came in. "Dex, do you realize how many bad guys you've got on your tail?"

"What the hell is that?" Lacy called.

Jaskek looked out the window, then quickly back at Dex before he could be caught off guard again. An imperial transport ship was hovering over them, with starfighters pouring out. "Those aren't Zar-Mecks. You've got some friends, huh?"

Unable to hold herself back anymore, Lacy jumped from the controls to Jaskek and pulled him off Dex with her arm around his neck.

Jaskek thrashed at her, trying to pull her off, but Lacy was so full of rage toward everything to do with the Empire, and reveling in her chance to get some payback, nothing could pull her off of him.

Dex struggled to regain his breath.

With what little focus he had, Jaskek reached for one of the blasters on the floor under the ship's console. He was going to risk getting to Earth without either of them.

Dex grabbed the first thing he could find. The small object that hit his head during the barrel roll.

The jarrmin box.

Dex pulled himself on top of Jaskek and slammed the box on his face. The force alone was enough to shatter bone, and the pain shot through all of Jaskek's being.

Jaskek aimed the blaster at Dex.

Lacy pulled tighter on his throat.

Dex activated the box.

As the medical device numbed and pulled back the flesh on his face, Jaskek pulled the trigger of the blaster.

Dex fell back in pain, ripping the jarrmin box off of Jaskek's face.

Within seconds, Jaskek went from feeling incredible pain to shock to death. He lay fleshless-facedown on the floor of the *Silent Horizon*.

Dex and Lacy were both sweating hard in the rush of the action. Her body paint was starting to wash off and run. She wiped it off her face, unsure what to say next.

Looking down at Jaskek's corpse, she thumbed the transport ship just outside. "Um..." she tried to say. "That. You should look."

Dex pulled himself up, then helped Lacy, and they returned to their seats.

Again, the voice over the radio. "Dex! Are you there? Fix your flight path, you're headed straight for me."

Instinctively, Dex angled the ship away from the transport, then responded to the call. "Korr? Is that you?"

"Who in Maoul else would it be?" Korr responded enthusiastically.

Dex and Lacy looked out the window and at the rearview feed. Small unmanned fighters from Korr's ship were fending off the Zar-Meck starfighters.

Dex laughed, "What changed your mind?"

"Don't get me started. But I will say, if I'm gonna die, might as well be for the right reason. And a blow to the Emperor himself seems like a pretty good reason."

Lacy took over the radio. "I don't know who you are, but thank you!"

"Appreciate it," Korr said. "Now let's catch up later. I have a hangar open, and not a lot of fighters left on the battlefield. So get in here and we'll be off."

"You got it, Korr," Dex said, then gave a command to Lacy. "Power down the hyperdrive engine."

"Hyperdrive?" Lacy asked.

Dex shrugged. "Call it an anniversary present."

The *Silent Horizon* flew around the perimeter of

Korr's ship, looking for a hangar entrance. Zar-Meck fighters pursued them, which were pursued by Korr's fighters.

"There it is!" Lacy called, pointing to a small opening in Korr's ship. "The hangar."

"I see it, diving now!"

Dex angled the ship down and began a fast approach to the hangar. It was going to be a close call, but the Zar-Mecks on his tail were too close.

Just a few seconds to freedom, when out of nowhere, a Zar-Meck fighter made a suicide run across their path. Dex had to pull up sharply to avoid a crash.

"Korr, I missed my chance!" Dex called through the radio. "I'm coming around for another pass!"

"No!" Korr called back immediately. "I'm too low on fighters. We've got two imperial battleships approaching from the city. I can't cover you much longer. Just get out of here!"

Dex wanted to argue, and he could see in Lacy's eye that she did too, but they both knew they weren't going to last long enough for another run. Alarms were blaring left and right in the cabin, screaming at them that the *Silent Horizon* had taken too much damage.

"We're sorry, Korr," Dex said. "Lacy, prime the hyperdrive."

Korr's remaining fighters were doing all they could to hold the Zar-Mecks off.

"Lacy, what are you doing?" Dex shouted.

"Just wait! We need something for this!" Lacy raced to find something in the computer's library. "Here!"

Throughout the ship's speakers, "Pines of Rome" picked up where they had stopped after crashing on

Prullen-1.

"Lacy, are you serious right now?"

"Trust me! I have an idea." As the triumphant climax of the song played, Lacy rerouted the output to play through the radio as well.

From the other end of the radio, Zar-Meck transmissions argued with each other about what they were hearing.

"That should throw them off for a moment."

Dex scoffed playfully. "All right, enough of the games. I need you to prime the hyperdrive."

"Roger, Captain," she said, almost with a laugh. "I'm ready to be out of here."

The *Silent Horizon* raced across the top of Korr's ship, while on the underside, the Empire battleships drew in closer and began opening fire on Korr.

Korr abandoned his ship's bridge and fled for the nearest escape pod. The ship was shaking violently under the heavy cannons of the Empire's fire. He could barely stand as he dragged himself through the halls.

Dex angled the *Silent Horizon* upwards again toward space.

"Engine ready?" Dex asked.

"Ready."

A thought struck Dex suddenly. The ship's fuel levels. "Wait!"

"We don't have time to wait, Dex!"

"Lacy, we only have enough fuel for one jump. Wherever we go, we might not make it back to Earth…" His voice began to die out, not just fade away.

All around the ship, Zar-Meck starfighters and drones from Korr's ships blasted away at each other. Laser beams crossed the *Silent Horizon*'s viewport. It would take only one unlucky blast to blow them out of the sky. Yet the only thought in their minds was the choice between safely escaping to an Earth they would doom, or flying off into the further reaches of uncharted space, where any sort of peril and adventure would await them.

Korr's ship met its ultimate fate in the skies of the Heart of the Void, with flaming debris raining down around them, crashing into Zar-Meck ships before assaulting the ground below. The pieces missed Dex and Lacy as if only by fate, and in that moment, the answer was clear to both of them.

Without plotting a course, Lacy reached out to the center of the console and activated the drive to propel them in whatever direction they were meant for.

The universe slowed, then froze around the *Silent Horizon*. Light began to wrap around the ship. The music swelled triumphantly.

Dex looked into Lacy's eyes.

Lacy looked into his.

He put a hand on her cheek, and they leaned into each other.

As their lips met, the *Silent Horizon* made its jump into the unknown infinity of space. Captain Dex and Lieutenant Lacy Prullen, two astronauts from Earth, began their next adventure together, happy again in each other's love.

Epilogue of Book 1

Tarnascus entered the throne room accompanied by a taourun, Romek Amari.

The two of them fell to their knees by the pit's ledge. They bowed and gave their salute to the Emperor.

"How may we serve you, my Lord?" Tarnascus spoke for the two of them in a bold and respectful tone.

The Emperor appeared on the platform above the center of the pit. His voice boomed through the Pyramid as he spoke. "You and the Zar-Mecks have failed me, Tarnascus."

"My Lord," Tarnascus' voice trembled slightly. "He was given aid by a traitor. He had help fro-"

"SILENCE!" The Emperor's voice rattled the entire palace-city. "I care not for your excuses. For three hundred years, you have served me. It seems as though your service has run its course. Step forward, and show your bones."

Tarnascus rose slowly and stepped closer toward the ledge. His legs were healing fast from the shots the earthling had taken at them.

To the side of the Emperor, a phantasm resembling a horrifyingly disfigured Child of the Void appeared.

"Please... my Lord... I... I beg you." Before him, a platform from the pit below rose to the ledge.

"Tarnascus, I condemn you to suffer in Maoul."

Tarnascus stepped onto the platform, tears streaming down his face. "I only wished to serve you..."

Romek continued kneeling, eyes to the ground. Unless the Emperor commanded him, he did not wish to witness the suffering Tarnascus had begun to endure. The screams of pain and holy terror were enough to last an eternity in his memory.

When the screaming stopped, the Emperor shifted his attention to Romek Amari. "The Earth beings have escaped, and I now task you to hunt them down."

A tear fell from Romek's cracked green eye. "I am... honored... Lord, that you would choose me for this holy mission. I will be merciless in my hunt, Lord. I will earn this duty." Romek let his hands fall to the ground and looked up at the Emperor's imposing golden head. The platform with Tarnascus' body had been replaced with a clean one.

"RISE!" the Emperor commanded.

Romek was on his feet quicker than he realized and stepped onto the platform. Almost instantly, his muscles began to ache, and his head felt like it was about to cave in.

"I grant you my powers, Romek. Fail me, and you will never pass beyond this universe. You will be lower in my eyes than the multitudes of worlds I have obliterated, and you will suffer more than all combined."

Romek screamed. His bones cracked. His muscles spasmed and exploded under his skin. He wanted to claw out his eyes that had felt like they were melting, and leaking into his nose, mouth, and lungs. Romek tried to fall to the ground, but the Emperor commanded him to rise, and through all his pain, Romek couldn't say no to his god. He stayed on his feet, which stung as if he were standing on molten glass shards.

Romek wanted to die. He wanted to throw himself off the ledge and dive headfirst into the abyss, obliterating himself on whatever lay however far down there, but the voice of the Emperor bade him stay standing where he was.

As quickly as the pain came, it left him. Romek was allowed to fall back onto his knees. His body was intact, eyes whole where they belonged, but something was different about him. In his core, he felt new energy welling up. His muscles were bigger, and he had a greater sense of his surroundings. In fact, all of his senses registered much more than before. And more so than that, he had a craving.

Looking at the ground around him, he saw the dust and dirt vibrating.

Romek brought his eyes back up to look upon the Emperor's magnificence.

The thousand voices of the Emperor ripped through Romek's mind. "Go now, my servant. Do what must be done for the sake of my Empire!

Thank you for reading "Empire of the Void," and now please check out this special look at the sequel, out now!

Lost World of the Void

The Empire Marathon: Book 2

By Andrew Valenza

15. Flight of the Silent Horizon

Fire erupted from the engine room and began to spread throughout the rear of the *Silent Horizon*.

"Robbie! Help us out!" Dex barked orders at the small ash-black robot. The two of them held back the flames of the overworked hyperdrive engine; Robbie with his extinguisher claw, Dex with the ships'.

Music blared over the crew's shouting. Lacy tried shutting it off so she could think, but one alarm sounded after another and got in her way on the computer. *Fire in the engine room! Fire in the airlock! Life support critical! Fire in the greenhouse! Engine critical!*

"Dex, hurry up! This whole ship is about to blow!" Lacy cried.

Any moment now their atoms would be dispersed into the universe, flying at the speed of light in a million different directions. Dex and the robot pushed on, holding back the flames.

"Dex! The engine!"

"I know, I know! Vent it!" Dex called back.

"Vent is offline! System's totally fried!"

"Damn! Can you shut off the airflow?"

Lacy checked the few remaining controls they had. Sweat dripped from her brow into her eyes. "It'll have to be a complete life support shutdown."

"All right, I'm getting there!" He shoved the robot closer to the engine room door. "Go on, you worry about the engine, I'll get the hall!"

"It is too hot in there." The robot said mat-ter-of-factly.

"You'll be fine!" A burst of flames shot out through the doorway, inches from Dex's face. The heat was over-whelming. "You're strong, you got this! Just go! Fast!"

"I am not." He tried to back away, but Dex pushed him further in.

"I believe in you, go!"

Robbie processed the chances of success. He had a light but tough metal shell. There was a high chance his circuits would melt, but there was also a guarantee that the ship would be destroyed if he didn't act.

"I will g-"

"Great!" Dex cut him off. "Shut it down, Lacy! And hold your breath!"

Robbie wobbled as fast as he could into the engine room and flailed his extinguisher arm every which way, at-tacking the flames with extreme prejudice.

Lacy deactivated the life support and rushed to grab an oxygen tank from their space suits in the rear of the cabin.

The flames ate up the remaining oxygen in the ship. Dex held his breath as he and Robbie fought off what remained of the fire. When he couldn't hold his breath any longer, Dex rushed to join Lacy. They took turns breathing through the tank and prayed Robbie would be able to clear out the room.

Between breaths, Dex called out to the robot. "Robbie, how's it looking?"

"Fire is out. There is no air. I cannot breathe."

Lacy's eyes went wide and rushed to save him. "Robbie!" She screamed and dropped the tank into Dex's hands.

"Lacy, wait!" Dex grabbed her by the arm.

"He's going to…" she struggled for air, "die in there!"

Dex took a deep breath from the tank, handed it back to her then held up a finger, telling her to wait.

Robbie stepped out from the airlock hall. "It is a good thing I do not need to breathe. The fire is clear."

Dex gave the robot a thumbs up, then patted Lacy on the shoulder, signaling her to turn the life support system back on before his face could turn a deep blue.

The crisis was averted for the time being. Battle scars from their escape from the Empire displayed themselves proudly on the *Silent Horizon*. The outer hull was heavily damaged, streaked with laser burns from the Empire's Zar-Meck starfighters. Ash from the fire caked the ceiling of the airlock hallway, engine room, and the artificial greenhouse. The newly installed hyperdrive had been activated too frequently and it was taking its toll. In the main cabin lay the corpse of the faceless Imperial officer, Jaskek Dreed.

Robbie offered to move the body out of the way. He'd been freed from his Imperial programming by Lacy, but still felt discomfort at seeing the body.

"Where would you like me to put this?" Robbie asked, holding up the foot of the corpse.

"Over in the hallway, buddy. We'll dump him when we pull out of hyperspeed."

Robbie nodded in acknowledgement then struggled to pull the corpse into the *Silent Horizon*'s hallway.

"What do you say we get this…stuff…off you, dear?" Dex traced the backs of his fingers down Lacy's scarlet-painted cheeks.

She was adorned in a magnificent scarlet sacrificial dress, with beautiful jewels around her neck and in her hair, and her skin was painted in such a way as to exaggerate her bone structure. She didn't know for certain, but in seeing phantasms of the Emperor's court, and the way the alien Rassmenda talked as she prepared Lacy for sacrifice, Lacy believed that the dress, jewels, and painting were meant to merge into her being, decaying her natural beauty into a horrible skeletal image.

"Yes, please," she faux-pleaded Dex, then laughed. "It's a lovely dress, but I don't think red's my color anymore. And I could do without all the extra."

Dex held a smile but was still unnerved about the circumstances of the escape. Lacy's eyes had always been blue, but they were strikingly different now, and Dex didn't think she had yet realized this.

She stood up to walk to the head to change, but Dex, staying seated, gave her pause. "Are you feeling all right?"

Lacy turned slightly, with a quizzical smile. "Perfect, darling." Her starry eyes shined brightly. "Why do you ask?"

They'd escaped the Empire but the lights swirling in her eyes told him they hadn't left it behind. These moments should have been sweet between them, and as much as Dex wanted to let them be so, his better judgment told him this should be addressed.

"I need you to see this," he said as he jumped from his seat, closing the small gap between them, then took her by the hand and walked with her into the head. "Do you see?"

They stood in front of the mirror together. Lacy leaned in and raised a hand to her face, touching the cracking paint, too distracted to notice her eyes.

"See what? Do you think I'm having a reaction to this stuff? I don't feel irritation or anything."

"No, I mean your eyes. Look." Without giving her a chance to look deeply, Dex grabbed a face towel that hung next to the sink, ran it under the water, and handed it to her. "Maybe it'll be easier to see without all that crud off your face."

Lacy took the towel and wiped. With the paint gone, she was now able to see what Dex had been talking about. To her, it didn't pop out as much as it had for Dex, but the stars in her eyes couldn't be ignored.

As she inspected the abnormality, Dex asked her again, "You sure you feel fine?"

"Yes," Lacy said, slightly annoyed at his insistence, but still patient. "I'm sure it's nothing, just… I don't know. Something in the food maybe."

Deep down she knew that wasn't it. As strange as this adventure had been she knew the most likely answer to this mystery had to do with whatever had been interrupted in the Emperor's hall. The failed sacrificial ritual.

"After you shower, I want to do a scan. Just to be safe."

Lacy nodded but didn't say anything. Now that it was obvious to her, she only wanted to ignore it. The thought of keeping a piece of the Empire inside her disgusted her. At least with Robbie, he had no loyalty to the Emperor. But this… thing… she knew was a piece of the Emperor himself.

Dex gave her privacy as she undressed and cleansed herself of the previous days. They both knew how precious those moments were after coming out of the field from a training event and how necessary it was to have a warm shower and soft bed all to themselves for a few minutes. This had been much more stressful than any training event.

As she showered, Dex turned his attention to the corpse in the hallway.

Robbie had been busy cleaning the blood off of the floor and struggled to comprehend why more continued to slowly leak out of Jaskek's torn-open face. The smell of dead flesh was beginning to seep through the doors and would have to be dealt with quickly.

"Move over little guy," Dex said as he knelt beside the robot.

Dex looked the body up and down. Their sizes weren't far apart. Dex was slightly bulkier and an inch or two taller, but a spare Imperial uniform wouldn't be bad to have in Dex's wall locker. Just in case.

Robbie had also placed Jaskek's blaster on the corpse's chest.

Dex reached for the blaster and held it up for Robbie to see. "We don't want to get rid of this kinda stuff, got that?"

Robbie shifted his weight to the left. "Why?"

Dex felt like he was talking to a child. "Because things are probably going to get harder from here. We have to conserve whatever gear we can. So, when we find stuff like this, tools or whatever, we might need to keep it."

"But it is not ours."

"I don't think he's gonna miss it." Dex looked down at Jaskek's skinless face. Another small stream of blood trailed down his neck and the side of his head. The shock alone must have been enough to kill the Imperial officer.

Robbie reached out to put his claws over Dex's hands. "You should give it back. He might want it when he wakes up."

Dex almost laughed, "Robbie, do you think he's…"

"He might still be alive. He is still making fluids." Blood pooled around the robot's feet.

Although Robbie couldn't directly show any emotion, Dex could see the look of innocence in his lenses.

"All right, how about this? We'll drop him off as soon as possible, and if he's somehow still alive, I'll give him all his stuff back. Okay?"

Robbie straightened. "That is fair."

"Now you just, um… go stand guard outside the head and make sure no one hurts Lacy."

The robot saluted Dex and shuffled away.

"And don't salute me!" Dex called after Robbie as the door shut between them.

With the robot gone, Dex slipped the blaster into his waistline then picked up the medical device Korr had called a jarrmin box. It was still open and active from their fight. Having a strong idea of what would happen next, Dex mentally prepared himself for the horrific sight to come, and then deactivated the medical device. Jaskek's face fell from the device, onto where it belonged on his head, though, rotated almost a full 180 degrees.

Dex wanted to vomit but knew the look of his vomit seeping into Jaskek's bloody skull and facial muscles would only make him sicker. But that thought also made him want to vomit.

From the shower, Lacy thought she heard Dex shouting in the hall.

"Dex? You okay?" She shouted through the walls.

"Fine!" He called back, wiping the bile from the corner of his mouth. The body had to go. Fast.

He stood back up, jarrmin box in hand, and was about to leave when he noticed another object on Jaskek's hip. It was one of the data tablets Imperial officers carried on them. Dex made a quick pass to grab it then rushed out of the room, escaping from the rank smells before a headache could overcome him.

"Is he awake yet?" Robbie asked.

Dex walked back to his seat at the console and answered Robbie without looking at him. "Not yet buddy. But I'm sure in a few hours he'll be just fine. Get on back to the controls. I want to find somewhere to touch down before we don't have fuel left to even land." He followed close behind Robbie back to their seats.

The *Silent Horizon*'s radar wasn't programmed to detect anything while moving faster than light speed. Dex hoped though, that with the new antenna Korr installed, they wouldn't have any issues.

Lacy finished showering, dried herself, and dressed in her skivvies. Her Planetary Exploration Suit and olive jumpsuit had been confiscated by the Empire. Save for the scarlet dress, her wardrobe wasn't carrying many options.

"Hopefully wherever we land has a Macy's." She joked with Dex. "Let's see what we've got," Lacy scoured through the storage bin above their bunk. "This could be a nice outfit." She pulled out a light blue nightgown that fell just below the knee and held it up in front of herself.

Dex spun in his chair and traced her figure with admiring eyes. "Lovely, darling. But not quite the right outfit for going out."

Robbie turned as well and gave Lacy a once-over. "Dex is right. That won't give you any protection in space."

"Thank you, Robbie," Lacy laughed, then to Dex, "It's this, that hideous red dress, or I go out in my undergarments."

Dex considered the dress but remembered the words of the Zar-Meck when they were first captured.

The Emperor's colors.

"The nightgown should be all right."

As if on cue, a beeping rang from the console.

Lacy draped the gown over herself and asked, "Are we coming up on something?"

"Looks like it," Dex said, reading off of the computer. "Can't make out any details. The ship can't tell if it's a planet or some floating debris."

Lacy walked up behind him and put a hand on his shoulder. "Think it's worth it to check out?"

Dex took a deep breath and thought. "Way I see it,

we've got three possibilities. One, it's nothing. Not enough gas left in the tank to jump again, and we've burned too much to get back home off of just cruising. Dead in the water. Option two, my preferred option, it's a habitable planet. We land safely and start an early retirement."

"And the third option?"

Dex opened his mouth, but it was Robbie who answered. "The Empire is very large."

Lacy watched Dex, waiting for a response. He only shrugged in agreement.

"So do you think it's worth it?" She pushed again.

"If it's even a five percent chance of that early retirement, it's one hundred percent worth it. All right crew, please ensure you are strapped in safely as we are beginning our descent." Dex flicked some buttons on the console.

"Mind if I sit here, Robbie?" Her graceful aura made it impossible to deny any request.

"I will not be able to see if I move."

Lacy rolled her eyes. "You can sit on my lap, how about that?"

Without waiting for a response, Lacy picked up the robot and sat down placing him on her lap like a child.

"Coming out now. Who wants to put bets down? I bet retirement."

"I second," said Lacy.

"I do not know what any of that means," said Robbie.

The *Silent Horizon* dropped out of light speed.

"What is that?" Dex and Lacy asked.

"What is it? I cannot see." Robbie attempted to pull himself up on the console for a better view. "Oh, that. That's a spaceport. Private. Non-military by my data."

"Is it safe?" Lacy asked.

"It is for me."

Acknowledgement

First off, I have to give thanks to **God** for the gifts he's given me in life that allowed me to write this book.

I owe thanks for this book to too many people, most of whom I've never met, but thank you for creating such incredible films.

My graphic designer **Matthew Gunther** was incredibly patient with me and all my nitpicking, and I never once doubted his ability to translate my vision into a reality.

The first person to read any of this was my high school creative writing teacher, and now writing partner and good friend, **J.T. McGee**. Your feedback gave me all the confidence I needed to carry on writing this book.

My brother **Mitchell Valenza** gave me the best feedback, and if this book is at least halfway decent, it's because he cleaned it up for me. Thank you, Mitch.

Since this is the second edition of the book, I have to thank as well my editor, **Dr. Stephen Hull**. You taught me all I know about publishing, and you made this version of the book I can truly be proud of.

My wife **Lexi** was so supportive thoughout the writing process, and incredibly patient with me through this publishing journey, and the obvious inspiration for the character and beauty of Lacy. Lexi, I'd cross the universe for you.

And finally, thank you to my **Dad**, for not only introducing me to all the best movies, but for letting me share in your childhood. You told me once that you believed if we had grown up together, we would have been the best of friends. At the very least, we would have been able to see Star Wars in theaters. And that would have been cool too.

About the author

Andrew Valenza is an Author, veteran, and newspaper editor from upstate N.Y. He published his first novel, "Empire of the Void," in June of 2023 and soon after founded Valenza Publishing.

He is a major movie collector, much to the chagrin of his wallet. But hopefully his love of film and storytelling made this book more enjoyable for you. Thank you for reading!

Please leave a review on Amazon or Goodreads!

Follow us on social media!

Andrew Valenza
@avcollecting - Instagram/TikTok

Valenza Publishing
www.valenzapublishing.com
@valenzapublishing - Instagram/Facebook/Threads

And support indie authors by checking out these
incredible books!

"Fate's Tether" by Jade Nioma

"The Chosen" by J.M. Gokey

"Goodwill's Secrets" by Christopher Mele

"Witness to the Revolution" by Kiersten Marcil